It's my time

THE FOOL'S ERRAND

Reach for me when it's yours.

KATHERINE CARTER

Dedication

To six-year-old Katie, who thought her dreams of writing were too high for her to reach. I'm so proud of you.

(Don't tell her about the smut)

Copyright © 2024 by Katherine Carter
First Edition May 2024

All rights reserved. No part of this publication may be reproduced, stored, or transmitted in any form or by any means, electronic or mechanical, photocopying, recording, scanning, or any other information storage or retrieval system, without written permission from the publisher. It is illegal to copy this book, post it to a website, or distribute it by any other means without permission.

This novel is entirely a work of fiction. The names, characters, and incidents portrayed in it are the work of the author's imagination. Any resemblance to actual persons, living or dead, events, or localities is entirely coincidental.

Cover Art by Giulia F. Wille
Map by Rusty Maps
Edited by Emily Marquart and Katie Bucklein
Typeset by Lorna Reid

ISBN 979-8-9902904-0-2
ASIN B0CVVHDGTZ

Content and Trigger Warnings can be found on page 281

Contents

Link to the official Spotify playlist: ix
Map x
Prologue 1
Chapter 1 5
Chapter 2 17
Chapter 3 24
Chapter 4 30
Chapter 5 37
Chapter 6 43
Chapter 7 47
Chapter 8 49
Chapter 9 52
Chapter 10 70
Chapter 11 80
Chapter 12 82
Chapter 13 86
Chapter 14 88
Chapter 15 93
Chapter 16 97
Chapter 17 103
Chapter 18 108
Chapter 19 118
Chapter 20 129
Chapter 21 135
Chapter 22 142
Chapter 23 151
Chapter 24 156
Chapter 25 164
Chapter 26 172
Chapter 27 178
Chapter 28 182

Chapter 29	189
Chapter 30	192
Chapter 31	195
Chapter 32	199
Chapter 33	206
Chapter 34	216
Chapter 35	219
Chapter 36	223
Chapter 37	227
Chapter 38	230
Chapter 39	232
Chapter 40	240
Chapter 41	245
Chapter 42	250
Chapter 43	259
Epilogue	265
Acknowledgements	275
About the Author	277
Content & Trigger Warnings	279

Link to the official Spotify playlist:

ERALYN

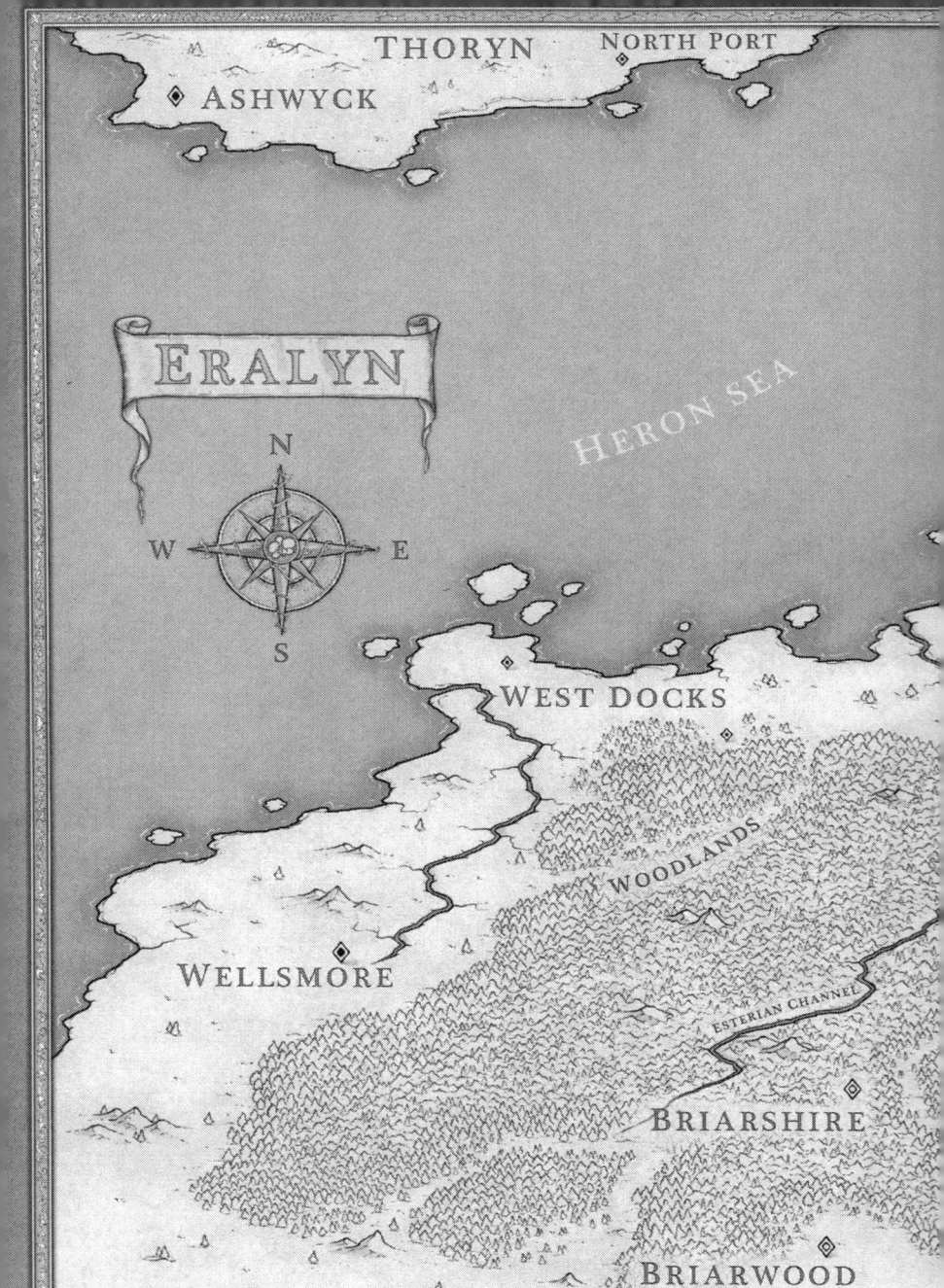

THORYN

- ASHWYCK
- NORTH PORT

HERON SEA

- WEST DOCKS
- WOODLANDS
- WELLSMORE
- ESTERIAN CHANNEL
- BRIARSHIRE
- BRIARWOOD

WILDLANDS
SILVERMIST
NORTH FOREST
MISTWOOD
THESTON GULF
SOUTH FOREST
WINDBURNE
BRIARSTONE
MT HALEBURNE
CLOUDBURNE
THORNEBURNE

Prologue

The Wraith of Wells

ONCE UPON A TIME...

A scream tore through the air. His head whipped around and he scanned the docks around him, but the air went still once again. A bitter and harsh scent wafted over him, blanketing the usually pungent aroma, and his hands curled into fists. He took several steps forward towards the boardwalk, passing by crates yet to be unloaded. He dropped his ledger onto the tallest and nodded to the burly man who stood next to it.

"Keep counting," he ordered, before swiftly moving towards where he'd heard the scream. The man trembled but picked up the ledger all the same.

His steps were hurried but silent as he crouched along more crates, searching the West Docks for anything amiss. A large ship was docked at the main ramp, due to set sail soon. A few people milled about, most passengers having already boarded the ship. It was enormous and could fit many wares, even when filled to capacity with travelers. It was one of his favorites, for just that reason.

A light in one of the houses along the shoreline flickered against the darkness, catching his attention. Inside he saw two massive men speaking and gesturing wildly, angrily. He stalked towards the small wooden home to peer in through the nearest window. Even with his abnormally gifted hearing, he couldn't quite make out their words through the glass.

THE FOOL'S ERRAND

It didn't matter, for the men stormed out the front door, stalking towards a smaller, infrequently used dock. While they didn't speak again, their hefty feet crunched over the thick pebbles of the shore, and he followed closely behind, cloaking himself with his shadows.

No one ever knew The Wraith was behind them until The Wraith wanted them to know.

He followed the men to the far side of the docks, reaching for the dagger strapped to his thigh. Out here, no one would hear their screams. His gut told him they wouldn't live long enough to have the chance to, anyway.

The men crossed over the wooden gangplank, and knocked on the hull of a small boat. A moment later, a third man—this one greasy and thin—climbed out from under the deck, wrenching a petrified woman along with him. The third man dragged the woman behind him as they crossed the gangplank to huddle on the wooden ramp. Her long hair was disheveled and a gag in her mouth muffled her cries. He bit back a scoff, frustrated with how callous the Cosmic Fates were to have allowed this to happen, to only care about silly quests and trials when real people were being injured across the lands. As if the Fates heard him, the dagger in his palm warmed.

The woman looked frantically around the space, still screaming around the cloth as her bound hands strained in front of her. It was a terrifying sound, one that burrowed deep into his soul, feeling as though it were made from the nightmares he'd been plagued with recently. He stood behind the first two men, and cleared a space of shadows in front of his face, and when he caught her attention, he motioned for her to be silent. Still she trembled, but in her confusion she grew quiet.

He replaced the shadows, slipping into the space between air, as he approached the men. The third—the one who held the woman by the back of her neck—paused, glancing around the space. He wouldn't find anything. His curiously red eyes shone as they skipped over his presence.

The Wraith slipped behind him first, slicing his throat with his dagger, silencing him forever. He wrapped shadows around the woman, covering her completely, before stepping out of his own darkness, tilting his head eerily at the two who remained.

"Who told you that you could hunt on *my* docks?" His voice was chilling, and an acrid scent wafted in the air. He laughed bitterly, before lunging forward and stabbing the bloody dagger through the left man's neck, twisting it violently as he ripped it out. The man gurgled, reaching for his neck even as he fell off the side of the ramp and into the frigid waters.

The Wraith darted forward, grabbing the final man and wrenching him forward by his tunic. The man was frozen in fear, though whispered pleas fell from his lips. The Wraith chuckled darkly, enjoying the fear saturating the man's maroon eyes.

"Tell your *master*, whoever you bow to, never to step foot in my docks again. I won't be so lenient in the future."

The man audibly swallowed, frantically nodding his head.

The Wraith smiled menacingly. "Run."

The man took off, kicking up pebbles and rocks as he raced off the ramp and into the darkness of night.

Turning, he dispelled his shadows, freeing the terrified woman from their control.

"Are you all right?" he asked, voice gentle, a stark difference from his usual tenor, as he cut her loose from her ties.

The woman just nodded, eyes glassy as she ripped the gag from her mouth. "I'm fine," she said. "They'd only just grabbed me." The horn of the ship rang through the night, birds launching into flight over the startling noise. She looked around the docks and must have seen how far they were as her face visibly blanched.

"I take it that's your ship?" he asked.

"Yes." Her voice shook.

"They'll wait," he assured, gesturing with an outstretched hand for her to move along to the shore. The Wraith walked her to the ship, the pebbles crunching under their feet the only sound between them. This wasn't the first attempted abduction he'd heard of late. A rotting energy seemed to be spreading through the city, causing a surge in violence and cruelty. He'd need to keep an eye on it.

Once they reached the ramp, the woman turned to him. The emotion had cleared from her face and only fierce courage shone back at him.

"Thank you," she finally said.

The Wraith stuffed his hands into his pockets and nodded curtly. A breath later, she nodded back, mumbling something under her breath about never returning to the damned south again.

He watched her board the ship, and remained standing on the shoreline for several minutes, even after it departed. He couldn't get the haunting look of those maroon eyes out of his head.

Shaking off the past hour, he stalked back to the crates to resume the task he'd been so rudely interrupted from.

Chapter One
Emelle

SEVERAL MONTHS LATER

"And then he drove his dagger through the beast's softened belly and ripped out its bowels!"

Boisterous laughter rang through the dimly lit tavern, jesters and fools cheering for the man feigning humility as his companion relayed his most recent act of heroism. As light from the roaring fireplace flickered against his skin, she supposed he was attractive as he lifted his stein and took a large gulp.

The knot in his throat bobbed as he swallowed, and her eyes followed in a daze as a drop of ale trickled down onto his filthy tunic. White teeth flashed in a knowing grin just before he took another drink. She knew it was foolish, but as the light flickered on his flesh, the smallest part of her felt jealous of the heat.

Or maybe she just needed to get laid.

Yeah, that's probably it.

Feeling a tingle of awareness, her cheeks flamed as her gaze snapped back up to his face, her gaze crashing into his. She'd been caught. All she could focus on was the glint behind his light eyes igniting a slight twinge of apprehension in her gut. She knew what that look meant.

Turning away from the poorly concealed posturing, Emelle St.

King of the remote village of Silvermist, scanned the bartop for spills and drink orders.

Despite her regal-sounding name, Emelle knew she was the furthest thing from royalty. Her village, snuggled in the North Forest of the rural lands of Mistwood, may be the last town between the Wildlands and the rest of Eralyn, but still they were quaint, not royal. She gave a small shake of her head in annoyance at the sole copper left as a tip by her most recent patron. *All those spoils and yet no one knows how to properly thank the barkeep.*

Huffing to herself, Emelle collected the measly coin before moving past the raucous group still seemingly enthralled by the latest Hero recounting the obviously dramatized tales of his travels.

She wondered if they'd ever noticed that it was always some variation of the same three stories: man slays mythical beast, man solves harrowing puzzle, man rescues woman from certain death...

Once the prince completed whichever trial they'd been bestowed, the newest Hero was always awarded a woman at the end of his journey. Sure, the Cosmic Fates said they were soulmates—gag—and the man just had to prove his worthiness before the bond snapped into place. They said the union restored some innate magic that nourished the earth. *Yeah, right.*

All it seemed to do was give the men an ego the size of Eralyn itself, their chests puffing out as they sneered down on those around them. It was always too easy to clock a Hero amongst the groups. They all shared this air of confidence, carrying themselves as though they were owed the dirt underneath their feet.

She glanced up from the stein she was polishing to the blond Hero finishing the last of his ale. The golden band denoting his status gleamed atop his hair and was glaringly obvious, even to her.

The diadems and jewels also helped.

The jesters and fools could never seem to replicate the exact air of smug pretense, always averting their gaze too quickly—the fools, especially. They seemed to be more than happy to ride the coattails of the Heroes, getting kicked and berated as they yipped at their masters' heels. The jesters were more subtle, and usually a little more clever, as if they understood their precarious rank and did what they could to not slip down a rung.

They all drank the same, though.

A heartbeat later, Vivian grabbed the stein Emelle had just poured with a wink, and prowled up to the Hero. Offering the fresh drink, the older girl charmed her way closer and closer, until she had a hand permanently resting on his filthy forearm.

It was hard to believe the romantic notion of soulmates when Emelle had seen how these men acted in her tavern, The Flushed Finn, once their stories had been told and the candles had dimmed. It wasn't every man, but it was certainly the majority. She doubted the random women following the newly appointed Heroes into their rented rooms knew they were spoken for. The jesters and fools were certainly aware.

How wonderful and generous are the Fates.

She scoffed under her breath. There was always another kingdom she'd somehow never heard of. Always another missing princess in need of yet another Hero. Always another beast to be slain. And there was always another white knight finally stepping into his destiny as a Hero, as if it were prophesied by the Fates themselves.

She supposed it was.

Yet Heroes were too common to be special anymore. Princesses were a copper a palmful and plucked from seeming obscurity. She could've sworn the crumpled letter in her pocket warmed, as though reminding her of this very fact.

Four months ago, Emelle watched her oldest and greatest friend, Greer Wrenly, fall into her destiny and leave their village on the back of a primly groomed, speckled white horse. Clutching the back of her recently betrothed, the newest Hero of the month, she never looked back.

Emelle didn't blame her. Prince Elwood was certainly one of the more handsome Heroes she'd seen, and his dazzling smile effortlessly balanced Greer's fiery personality. His rich brown skin had glistened with perspiration when he found Greer, and his chest heaved while he tried—and failed—to catch his breath, which only seemed to heighten his obvious beauty. Greer's fair complexion had flushed deeply—something Emelle almost never saw—and Emelle knew they were a match.

It also helped that he looked at her like she hung the moon. He was one of the good ones, Emelle had noticed. While he still had a confidence that couldn't be shaken, his heart was pure. And it was held in Greer's wild hands.

The letter in Emelle's pocket was one of the last she'd read from her friend, and a pile had been accumulating on her desk over the last several weeks. This one was on the shorter side, Greer sharing that she and her betrothed had made it to the north, and remarking on how beautiful his kingdom was. Whenever Emelle needed to feel her friend she missed so dearly, she pulled out this letter and read it. It was crumpled and warped from countless secret tears, but the weight of the letter in her hands grounded her. Knowing Greer was safe and happy bolstered her for another day at The Finn.

Making the weeks-long ride to the nearest docks in the west and then the full three-week journey across the Heron Sea to Greer's new palace in Ashwyck was never going to be feasible for Emelle, but Greer spun a story of a whirlwind romance and Emelle found herself caught up in the passion of it all. How could she not be happy for her oldest friend, even if she was an ocean away?

Emelle assured Greer she would be fine, and vowed to visit when she could make it work. Even so, she wasn't sure how her longest friend couldn't see her heart break with every word. But that wasn't fair to Greer, so she swallowed her pain.

Emelle shuddered, a breeze through an open window wrapping around her heated body with relief. She rolled her neck, wiping away sweat with her sleeves, and glanced to her left out of habit—only to find no one there.

As the seasons changed, the chill freezing her bones, Emelle still found herself turning to where Greer would've been. Before Greer had left, they had spoken about running the tavern together one day. Emelle had never wanted to run it on her own. Well, she didn't want to run it at all, but it had been in her family for generations. Her father all but locked the cuff around her ankle himself, a familiar glimmer sparking in his eyes whenever he spoke about her taking over one day. She swore she felt the heat of the metal clamping her bones even now. So who better to be there with her every day than Greer?

Greer's absence gnawed at her, as she mindlessly continued with her duties, refilling ales and ignoring the rising volume as her heart throbbed. She could run the tavern in her sleep, though the thought scared her. She wiped at yet another spill on the bartop and the bitterness towards her father reared its ugly head yet again. No matter how hard she fought to let her resentment go, having known her destiny from the day she was old enough to understand what the word even meant, it still broke something in her when her father laid into her about duty, about keeping the family legacy alive.

Her hand stilled on the bartop as she peered around the tavern, the place she'd spent her entire life in, the duty her father had shuffled off to her. Only the flickering candles and fireplace provided any light, mostly because her father hadn't wanted to draw attention to the cracks in the walls, the stains in the floors. The long tables taking up space near the back of the room had mismatched chairs and grease stains that wouldn't come out no matter how hard she scrubbed. And those damned stairs, the ones a traveler first saw when they entered The Finn and led to the rooms she rented out, the ones she'd run up and down countless times—every other step creaked. She still hadn't forgiven them after she'd tripped in front of a handsome boy with a charming, toothy grin. How she hated those stairs.

Her quaint office to the right of the bar stayed shut whenever she wasn't working at her desk, but it bore stark similarities to the tavern on the whole.

Aged. Broken. Desolate.

Those three words echoed in her soul each month as she paid the taxes, forgoing any coin for herself. When Greer was here, she paid her as much as she could spare, and Greer was happy to pretend it was enough. Everything they made went towards the tariff or paying vendors. And despite the fact they had a revolving door of guests, somehow there was never enough for th*e badly needed* repairs. So she settled for rugs to cover the stains and cheap art and tapestries to hide the holes in the walls. Each time she saw one of the canvases, her anger rose.

Greer would somehow spin her mood around; her lighthearted jokes about the state of the tavern being a reflection of her overworked mind always seemed to bring Emelle out of her fog. But as the sounds of the rowdy crowd suffocated her, the familiar resentment bubbled up inside of her without Greer there to quell it.

Emelle's father had long since retired after he injured his knee from breaking up a tavern brawl, and her mother was off raising her second family as if her first didn't exist. Emelle hadn't spoken to her in years. But Greer was *always* there, and Emelle had grown dependent on her presence. They could have entire conversations with just a single look, a secret language they'd perfected when they were just girls. How was she supposed to just let that go?

She missed her so much her heart ached. The letters that arrived every other week eased some of the pain but each time it took longer to read them, took longer to respond. She didn't want to admit to herself the truth of why that was. The latest arrived only two days ago. She'd tossed it into the pile on her desk. She wasn't ready to read the words quite yet.

Greer deserved to be happy, so Emelle had decided she wouldn't tell her the secret truth she harbored deep within the dark corners of her soul. The painful truth that she wished Greer had asked her to come along, to escape the tavern together. To escape this *village* together. But Emelle knew that was a fool's errand.

She sighed. Chasing dreams was for people who could run. And she never even learned how to walk.

In her small village of Silvermist, all they had were a couple hundred folks and certainly no missing princesses. Greer was a happy accident, the town had decided.

Many people passed through Silvermist, stopping only for a hot meal and a bed to sleep in. They lounged in her tavern for a night, spilled their ale on her tables and floors, sang rowdy songs of bravery and perilous exploits, ruined her sheets and dirtied her lavatories, all before eating a hasty breakfast and mounting their steeds to leave Silvermist behind. They'd never think of the small village that served as one of several stops along Eralyn during their journey again. Or the nameless barkeep who served their ale, cleaned their rooms, brought them a hot breakfast.

The sight of Vivian, now whispering in the Hero's ear, soured what was left in her stomach. Surprisingly, Olivia was absent. At least she only had to watch one of the sisters flirt with her patrons tonight.

The night before her seventeenth birthday, Emelle had watched the older girls float around the latest Hero, subtly shooting looks at each other claiming their stake. She'd seen Olivia sneak into a darkened corner before returning flushed and fixing her skirts. Later that evening, she'd caught Vivian leading the Hero up the stairs to his room. They didn't come back down.

Rumors around the village said the Sable sisters were trying to fall into any destiny as a mate, to whichever Hero who could whisk them away from this small village. Unfortunately, all they snagged that particular night was a case of lumps requiring a visit to the local healer for a foul-smelling cream—and it must have been effective, as they were back only a few days later. It had now been over ten years of the sisters' antics. When would they learn that they couldn't force a destiny not blessed by the Fates?

Her head shook of its own accord. The Cosmic Fates—she rolled her eyes—were certainly too busy weaving destinies for the princes around the kingdoms to bother with the common folk who were barely worth a thought in their divine minds.

Shaking herself from the memories, she gathered her wits and moved along. But a pang had her pausing mid-step as she fought a tear gathering in the corner of her eye.

She took a moment to remind herself: he's just passing through and would be gone by morning. He had likely already found his soon-to-be-bride. He was moving onwards; he'd fulfilled his prophecy.

A tiny voice sounded in her head: *And you will be here.*

She straightened in resignation and raised her chin with false bravado. Yes. She would be here. Night after night. Week after week. Year after year. As it has been. As it would be. As it was with her father, and her father's father, and her father's father's father, and so on.

Yes. This was her home. Even if she secretly dreamed each night of the lives that were lived beyond her four aging walls.

A hollering jester yelled for a refill. She went back to work.

☽✻☾

As Emelle prepared for last call, she scanned the tavern once again. She was hoping the men wouldn't push back tonight and that she could be in her bed soon.

Walking up to the bartop to clean yet another spill, her attention caught on a new face. She stopped, breath sticking in her throat. Light appeared to leach around him, darkening the already shadowed corner. His eyes appeared so dark, almost as if they hid in their own shadows, storing secrets and spelling misfortune.

He stood alone, and she couldn't help but thank the Fates that Vivian had already taken the blond Hero to his room. Her sight flashed green at the thought of another woman leading this stranger up her stairs and into a room that wasn't hers.

Leaning against the shoddy wall, his frame appeared lethal with impressive stature and a gleaming sword strapped across his back. A matching dagger was strapped to his thigh, and the glint of the blade meant it was sharp. Rugged fingers wrapped around his stein threatened pain, and she worried for a moment that with one wrong movement the glass would shatter in his palm. His armor was molded to his frame, muscles and power visible even through the leathers. He looked out of place next to the damaged plaster and the fraying tapestry that covered the largest of the cracks. She prayed the wall held steady against his sizable form.

Head cocked, she noticed a distinct lack of emblem declaring which kingdom he came from on his armor. This piqued her interest, and she found herself mindlessly taking a step forward only for Fate to intervene as she bumped into the bar, jostling her back down to earth. Schooling her features, Emelle reminded herself that he would only be here for the night.

No one ever stayed longer than a night.

She decided he must be at the beginning of his adventure. His leathers were too clean, skin too smooth and free of fresh cuts and bruises. He wasn't looking in her direction, but she knew that would change any second as he keenly scanned the room.

Rain hammered outside as she waited with bated breath. Straightening her back and inhaling slightly, she parted her lips into an innocent smile and lifted her chest ever so slightly. Vivian may already be upstairs, but she wasn't.

Yes, she really needed to get laid.

His head turned, and she saw him straight-on as they locked eyes for the briefest moment. A moment which seemed to be carved out in deafening slow motion. His gaze was focused, and she swore she saw a hint of surprise flash through his features, too quick for her to be sure. How easy would it be to fall into those depths?

A thousand images flashed through her mind, too fast for her to catch onto the slippery wisps, as they stared at each other from across the room. Looking at him felt resoundingly like peace and comfort and *home*.

In the distance, a sharp clap of thunder crashed and, like that, the spell broke.

Sound flooded her ears, overwhelming her senses, as her attention was yanked to a patron shaking his near-empty stein in the air and whistling a sharp note to catch her attention. The earth resumed its rotation as she forced her body towards the drunkard.

Each step away from the newest stranger echoed in her blood. The heat from each pulse had her glancing over her shoulder, needing to know if she'd imagined the imposing man, or the shadows that seemed to spill from him.

But she saw nothing. Where had he gone?

She continued over to the jester.

His ruddy cheeks and droopy eyelids told her that while he certainly didn't need another ale, that wasn't going to stop her from pouring the drink. She'd learned it was best to just serve the patrons and hope they passed out instead of starting another tavern brawl. She couldn't afford to replace all the chairs again.

Pouring the ale from the tap of the barrel, Emelle placed it roughly in front of the man, eyebrow raised in challenge. The jester was undisturbed by her warning, his disheveled tunic suspiciously stained as he reached into his pocket. Before she could even open her mouth, he had already flipped a silver coin onto the bartop, grabbing the stein while spinning away.

She blew out a short breath in annoyance, collecting the now wet coin. Grabbing her damp cloth, she wiped the drops of shit ale the man spilled on the surface of the bar, probably on purpose.

"Last call!" she hollered at her patrons, sneaking glances towards the now-empty corner.

A few grumbled but stayed put. Disappointment singed her chest as she surveyed the room and came to the conclusion that he'd already left. Or perhaps her tired mind had simply conjured him out of shadows.

But the thrumming in her soul told her she hadn't.

As several men ambled up to the bar, she did what she did best: she poured their ale. Once again, a few sad coins were left behind as the Heroes and jesters resumed their revelry, promptly forgetting her presence. Retreating into obscurity, Emelle St. King did what she did second best: she listened.

Close to an hour later, Emelle swept the last bits of rubbish into the bin. She put the broom away and clasped her hands together behind her back and pushed up, hoping to ease the ache in her shoulders.

All but one candle had been snuffed as she'd cleaned her way through the tavern, so she grabbed the chamberstick by the round notch on its worn holder and made her way upstairs, her back aching with each step. The fireplace would bank overnight and she paused on the first step as she thought about throwing another log in before hastily dismissing the idea. Had she mentioned she hated these stairs?

Though she was only twenty-eight, she felt much older as she yawned, her body growing tired as her mind raced, piecing together what she heard tonight and how it fit with the news from the past few weeks. The circulating reports were certainly interesting but nothing new. Unease rising in the kingdoms to the southwest, royalty raising taxes and tithes—she was intimately familiar with this topic—mercenaries being recruited by the various crowns, a few magical beasts slain in the south, and one Hero who perished during his trial. A trap had suffocated the prince. He was likely too pompous to see death right in front of him. She didn't feel bad for him. The webs wove and overlapped in her buzzing mind as she made her way to her room.

Quiet grunts and soft moans rang out as she passed the latest Hero's room. The floor creaked faintly as she froze, eavesdropping on the not-so-private moment. A heat gathered in her lower abdomen as the groans grew deeper and the breaths came quicker. She knew what was coming.

Or rather, *who* was coming.

She listened as he crested, never wavering from her spot, never looking towards the door. Her pulse quickened as her undergarments grew damp. But after a moment, the silence became noticeable. Emelle steadied herself with a shaky inhale before continuing toward her room on silent feet.

It had been months since she'd felt that euphoric peak by

anyone or anything other than her own hand. She'd bedded a man who was passing through a few weeks back, but he hadn't managed to push her over that edge. He'd barely even tried.

She thought of the stranger in the corner from earlier. He looked like he'd drag her over that edge if it was the last thing he did. And she would let him. *Cosmic Fates, she would let him.*

As many times as he wished.

Letting herself into her dark room, Emelle placed the dying flame on the small chest next to her cot and dressed for bed. After quickly jotting a few notes of the information she learned on a piece of parchment to add to the ledger tomorrow, she laid down on her cold, worn bunk. Closing her eyes in regret, Emelle momentarily let herself wish she had approached the mysterious man. That she'd somehow gotten his attention.

But that kind of thinking wouldn't help her.

Come morning, he'd be gone. They always were. Tomorrow he would be just another Hero from the masses, passing through to fulfill his destiny. By next week, his face will have become lost in the sea that plagued her village. A fluffy mass curled up behind her back and siphoned some of her hurt. Her cat always seemed to know when she was needed.

Somewhere in the deepest part of her soul, she knew she was lying to herself. Knew she was simply in denial of the planetary shift that had thrown her into some parallel universe. One where someone noticed her. *Saw her.*

Everyone she served looked straight through her, never taking a breath other than to order a drink. But he...He stared *into* her very soul.

Though she only saw him for a few seconds, she'd felt a tug. It was so light she thought for a moment that she'd imagined it, trying to rationalize that her pulse had simply jumped from the thunder that crashed just moments after. But somehow, as she drifted off in a restless slumber, she knew in her bones that was a lie.

Chapter Two
The Wraith of Wells

Making his way to Silvermist was easier than he anticipated. Though he'd trained for the majority of his life, he hadn't spent much time outside his kingdom borders. He'd taken a couple extra weeks to travel through the Woodlands of Eralyn, visiting the small villages to see if they were plagued with a similar evil as Wellsmore. So far, it seemed as though the rot hadn't spread past his kingdom yet. He was grateful for it; the screams of the woman he'd saved a few months back from the man with strange eyes still haunted him.

Walking around the corner of a building that had seen better days—*years, even*—he spotted his mark but didn't approach. Moving into the tree line, he watched the entrance of the tavern from the coverage of the dense copse of pines. The falling rain gave the night a chill that crept into his bones, but he didn't budge until the last candle had been snuffed.

As the first rays of dawn appeared on the horizon, he cloaked himself in his shadows to make his way back to the secluded room he'd secured for the next few evenings. The man he'd rented it from ceased all questions once he tossed him a small pouch of silver coins.

He had waited for over two decades for the chance to overthrow his king. He could be patient a few more days.

☾✷☽

After spending a few hours in Silvermist, he thought the town appeared rather unassuming. For years, he'd heard rumors of the tall tales people shared in the rural village of Mistwood. As the only town in the North Forest, the bottlenecked land between the Heron Sea and Theston Gulf led through to the Wildlands where many celestial trials had been rumored to be found. Countless Heroes passed through, either just starting or finishing such a trial, fulfilling their prophesied destiny. Others traveled in search of any adventure they could find. Not all returned.

There was excitement here. He just had to know where to look.

As he explored the small village, he listened for any sign of celestial quests being shared. Throughout the various establishments, he'd heard only a couple of rumors. Ones probably juicy for the folk who lived in the village, but nothing of the caliber he searched for. He figured most stayed inside to avoid the rain.

The town seemed to still be buzzing about a woman who'd recently moved away. He supposed that was a big deal for a remote village like Silvermist.

Typical rowdy sounds that came from a place of festivity drew his eyes, his ears, once again. He would find what he needed. There was no alternative.

He swore even the ground shook in agreement as he crossed the gravel street. Under the cover of night, he opened the tavern door on loud hinges. Shaking the water off his wool cloak, he entered the lively room.

The tavern was busy, as usual. He'd noticed a pattern after a few nights of surveillance. Inconspicuously, he found a spot in the corner to survey the patrons.

Tonight, there was a newly minted Hero sharing his grandiose tale quite intensely. His ears trained on the man, listening for clues. Other men spoke loudly and without care for who wasn't listening—or more importantly, who *was*. They didn't seem to mind as long as they could hear themselves talk.

Drinks were refilled promptly and spilled equally as quickly while conversation grew louder and lips became looser. He scoffed sharply as he judged the prince in the room, knowing he was only Hero because of the Fates.

It was expected to follow destiny; it's physically the easiest choice you can make, as it's written—predestined even—by the Fates. True valor drags your very soul through sacrifice after sacrifice and yet still asks for more. When you think you have nothing left to give, still you must yield the final dregs of your mangled soul.

These Heroes know nothing of sacrifice.

He was grateful he'd already been dragged through the shattered remains of his soul long ago. Broken and bleeding, he knew there was nothing in this world that could faze him anymore. He dared the Fates to test him.

It was even more laughable knowing many Heroes sent scouts ahead of their travels, forgoing the legwork and letting the jesters and fools risk the Wildlands in exchange for a place of prestige in their guard upon ascending their throne. Fates forbid they actually made something of themselves on their own. Leveraging the promise of status and coin to keep their hands as clean as possible. It was comical how much effort most Heroes would go to so as to avoid shouldering any of the real work.

And these were supposed to be the next leaders of their kingdoms? Surely, it must be a farce. Oh, how he wished to have just *one* conversation with the pompous Cosmic Fates. His upper lip curled in disgust. The conversation would be with the business end of his claymore, but one conversation would be all he needed.

The wood groaned under his feet as he shifted further into the corner.

If anyone noticed, no one showed it by acknowledging his

presence. He preferred to blend into the shadows of the tavern. And though he wanted none of the piss water masquerading as ale, he held a stein so no one would look twice if they somehow spotted him lurking in the corner.

He wasn't looking for a drink. He thirsted to plot. He knew he was dealt a rotten hand at birth, but he was determined to change his course. To change the course of his kingdom.

Fates be damned. He would craft his own destiny.

☽✶☾

A flash of strawberry hair caught his eye, drawing his attention, once again, to a curvy woman expertly carrying several large ales in each hand as she sped through the aged bar. She cloaked herself behind a demure mask of innocence, as she floated around, as if anticipating her patrons' needs before they could even ask.

Not one person acknowledged her presence after grabbing a fresh stein from her. Whether that was because she was so efficient and was already on to the next order, or because she didn't give them the chance in the first place, he wasn't sure.

Light spilled from her hair, her smile, her... well, from everywhere. The worn wood creaked beneath her boots as she deposited steins onto the bartop, collecting payment as she went.

He couldn't fathom why no one was sparing this captivating enchantress a second glance. Her keen attention and quick hands were an obvious tell there was more to her than met the eye.

How does one not see her?

Even from across the lively pub, she was all he could behold. He tried to focus on the tales, to gather his desperately needed intel on where he could find a trial, *any* celestial trial, but she unknowingly demanded his every attention with each swish of her hips.

Enthralled by the way her eyes appeared coy, her delicate ears always seemed to be trained towards her customers. *What was she listening for?*

He felt a flicker of protectiveness over the woman as he detected salty tears mixing into her scent. Her brows furrowed ever so slightly as a singular tear escaped. Fighting against that primal instinct, he rooted himself to his spot, doing nothing as her steps faltered. Scanning the room, he searched for any indication of what was causing her tears. *If one of these drunk fuckers did something...*

Already, he knew he would eliminate whatever, *whoever*, threatened this tiny enchantress's happiness.

Fortunately for those in the room—and the pub itself—his newest obsession quickly gathered herself and went back to serving her patrons, blank smile fixed once again. One that seemed *mostly* natural to the untrained eye.

Surveying the crowd for the cause of his little enchantress's tears, more than a few men seemed to feel the weight of his gaze on them, shifting uncomfortably where they stood. He smirked, knowing they'd soil themselves if they turned around. He wasn't known for being gentle.

Feeling a tingle snaking up his spine, he was acutely aware of a new gaze on him. He scanned the room again, before his line of sight crashed into the curious woman's.

For the first time since he was nine, he was entirely stunned.

Frozen, he was consumed by her eyes. He'd never seen a color quite like hers. Twinkling emerald irises stared back at him as time slowed to a crawl. In her gaze, he saw warmth and acceptance and a *future*. Flashes of a life he'd likely never have the chance to know taunted him from afar. Her breath hitched and her pulse quickened at the base of her delectable throat.

Oh, how that neck would look even prettier with his teeth marks imprinted for any man to see.

Surprised by the force of his desire, his eyes widened slightly.

But as quickly as it began, the moment broke as a *crack* of thunder spurned the little enchantress back into action as she filled another stein and called for final drinks. She was even more captivating from the front, her heart-shaped face screaming innocence while her eyes shimmered with lightly veiled mischievousness.

Slinking around the corner, he cloaked himself with darkness and continued to observe the bewitching barkeep resuming her duties as if his entire world hadn't just been tilted on an axis. The roar of the fire in the hearth rushed through his ears as he shifted next to the wall, attention focused on the woman fading in and out, almost as if she had control over the darkness, too.

He'd never discovered the source of his shadows, but he was grateful for the influence he held over the darkness. It was handy, slipping into the space between the air more times than he could count, as he did now.

A handful of grubby men approached her bartop and he monitored them as she took their coin and filled their steins. Settling into his new spot, he watched over his newest interest with rapt attention. He still didn't know what made her cry and he didn't want to leave her on her own just yet.

So he stood sentry, and waited.

☽✷☾

Another hour crawled by and his bold little barkeep finally pushed everyone either out the door or up to their rooms. A man who had seemingly passed out on the bar was carried out by his friends, and she shook her head at their retreating backs. Her fake smile dropped the moment she shut the door behind them.

Pushing further into the shadows, he waited as his enchantress swiftly collected empty glasses and wiped down tables. Glancing around the room every so often, she blew out every candle but one. *What are you searching for, little enchantress?*

The final candle she took upstairs with her. Halfway up, she turned towards the fireplace, gazing blankly into the dying flames, unfocused in thought.

But her eyes cleared, head shaking off whatever had captured her momentarily, before she ascended the stairs. He knew he shouldn't, but even the damned Fates couldn't stop him as he followed her up to the second floor on soundless feet. He followed as close as he dared as she made her way down the hallway.

But something, a soft moan by the sound of it, had her pausing next to one of the occupied rooms. Her thrumming pulse was the only part of her that dared to move. His nostrils flared and he detected another scent on her this time, something headier.

Something...entirely too tempting.

Soft pants escaped from her plump lips as she listened to the show on the other side of the wall. But a few unsatisfying moments later, the room went silent and his little enchantress inhaled sharply before moving on.

Following her to what he assumed was her room, he slipped inside just as she shut the door. Despite knowing a good man would, he didn't dare look away as she removed her shoes and changed into her shift before jotting something down in a small journal and climbing into bed. Fates, she was beautiful.

Her room was plain and tidy and his gaze flitted around quickly, trying to catalog any detail he could about this fascinating woman. But the bare walls and simple furniture gave nothing away.

Her desire still coated the air and suffocated his senses. Swallowing the saliva that had gathered in his mouth, he vowed to taste this stunning woman one day. Fates be damned, he would drench himself in her scent and wear her release as a badge of honor.

For the third time that night, he stood sentry to watch his newest obsession, this time as she fell into sleep.

Moments later, a fluffy white, orange, and black patterned cat hopped up next to his little enchantress's back and stared at him warily. He fixed an earnest look at the cat, one that promised he wouldn't harm the stirring woman. The cat meowed softly in what he hoped was understanding, before closing its eyes and falling asleep.

He wouldn't let this enchanting woman keep him from his destiny for too long, but one more night couldn't hurt.

Chapter Three
Emelle

Gasping, Emelle reached for her toes as she stretched her lower back. After sleeping a mere four hours, she was awoken by the too-bright morning sun streaming into her room. Her calico cat, Evie, mimicked her stance as she yawned and presented her glorified servant with her rear end. Emelle just laughed and gently swiped the fluffy tail out of her face.

Glancing at the position of the sun, she groaned, knowing she needed to start her chores to have any chance of finishing them all before the dinner rush. Her knees ached on the hard wooden floor, and for the millionth time, Emelle missed Greer, but this time for a more selfish reason: Emelle hated breakfast duty. Well, she hated *waking up* for breakfast duty. Even after all these months, she still wasn't a morning person.

With a final glance at the sky, she spurred into action. Moving to the chest at the foot of her bed, Emelle pulled out her clothes for the day. She donned a thicker, olive-toned wool skirt that fell to her ankles over a lighter shift. Gathering a section of the fabric near her right thigh, she tucked it into the cinched waistband so she wouldn't trip on the length.

Binding her breasts was no longer pleasant—not that it ever really was since they'd grown—but she did what she could to keep them from giving her a black eye every time she ran up and down the stairs. A breezy, though plain, cream-colored chemise with long billowing sleeves cuffed at her wrists followed, and she tucked the hem into the waistband. She finished by putting on her socks with the least holes and her mud-flecked leather boots. If they could last a few more weeks, she would have gotten through almost the entire winter having only mended them twice.

Brushing her hair back, Emelle wished her wispy bangs looked presentable in the morning without getting them damp and drying them with a cloth. She was glad she always kicked the men out in the dark of night so they wouldn't see the rat's nest that took over her head in the revealing morning sunlight. While she didn't want any repeat customers, she certainly didn't need them running from her bed before she could even make an excuse for their leave.

Emelle sighed as she stepped into her private lavatory, a perk that came with being the owner of the tavern. After quickly using the facilities, she pushed up her sleeves and washed her face and teeth. She then reached for a patterned handkerchief that was delicately folded on a shelf over her basin. The shelf held several, and they were all precious to her. Emelle likened herself to a collector of the expensive cloths and often made...unsavory trades when she saw a new one that pulled at her heartstrings. Grabbing one of the few luxuries she afforded herself, she tied it around her head in her usual style to keep her hair back, leaving only her bangs and two wispy front pieces out.

Making her way down to the tavern, Emelle shut the few windows that were left open overnight, noticing a nasty storm brewing in the distance. The rain would likely send everyone indoors. She might even sell out.

Her spirits lifted at the prospect of having no vacancy. It had been too long since she was able to turn someone away. She didn't enjoy it, but she secretly held onto the hope that she could fix the leaking roof and replace the creaking front door soon.

The sounds of the rusted hinges had begun to invade her

dreams, forcing her, even in sleep, to remember her duty to this place.

Emelle righted chairs and pushed them into the long tables, attending to her usual morning duties. Placing a fresh log in the fireplace, she struck her flint to bring the flames back to life. She tossed a few pine needles from her dwindling stash into the budding fire and hoped the mist would let up before the storm arrived. She was running low on dry kindling.

Pushing through the swinging half-door to the right of the bar, Emelle entered the small kitchen and gathered the quail eggs and her least-ugly spuds and began preparing breakfast. Most guests requested breakfast in their room, still recovering from the revelry of the night before, so she found herself going up and down her stairs too many times to count. Falling into the familiar routine, Emelle set on her day.

☽✻☾

By dinner, Emelle was short of breath and her bangs stuck to her temples with a thin layer of sweat. Swiping her sleeve across her forehead, she wiped down the wooden surface of her bartop once again. While the storm hadn't reached her village quite yet, the air was more humid than usual and she felt *sticky*.

Her heart sank as she counted the patrons renting a room. There were rarely any repeats, and after seeing so many faces over the years, almost none were remarkable enough to remember.

Last night was the exception. Tonight was not.

Olivia Sable sat at a table, speaking demurely with an attractive jester while finding small ways to touch his arm, his shoulders. There weren't any Heroes here tonight, so Emelle assumed Olivia picked the most attractive man present and figured he might have a connection. She didn't fault the Sable sisters for using their obvious beauty and witty charms to bed the Heroes—she just wished she didn't have to see it every other week.

Once again, Emelle was reminded how much she missed Greer. If Greer were next to her, Emelle would widen her eyes ever so slightly and Greer would hear every silent word.

As the hour grew late, Emelle's few patrons made their way upstairs without any prodding and she found her tavern surprisingly empty before midnight. The dying candles flickered against the darkness, reminding her once again of the warmth that curled in her abdomen, the heat licking against her spine.

Serenaded by the rain pattering against the wooden structure, Emelle decided to clean a little *too* quickly so she could escape to her room.

All day long, the feverish moans she'd heard from last night infiltrated her thoughts, and the heat growing in her core was nearing explosive. Emelle extinguished the last of the candles and rushed up the stairs, excitement bubbling in her chest as she grew eager for release.

Slipping into her room, Emelle threw a quick kiss to an uninterested Evie, and undressed without care. Her skirts and chemise landed in a haphazard pile by her washtub, but Emelle wasn't worried about the dirty clothes. She *was* worried, however, about her hair, and gently took out her handkerchief, placing it back on the shelf with the others, before throwing her light strands into a messy knot atop her head and turning the faucet on. She knew she would be miserable tomorrow if she wet her hair this late at night. Needing to cool her overheated skin, Emelle bathed quickly without waiting for the bathwater to warm.

Once she felt clean, she haphazardly dried her body and slipped under her blankets, wiggling her body into a comfortable position. The muffled moans she heard the night before sounded in her head once again.

An image of the gloating Hero from last night flashed in her mind and she visualized him coaxing those same noises from her. He would start by sneaking up behind her and licking the bead of sweat that always seemed to trickle down her neck as she served her patrons. Wrapping his arms around her waist, he'd pull her into his chest, molding their greedy bodies together. On a laugh, she'd quickly check on her customers before allowing him to pull her into a shadowed corner. Eyes dark as night would hold hers hostage as he spun her around.

Releasing a sigh, Emelle imagined the Hero dipping his head to suck on the soft spot behind her ear. Her needy panting would only spur him on as he gripped her hips and ground her into his hard cock.

Fates, she needed him inside her. Fingers gripping her hips. Cock filling her. Emelle audibly moaned as she lost herself to her fantasy.

Sliding a hand down to her slippery entrance, she teased the sensitive bud as her opposite hand tweaked her pebbled nipple. Glossy hair that smelled of danger and pine filled her senses before she gripped his head and pulled him off her neck.

She needed a taste and couldn't hold her desires back any longer.

He chuckled darkly as she tugged his head back by his hair, running her nose along the column of his neck before darting her tongue out to flick against his searing skin.

Deciding to be bold in this fantasy, she'd bring her hungry lips to his ear and whisper what she wanted him to do to her. *Filthy, wicked things.*

Leaving him momentarily speechless, she'd release his hair and smooth her palms over his rough leathers. Hands traveling down to his manhood, she gripped him. Hard.

Look at me, he'd command, and her gaze would snap to his. His pupils would dilate, until she was sure she'd fall into his abyss.

Her mouth watered, consumed by thoughts of the solid length she needed to fill her, core clenching with wanton desire. Plunging her fingers into herself over and over, she built a rhythm she knew only he could deliver.

Lost in her fantasy, Emelle heard his deep voice whisper in her ear.

Come for me, princess.

Leaving her nipple to the cool air, her now-free hand ran down her body to push on her lower abdomen and ground her clit in quick circles with her outstretched fingertips. Succumbing to the fictional man, Emelle threw herself over the edge as her fantasy dissipated on a phantom shadow into the cosmos.

Gasping for breath, she gulped in the cool air.

The Hero from last night had blue eyes.

Chapter Four
Emelle

The days passed and the storm still lingered just on the horizon. The rare humidity had dried up, and a constant chill pierced the walls of her tavern. Emelle found herself going through firewood quicker than she was prepared for. At least the mist had temporarily lifted and she used the chance to scavenge some dry pine needles to replenish her measly stock.

A near-constant rotation of Heroes, jesters, and fools kept her rooms half-full, but she found herself willing the storm to finally breach their small town.

Not for the first time, she thought of the stranger from last week and wondered if she had imagined the depths of his eyes, the strength in his hands. Her dreams had been filled with the ghost of his touch and each morning she woke up needy and empty.

She chided herself for being disappointed each night when she scanned the room for him. She knew better, so why did his absence send a pang through her chest?

She didn't have time to think of a logical answer as a drunken Hero demanded her attention, pounding his stein on the bartop. Though there were only a few sips of ale left in the large glass, he somehow managed to spill the rest. The scene was hauntingly familiar, and her memories flashed with the countless times a puffed-up man demeaned her because of her station.

Biting her tongue, Emelle plastered a placating smile on her face and took his stein.

☽✻☾

It hadn't stopped raining for three days. Emelle cursed her three-day-younger self who'd wished for the storm to grace their village. Her leaky roof dripped in a constant, maddening pattern that she wasn't sure she'd survive with her mind intact. At least her rooms were filling up. There seemed to be more Heroes passing through than usual. A few Heroes passed through just this week.

She wasn't sure what that meant. Were the Fates not pleased enough with the hordes of Heroes they groomed?

But she continued to listen, not looking for anything in particular, but rather, to hear about life beyond her tiny village. Everyone was living out their destinies and she—A throb in her chest interrupted her thoughts. Emelle wasn't surprised at the familiar ache.

She shook her head to dispel her depressive rambling. Making her way back to the bartop, she stopped short at the familiar head of inky waves that had been the subject of her private fantasies of late. A curl—that was somehow both frustratingly adorable and incredibly attractive—fell just over his right brow.

The stranger looked up from his place at the bar, his sight crashing into hers. She inhaled sharply. Black irises searched her face, and his brows furrowed as he took in her features, though she couldn't be sure why.

Somehow, she knew she hadn't imagined his violent aura, the inhuman power that rolled off him in waves. She wasn't the only one, either: the stools on either side of the stranger remained noticeably empty. Even Olivia Sable, who was currently subjecting one of the newest Heroes to her feminine wiles, kept her distance.

As if she'd heard Emelle's thoughts, Olivia threw a wary glance at the brooding man.

Emelle closed her mouth and took a step towards the stranger—only for a jester to reach over the bar and grab her around her waist.

"'Nother ale, pretty miss," he slurred, drooping eyes focused on her chest.

Warm breath rolled over her and she fought from cringing at the foul smell. Darkness seemed to cover the tavern, candles flickering in the charged air.

"Coming right up," she responded through a tight grin, smoothly extracting herself from his hold. As she poured the ale, she glanced back at her stranger, but he was no longer looking at her.

Instead, he was glaring a hole into the side of the drunkenly oblivious jester's head. Heat gathered in her core as his jaw clenched and his fingers tapped on the bartop, seemingly in irritation. It was need, not want, that had her wishing those hands were touching her, caressing her. She wondered idly, once again, how much pain those hands had inflicted.

She also wondered how much pleasure they could wring.

A twist of irrational jealousy choked her as she thought of the other women he'd given pleasure to with those capable hands.

Cold liquid poured over the hand holding the jester's stein and she snapped back to her task. Swallowing a groan, she poured a dash out in her drain before handing the stein to the jester, who swiped it and swaggered back over to his group.

Emelle's stomach dropped as she turned back towards her stranger, only to find the stool clattering from a swift exit. Then came the slam of the tavern door.

Without thinking, Emelle rushed under the bartop after her stranger and out into the pouring rain. She spotted him walking towards the copse of pine trees that marked the last of the North Forest. As the only village in the North Forest, Silvermist was the last stop a traveler could make before entering the Wildlands. The

Finn was their last look at civilization before braving the unknown. And the misty trees the mysterious man was about to disappear into were not a place Emelle could follow.

"Wait!" she shouted towards her stranger. Clouds billowed from her mouth as she fought the chill. The intimidating man paused mid-stride, and she waited for him to turn back towards her. Involuntary shivers racked her body as the seconds dragged on, and she began to worry he wouldn't.

After what felt like an eternity, but had surely only been a few heartbeats, he glanced over his shoulder. Wet strands of her hair stuck to her face. She was already soaked to the bone. His eyes narrowed just before he turned fully and stalked up to Emelle. She swore his swift and powerful gait shook the ground.

Lightning flashed, matching the sparks that jumped through his onyx eyes. Thunder crashed, echoing the pounding of her heart that was wedged in her throat.

She couldn't comprehend why he appeared to be angry with her. She'd only spoken one word—well, *shouted* one word—but that certainly didn't warrant his reaction.

"You're just going to leave?" she demanded, feeling her anger rival his.

Spellbound, his presence commanded her attention, his features illuminated by each sporadic flash of lightning. A faint scar she wouldn't have noticed if they weren't mere breaths away slashed over his nose. Dark stubble covered his angular jaw and his pink lips were deliciously full. She wanted to feel that mouth trace over every sliver of her skin.

A familiar heat swam in her abdomen, all thoughts of the downpour vanishing as she finally gazed upon the face she'd been touching herself to for these past several days. She tried to catalog and memorize each detail in case she never saw him again.

The stranger's nostrils flared as his sight panned over her body. "That was the plan," he finally deigned to say.

"Why?" she choked out.

THE FOOL'S ERRAND

He huffed a laugh and snarked, "You have shit ale. If I wanted to drink piss, I'd find a beautiful maiden to spend my evenings with."

Emelle gaped at his blatant insinuation.

Gathering herself, she took a chance and murmured, "No—" Her heart pounded and she gulped in an attempt to wet her dry throat. "*Why did you come back*?"

Unsure if it was from the icy wind or her anxiety, Emelle's fingers trembled as she waited for her stranger to understand her question. As she silently *begged him* to understand. To understand *why* it was the most important question she could ask him in this moment.

The bottomless eyes that held her hostage and whispered of carnal promises shuttered, and she felt the first twinge of fear of rejection. Did she just give voice to a hopeful, yet *completely false,* assumption and make an incredible fool of herself? His continued silence only heightened the growing embarrassment as blood rushed to her cheeks.

She edged one foot behind her as she prepared to make her escape. Throat burning, tears threatened to fall as he continued to flay her with his piercing gaze. Just as she was about to dash into the safety of her four familiar walls, she heard his gravelly voice break through the downfall.

"Because the ale is shit…but the food is even worse."

Emelle froze as she stared back at the stranger, knowing her confusion had to be written plainly in her features. Thunder crashed—*no*, it was laughter. The sound seemed foreign coming from the large man, whose shoulders were shaking with open humor. She glanced around and back to her stranger to see what was so amusing. Her cheeks flamed even hotter as the man laughed at her. The bricks she'd removed to peer over the wall she'd built so carefully slammed back into place. She felt each one pound into the other as she turned back to her stranger.

When their gazes collided once again, she noticed he'd grown quiet, and he smirked. Realizing he had made a joke—*a terrible joke, but a joke all the same*—she paused on the final brick. A heartbeat later, and she smiled slowly. He hadn't been laughing at her expense. His eyes dropped to her mouth and darkened with apparent heat.

Probably the same heat scorching her blood, begging her to close the distance. Her very soul was pulling her towards this stranger. Steam seemed to rise from his overheated body as the rain poured even harder, and she ached to share his warmth.

Stifling her grin, his gaze slashed to hers, all levity gone. Tingles in her hands clued her in to the newly charged scene. Fates, she wanted this man. The way he captivated her focus so intensely had her body thrumming, responding to his charge without a second thought. If that was the effect of only a few moments in his presence, what could he do with a few hours?

Realizing she still hadn't spoken, her tongue darted to wet her lips before she pleaded, "Don't...don't leave. It's—" She looked pointedly up at the stormy sky. "It's pouring. And I know for a fact there's not another inn you can reach before dying of a chill."

Emelle lifted her chin, staring the man down the length of her nose as she willed herself to believe the obvious lie that she was only concerned about his welfare. "Just—just stay until it's at least light out," she finished, voice surprisingly steady despite how tight her throat felt.

Her stranger took a step closer to her, towering over her five-foot-seven frame and blocking some of the biting rain. Fates, he had to be over half a foot taller than her. She peered up at him, the heat from his proximity finally reaching her shivering body. Desire pulsed deep in her core, and she was hopeful the storm would hide the scent of her arousal. His eyes searched hers, and whatever he found in them she was grateful for as he finally responded.

An exhale, then he nodded curtly. Gravel crunched under his boots as he made his way back to The Finn, each step echoing in her pulse. Emelle turned but her feet remained fixed as his deliberate stride ate up the distance. She hadn't realized they'd strayed so far from the taver*n. Fates, she needed to sink her teeth into that ass.*

Though they'd only been outside for a few minutes, the rowdy sounds from her inebriated patrons startled her as they filtered out the door he held open, jolting her from her trance.

Emelle quickly stepped into The Finn, heat flooding her cheeks. Embarrassment forced her attention towards the rambunctious crowd as she pointedly *didn't* acknowledge the man dripping in danger as she passed him.

As she crossed the threshold, a hand landed firmly on her sternum before dragging up her neck. Steady fingers grasped her chin, turning her face towards him, and carnal heat flashed through her body at the bold move. She'd never admit it aloud, but she craved a man who could handle her cheeky attitude, who could handle *her*.

Biting the inside of her lip to conceal her reaction, her stranger lowered his mouth to her ear and purred, "Little enchantress, do not walk past me like you didn't just beg me to warm your bed tonight."

Emelle jerked herself out of his grip, face now on fire as her mortification peaked. "That is *not* what I offered, y-you presumptuous brute!" she hissed through clenched teeth, eyes darting around the room to see if anyone had heard him.

Thankfully, the crowds were entertaining themselves, with raucous songs and cheers filling the quaint room, a familiar sight for this late hour. Emelle cleared her throat and returned her attention to the tactile man.

"No..." He paused. "I suppose it wasn't." His leisurely smirk only served to bolster the false annoyance she'd plastered on, in hopes that it covered her obvious arousal.

Slipping out of his arms with the grace of a newborn fawn, Emelle steadied herself and ducked behind the bar, earning several empty steins to fill. She fought to calm her heart, which was pounding so hard it threatened to beat out of her chest. She'd deal with him later, she decided.

Chapter Five

Lars

Following his enchantress into the tavern, Lars settled in a dark corner to wait as she resumed her duties. He eyed a few particular men who dared to look at her. His eyes narrowed when one fool stared at her plump ass. Fighting to stay hidden in his shadows, Lars shoved his hands in his pockets.

He chuckled darkly to himself. If only Willam could see him now.

Lars Winter was the bastard son of the sanctimonious King Wexley Winthorpe, ruler of the Kingdom of Wellsmore. Lars had been thrown to the wolves on the morning of his ninth birthday. His father—or rather, the king who sired him through one of his concubines—decided he'd fulfilled his duty of ensuring his survival long enough, and had the castle guard drop him into the streets that fateful overcast morning. Bastards were of no use to kings.

Lars had had to learn quickly how to survive out in the open of the city he'd only ever seen from a distance, behind the safety of the castle walls, and the first several years were certainly a testament to his dedication. After witnessing some of the most heinous crimes those first few months of living on the streets, he'd shed the last of the decorum he'd been browbeaten into while living at the palace.

THE FOOL'S ERRAND

Understanding the fragility of the current system, Lars became a master at manipulation and carefully honed his infamous image, perfecting a calm facade that could make a grown man soil himself with a single raised brow. Rising through the seedy underbelly of Wellsmore, Lars had wrestled control over The Den, the secretive meeting space the amoral men of Wellsmore used as a nexus for all their shady business dealings. Anything less than legal went through him. His hands were stained from the blood he'd spilt, from the lives he'd taken, either through brute force or toppling their target's entire lives with a well-timed extortion. Most deserved his wrath, but not all. Those few haunted him still, regret burning a hole in his chest at the part he played in their demise. Willam often reminded him of their golden rule: if it wasn't the Wraith, it would be someone else. And at least he could make it quick. Most times.

It was there at The Den where Lars operated for nearly the entire next decade, leashing the disorganized network of spies into a methodized faction he'd named the Sceptres. He'd cultivated profitable trades using the West Docks to incentivize the Sceptres to carry out his vision. Mostly, Lars channeled their dangerous skills into providing enhanced protection against the rising threat the capital presented. The crown was supposed to care for its citizens, not let hunger and disease run rampant. And with the increased physical violence against the people, Lars knew change was on the horizon with each report the Sceptres brought him.

His name was feared throughout the streets of Wellsmore, partly because Lars kept his more respectable affairs covert, ulterior motives carefully woven between dual-purposed orders. But mainly for his lethal abilities that he'd never shied away from demonstrating. For his unique abilities to slink into the shadows and remain impassive against any threat.

The Wraith of Wells, they called him.

His blank mask in the face of such morbidity was legendary across the kingdom. He'd never had an issue keeping his composure.

Until now.

The drunkards who sloshed over to his little enchantress, raking their filthy gaze over her unblemished skin, had his murderous hands curling into fists. Lars had to physically stop himself from eliminating one particular man, who was obviously not getting the hint from his barkeep that she wasn't interested. Shadows seeped from him, his control on them slipping.

As the evening finally came to an end, Lars stuck to the walls of the tavern, watching from the shadows as emerald eyes carefully scanned the darkness before pausing in his direction. Even from across the room, he saw them widen as she clocked his presence.

He was sure she had thought he'd left.

A light blush crept onto her cheekbones and Lars was enraptured. He wondered how he could make her whole body flush. *Oh, little enchantress, you are going to be such a joy to unravel.*

As if she'd heard his thoughts, she smiled timidly before she turned to her final patrons. The storm continued to thrash outside as she mindlessly poured one fool's ale and accepted his payment. Her hands slid along the bar, and she tucked the coin into her pocket with a barely visible flick of her wrist. A flash of a flirty smile towards the fool had the man flipping another coin onto the bar, which she collected promptly and moved on silent feet to her final patron. Lars was captivated as she completed even the most mundane of tasks. She was intelligent, and it was clear she hid it behind her mask of naivety. Only every now and again did he see a spark of agitation peek through her guise, but she hid it well.

He remained still, fighting against the urge to stalk across the room and seize the woman for himself. Only a few words were exchanged outside, but even in the storm he'd been consumed by the pull begging him to close the distance. His heart had thundered in his chest—an organ he'd thought was long dead—beating in time with the thrumming of her pulse. She'd been just as affected and her desire sang to him.

Moving with a savvy efficiency, she was almost ready to make her escape when the last of the steins were emptied. As he'd noted she did every night, his barkeep ushered those who were staying to the stairs and kicked the rest out.

Lars felt his trousers grow uncomfortably tight as she barked orders at the drunken men. What did he have to do to get her to bark at him like that?

Once the door shut behind the last man, his barkeep locked the door and slunk over to where Lars still reclined against a suspiciously damaged wall. She was flushed, and he couldn't help but innocuously sniff the air.

Despite their unintended shower in the downpour outside, Lars detected her clean sweat and a heady desire separate from his own. Stopping directly in front of him, the barkeep propped her hands on her lush hips and lifted her chin as she waited for...*something* from Lars.

Lightning flashed, briefly illuminating the dark space between them. He swore he saw more than heat simmering in her gaze.

"I think this is the part where you take me to bed, princess," he murmured suggestively, hoping to distract her from looking at him too critically. He'd already felt the stirrings in his soul, telling him to claim this inquisitive little enchantress all for himself.

He couldn't fight the pull *alone*.

A quiet scoff parted her lips and a sculpted eyebrow quirked in annoyance. "'Princess?'" she volleyed. "Not even going to ask for my name?" Curiosity dripped through her tenor. The storm continued to rage outside, but neither paid it any mind.

Lars wasn't sure how to respond when the answer was so glaringly obvious that he was too caught up in *her* to pay attention to anything else. Hell, he'd chased after two leads that he'd mixed the details on because his eyes couldn't leave her far too tempting hands wiping the bartop, or her bound breasts straining against her top, or the way her hair dampened with sweat from exertion. He hadn't been able to help imagining what other kinds of exertion would be far more rewarding for the both of them. The way she was generous and hid her intelligence behind a wall of naivety. The way her brows furrowed when she got lost in her mind. She was...captivating.

He'd found himself stuck in the middle of the Wildlands empty-handed, miserably waiting for a storm to pass before making his way back to the same damned tavern in hopes of trying again.

A foolish idea, he realized.

She didn't know that her presence demanded every morsel of attention he had and that he *still* didn't have anything to go on.

"Emelle," she stated plainly, extending her hand towards Lars.

He took in her soft features that starkly rivaled the spirit he'd seen come out to play a few times tonight, as her name settled deep into his soul.

"Emelle," he repeated, low and deep, just to see how she'd react. "Emmy...I like it."

She blushed prettily as her damp hair curled around her shoulders.

"Lars," he supplied, straightening his posture and capturing her hand to shake as he introduced himself to his future wife.

Was he delusional? Sure. Look at what he was doing, trying to weave his own destiny. Was that going to stop him from claiming this woman one day? Not a chance in the cosmos.

Emelle's head tilted as she scanned his body once more before her eyes came to rest over his heart, where the lack of emblem was glaringly obvious. His leathers warmed, as if aware of her scrutiny. A twinge of shame over his birth status bubbled in his chest, one he hadn't felt in a while. Ignoring the unspoken question, Lars cleared his throat and angled his head towards the stairs.

"Listen, darling," he drawled. "I would love nothing more than to follow you up those stairs again and fulfill *every* fantasy running through your mind right now, but you're dead on your feet. What I have in mind is going to take much longer than you can handle tonight."

Emelle's blush spread to her chest, but she didn't try to deny the desires that he so openly acknowledged. Nor did she appear to notice his slip. Lars looked pointedly at their hands, still joined, which spurred his lovely enchantress to jump and withdraw. A sharp ache in his chest told him he should've dragged her up those steps without letting go.

"Right. Let me go check my ledger. Wait here," she instructed, her eyes scanning him once more, before shuffling towards a small office at the back of the main room, twisting the knob with nimble fingers.

Disregarding her adorable attempt at ordering him, Lars instead followed her on silent feet. Entering only a few steps behind her, he watched her grab a large book that had seen better days off an overflowing desk. He stifled a chuckle as an amusing furrow deepened her brows when she found the correct date and scanned the page.

Her teeth bit the corner of her plump bottom lip in an attempt to veil her thoughts. But a few moments later, she released the offending flesh, a sigh escaping as she looked back at Lars. His enchantress finally spoke, breaking the charged silence.

"You'll have your own room at the end of the corridor on the second floor. Last door on the right. Breakfast is served from seven 'til eight, and since I'm closing up, you'll need to tell me now if you'll be taking it in your room." Her eyes sparked with an emotion he couldn't decipher quickly enough before it vanished.

"I'll be down," he responded gruffly. Like fuck would he leave her down here on her own after the behavior he witnessed tonight. Breakfast was usually a milder event, but those still drunk from the previous night could always make an unwelcome appearance.

Something akin to approval glimmered in her eyes as she nodded.

Retrieving a key from her skirts, she unlocked a drawer under her desk and scanned the contents until she found his room key. He let their fingers brush as he took the key, before tucking it in his pocket, watching her eyes widen in surprise.

"Lead the way," he prompted.

Chapter Six
Emelle

Stupid. She was *so incredibly stupid*. Her booking ledger was *almost* full. Emelle could have easily lied and said that the only room available was hers. It was the only bed she wanted him in, after all. Frustrated with herself, Emelle stood frozen in the hall as she stared at the closed door that Lars had shut on his way in without a backwards glance.

She hadn't been surprised he disregarded her order by following her into her office, but she wished her bravado hadn't disappeared as soon as his staggering presence filled all of the empty space in the room.

Never having been a good liar, Emelle had reluctantly offered up the truth that she had a room for him at the end of the hall—on the opposite wing from her own.

Like she said, *stupid*.

A muted groan escaped as she stomped her heel on the floor, her irritation spiking. Turning, she left his hall and made her way to her room on soft feet. She quickly changed into her night shift and brushed her hair before washing her face and mouth.

Evie hopped onto Emelle's cot and circled the same spot a few times before snuggling into herself. Placing some more food down for her furry friend before she forgot—not that the small creature would let her—Emelle lifted the covers and curled up next to her baby. Chuckling to the painfully empty room, she knew Greer would have had a field day with Emelle's stranger.

Lifting her fingers to her nose, Emelle inhaled deeply as thoughts of Lars overwhelmed her senses. His cedarwood and cypress scent lingered, and a tingle from the ghost of his fingers gripping her chin earlier burned with a low heat as though she could still feel his touch. Grumbling to the darkness, she did her best to ignore the growing dampness between her legs. Several minutes passed, and as she finally drifted off in slumber, she could've sworn she heard a muffled groan from down the hall.

☽✳☾

Preparing the same breakfast as always—the revolving door of guests ensured no one was complaining of a repeated menu—Emelle braced herself for seeing Lars. Would he come down already bathed and prepared to leave?

A spike of anxiety gripped her, but she forced herself to dismiss the question. No, she'd stop him if he tried. Would he sit down for breakfast and watch her as she ran food up and down the stairs? *Oh Fates, please don't trip,* please *don't trip.*

Emelle couldn't fathom why he had returned to The Finn, but she couldn't deny she was glad. She certainly wasn't going to kick him out anytime soon.

Grabbing several plates, Emelle stepped out of the kitchen and towards the stairs. But with quick reflexes only cultivated from a lifetime of working in the tavern, she stopped short right before crashing into a generously tall man.

The same generously tall man who had invaded her dreams last night, over and over.

He smirked, gaze dipping to the plates in her hands. "Need some help?" Lars asked impishly.

Emelle's eyes rolled in jest, returning his playful banter. "Yes, I do, in fact. I need you to *move*."

A spark flashed in his dark eyes, and Emelle began to lose herself in their depths. Rough chuckles rumbled out of his chest as he dipped his chin to hide his obvious amusement, and stepped aside.

Twinkling a smile up at him, she purred, "How gallant," and swept past him for the stairs.

"It won't always be that easy, princess."

Emelle paused on the first step, doing her best to ignore the nickname that unleashed ridiculous butterflies in her chest. He'd called her that last night, too. Steadying herself with a breath, she tilted her head towards the confusing man, brows raised to prompt him to elaborate.

A beat later, his dark eyes sparkled with apparent heat. "To command me, of course. You'll have to bark a lot harsher than that, Emmy."

Emelle's pulse accelerated as hazy images of her bending his imposing frame to her will, again and again and *again*, filled her head. Clearing her throat against the sudden desire, she merely hummed and hurried up the stairs.

After she returned to the kitchen, Emelle finished up the last few plates that were thankfully just going to one of the communal tables. All the while, she couldn't resist sneaking glances at Lars to reassure herself he was still there. He chose a seat in the back corner, opting to sit at a table by himself. She wasn't altogether surprised. He seemed the type to prefer being alone. And while there weren't quite *shadows* this early in the morning, somehow he remained cloaked in relative darkness. *How was that possible?*

A disturbing cough broke through her thoughts as a man choked on his food. His buddy slapped his back and the fool coughed up a chunk of potato, before popping it back in to chew again. Her upper lip curled. She turned back to her stranger, but Emelle found him missing once again. She groaned.

How does this keep happening?

A flickering light under the closed door of her office captured her attention. Placing her tray down on the nearest table, Emelle swiftly made her way over. She had a sneaking suspicion as to who was inside.

Opening the door slowly, Emelle peeked into her small office and spotted her intruder hunched over her desk, flipping through her ledger as if it *were* his own. Pushing the door the rest of the way open with a little too much force, Emelle crossed her arms over her chest. His hard gaze snapped to hers at the *slam* before he deflated imperceptibly.

"This isn't my room," Lars said roguishly with a sly grin, the lit candle on her desk now casting a warm glow against his suntanned skin.

"Why are you in my office?" Emelle asked, keeping her voice unaffected, as if it was no concern of hers. A singularly raised brow was the only indication she was bothered.

Dropping the thick ledger onto her overflowing desk, Lars straightened to his full, intimidating height. As the moments stretched in deafening silence, Emelle could only focus on the blood rushing in her ears and her quickened breathing. She began to draw wild conclusions as his gaze bored into her, seemingly sizing her up.

Just how dangerous was Lars? What—or who—was he looking for? And why was he looking at her like he wanted to eat her?

Chapter Seven
Lars

For the briefest moment, Lars was discouraged by Emelle's automatic retreat behind the wall she'd so carefully crafted. Last night, she'd peeked over the barrier, her curiosity winning over her apprehension. And while the brow she raised only served to deepen her thrall over him, he could admit he was hurt that she'd be so rash to judge him.

Unfortunately, her concerns weren't unfounded.

Lars weighed the benefits of telling this beguiling enchantress the truth. Her chest rose and fell faster with each breath, her panic visibly rising. Needing to calm her down, Lars gave a truth. Not his truth, but someone's truth.

"An old friend of mine left for his destiny," he began, the half-truth easy, "and I later heard from his mother that he planned to travel through Silvermist in search of his trial. He left a little over five months ago and I haven't seen him since."

Lars kept his expression carefully guarded. He hoped she would believe his words. "I've searched every village from my kingdom through all the Woodlands, and yet I haven't found any record of him even *making* it to Mistwood." Not exactly a lie: he did stop in the smaller towns on his way to check how far the rot had spread.

Soft eyes filled with pity met his. Most Heroes completed their trials within a month or two, at the latest, so she'd understand why he was worried.

"I would have preferred you ask for my help," she began, but stepped into the room to join him at her desk. Picking up the worn ledger, Emelle thumbed to five months ago. "But I'm happy to help with your search. What's his name?"

Lars sucked in a breath, somehow surprised by her innocent compassion. After he rambled off a name of an old acquaintance, his little enchantress scanned each line. But after only checking a handful of pages, she glanced up and visibly floundered with what to say.

"There's just...so many entries. This could take several days to get through," she murmured, a whisper of excitement he couldn't place lacing her words. No, that couldn't be right. Why would she be excited to spend days pouring over her booking ledger with him?

Nodding, Lars feigned reluctant understanding. "I can wait," he assured, despite the time crunch he was under. Abrupt satisfaction shone on her face before she schooled her features.

"We can look through the ledger after I finish my closing duties each night, if you agree?" she offered. "These are confidential files, though, so don't go ruffling through it again without my explicit approval." Emelle propped her hands on her plump hips, the picture of authority as a brow lifted in challenge.

Lars hid any hint of amusement. Any spare moment he could spend in his enchantress's presence he would take, greedy to just breathe the same air as her.

"It's a date," Lars said as he flashed bright teeth.

A matching grin fought past Emelle's adorable authoritative mask and he was, once again, stunned at her beauty. This close to her, he could see the rosy blush staining her cheeks in vivid detail.

Lars cataloged her long lashes framing eyes that shone with his new favorite color, and ached to feel her smooth skin. Needing to collect himself, he nodded once more before making his escape through the still-open door.

Leaving the tavern entirely, Lars lifted his face to the sunny sky and wondered when the storm broke.

Chapter Eight
Emelle

After being consumed by the sight of Lars's strong form and firm ass as he left her office—did his dark trousers have to cling so very tightly to every dip and curve while his black tunic with its sleeves rolled to his elbows have to showcase his powerful forearms?—Emelle busied herself with cleaning the tavern, washing the endless dirty dishes after the breakfast crowd filtered out. Her mind wandered as she scrubbed dish after dish in her soapy basin. After drying the final bowl, Emelle pushed out into the main room of the bar.

In the corner of her eye, she begrudgingly spotted Lonnie Leon, a boy from her village that she'd once naively thought she might build a life with.

A few days after giving him her maidenhead, Greer informed Emelle that she'd overheard Lonnie admit to his friend that she was just a fling. She'd long since gotten over the heartbreak, but sometimes she wished she'd saved her first time for someone who could at least make her see the cosmos.

Ducking out of Lonnie's view, Emelle moved towards her office, wanting to thumb through the ledger for a few minutes before she had to start on her next chores.

"Ellie, wait!"

She hated that he still used her childhood nickname. Only Greer and her father were allowed to call her that. Thinking of how Lars had called her Emmy, her heartbeat accelerated.

She quickened her pace, but his long legs caught up to her in just a few strides. She didn't even attempt to mask her annoyance.

His toothy smile dropped slightly before he spoke. "Hi, uh...Ellie. I've been meaning to catch you, but I can never seem to find you."

Of course you haven't, but have you ever stopped to think as to why *you haven't seen me?* Emelle wanted to say.

She didn't give him the satisfaction of a response. Even though she no longer held anger towards Lonnie, that certainly didn't mean she needed to give him any grace.

He searched her face, and whatever he didn't find seemed to crush the last of his hope. His shoulders slumped, but he still said, "I'd heard from Isla that you were running yourself ragged trying to manage this entire place."

Her jaw dropped sharply before snapping shut. The mention of Greer's mother sent a slash of pain through her chest. She hadn't seen her in a few weeks, too busy with The Finn to check in with her. But apparently Isla had seen her.

"Are you *seriously* telling me I look like a hag right now?" Emelle asked through clenched teeth.

Realizing his error, a sheen of sweat beaded along Lonnie's hairline. "No—no, I'm sorry, that didn't come out right," he said before looking away and mumbling faintly under his breath. Then he shook his head and amended: "I just meant, I wanted to see if you needed any help. Ever since Greer left, the village has seen you less each month and we're starting to worry."

"*We're* starting to worry, or *you're* starting to worry?" Emelle challenged with a raised brow, anger mounting with each second in his presence.

"The town, Ellie, I swear," Lonnie pleaded, hands raised pleadingly. "My mother wanted me to talk to you because..." A pause. "Because she was hoping you might hire my little sister."

She blinked, surprised, even as her heart tugged at the thought of Janie. To Emelle, Janie would probably forever be the ten-year-old girl with the freckled nose and toothy grin who liked to spy on Lonnie and Emelle after their classes were finished each day. She supposed Janie had to be in her early twenties now.

"Why does Janie want to work here?" Emelle asked.

Lonnie grimaced as he stared down at his feet. "Uh, well..." He paused again. "She doesn't."

"Well then why—" she started before he interrupted her, suddenly finding his spine again.

"You haven't visited Meggie's Place recently, have you?" he asked through gritted teeth. Meggie's was a smaller tavern on the southern outskirts of Silvermist. It had always garnered a tougher crowd, but never anything actually harmful. *How much had changed while she'd been lost to her grief and loneliness?*

At the sound of his sudden fury towards Meggie, Emelle regretted her recent decision to stay as reclusive as possible after Greer left to avoid the intrusive eyes of the village. Growing up side by side in Silvermist for almost thirty years would certainly be an excuse for nosy neighbors to try and glean some juicy gossip from Greer's departure. Emelle couldn't handle the stares, the whispers, the *questions.*

"No. I haven't," she rasped, trying not to voice the full weight of the shame that just slammed into her.

A cruel laugh she'd never heard from him before escaped his chest, as he propped one hand on his hip. The other reached up to pinch the bridge of his nose. "It's horrible, Ellie. The men..." He drifted off, amber eyes cloudy, as if he remembered some painful memory. "She needs to get out."

The mere thought was enough to compel her. She could afford a small wage to bring on some help, especially now that Greer was gone, and it wasn't like she really got paid anyways. Dipping her head in agreement, she conceded.

"Bring her by at six," Emelle said. "Let's see how she does with the dinner crowd."

Chapter Nine

Lars

Lars spent the unusually bright day touring the various establishments in Silvermist. So far, he'd perused a quaint market that held a few scattered vendors, one which sold books and wax candles, and another that sold fabrics and dyes. As he rounded the village, he also visited a butcher, a carpentry shop, and even passed by a small school that was currently in session. He'd hoped that the sun's appearance meant people would resume their normal routine.

He was right.

He still hadn't heard anything helpful, though not for lack of trying.

Leaving a small bakery, Lars gripped a bag of warm apple pastries he was told the entire village favored. He hoped that meant Emelle would too. Why he was buying her pastries, he wasn't entirely sure. He just knew he wanted to bask in another one of her magnetic smiles.

Truly, a purely selfish move.

Dusk had fallen about a half hour ago, so Lars made his way back to the tavern. He was certain things were picking up for Emelle and wanted to make sure he could keep a watchful eye on the men in the room. He didn't trust the pompous fools.

Slowing right before he opened the door, Lars cleared any lingering emotion from his face and opened the creaking wood. The offended screech surprised him, and Lars glanced at the rusted hinges, brows furrowing. He scanned the tavern, noticing details he'd missed before. Stained floors were hidden by large tables and worn rugs, while tapestries and odd art tactfully covered the cracked walls, with only the edges peeking out from under their coverings. It seemed repairs fell at the bottom of Emelle's list of priorities.

Dismissing the desperately needed maintenance for now, Lars ambled to the bar. His little enchantress hadn't spotted him yet as she filled several steins on the far end. Gently setting the bag of pastries on the wooden surface, he leaned one arm against the ledge, settling in to wait for his personalized service.

A *slap* of the swinging kitchen door to the right of the bar forced his attention away from his barkeep. A young woman walked behind the station, drying her hands on a discolored rag. Her brown hair was twisted into a braid that draped over her shoulder, nearly touching her waist. Her eyes were wary as she returned to work, scanning the bartop. Noticing her newest patron, the young woman subtly shifted her features into a coy mask as she looked him over. Lars cringed internally for what he knew was to follow.

She approached him seductively, moving her hips with an alluring swish that likely would've worked on any other man but him.

"Welcome to The Finn," she charmed, batting her dark lashes at him. Lars politely nodded back.

Glancing over to his little enchantress, he saw he now had her full attention. Still holding Emelle's gaze, Lars whipped out his most charming smile before turning back to the newcomer.

"Sorry, young one. I'm spoken for," he whispered with a wink.

Before the new barkeep could respond, Emelle appeared at her side and rattled an order that had the young woman's ears reddening at the chiding.

"Why are you flirting with my new barkeep?" Emelle gritted

through clenched teeth, as soon as the new barkeep went to help someone else, eyes sparking with vivid envy.

A chuckle fell from Lars. "Is my little enchantress jealous?"

Unable to hold his gaze, her eyes darted away before landing on the pastry bag. Her brows rose.

Not allowing the embarrassment over her shameless jealousy—which he quite enjoyed—he lifted her chin with his fingers and forced her to look at him. Searching her face, all humor left him at the sight of her thinly veiled fear.

"She certainly tried. She wasn't aware it was a pointless endeavor," he murmured. Let her draw her own conclusions.

Emelle ignored the calls for refills as she returned his assessment, taking in his words. Sound filtered out as onyx eyes met emerald. As she tried to turn her head, his fingers tightened to stop the movement, hazy shadows wrapping around them to offer the illusion of privacy. Emelle searched at them with open curiosity, but there was a hint of unease. No one else paid them any mind.

A question formed in her gaze and he dropped his hand to pick up the pastries. "I brought you a treat," he said with a sugary smirk.

Taking the bag from Lars, she peeked inside and a squeal escaped her perfect lips. Childlike wonder sparkling back at him, she opened her mouth before closing it just as quickly.

"These—" She cleared her throat. "These are my favorite. My best friend saved all year when we were kids just to buy me one for my birthday. I had them every year until..." She choked, pausing to take a breath.

A watery smile, then she continued, voice so soft he had to strain to hear her over the noise of her patrons. "Until this year. Greer moved away when her Hero finished his trial and found her. I haven't seen her in a little over four months." Her voice tapered as she finished. Sadness gripped him as he vowed to reunite Emelle with her chosen sister.

"Go," he ordered with a nod to the kitchen.

Emelle appeared confused, her brows adorably furrowing. "Eat it while it's still fresh," he instructed with a flash of teeth, challenging her to defy his order.

"I need to help Janie, it's only her first night," she argued feebly with a frown. Looking over in tandem, Lars dispelled his shadows as the young woman refilled steins and chatted with a few jesters. Clearly, she was capable of handling the bar for a few minutes. They both looked back at each other and his world slowed to a crawl as a small grin replaced her frown. As she hurried to the kitchen, Lars chuckled as he saw her tear into the bag.

Fates, he would do questionable things just to keep that light on her face.

Turning back to survey the tavern, he realized they'd been lost in their own little bubble. Covering his dopey smile with a blank look, Lars's blood rushed at the sight of a fool who stepped towards her, daring to stare at his little enchantress's ass as she retreated. The fool must've sensed his furious gaze, visibly gulping before returning to his group. His wisest decision so far. Lars stood and found a dim corner to listen from, keeping a vigilant eye on the group of drunk men at the bar.

☽✷☾

Watching Emelle round up the drunkards must have induced a chemical reaction for how considerably it affected him. He couldn't stop picturing her using that sharp tongue on him. A shiver rolled down his back as she locked the tavern door and passed right by him.

Emerging from the shadows, he fell into step with her. By her lack of reaction, he realized she must've known where he was—expected him, even. He wasn't sure why this comforted him.

Lars followed her into her small office and paused as she sat, noting a stool that must've been brought in from the bar across from her desk. Eyeing the weakened wood, Lars pointedly met Emelle's bold challenge. *Really?* he questioned with a raised brow. She barked a laugh but conceded, getting up to switch.

Lars marveled at their silent exchange. Most men balked at his stern looks, and this stunning enchantress just laughed in his face. Needing something, needing *more*, Lars crowded into her space and leaned over her body, wiping his thumb across her bottom lip where a few sugar crystals from the earlier sweet still sat. *Fates, was he envious of sugar now, too?*

Capturing her gaze, he brought his thumb to his mouth, parting his lips slightly as he slowly dragged the digit across his tongue. The temperature in the room rose with each heartbeat, sweat beading along the back of his neck. Her delectable lips parted in surprise as he sucked lightly on the pad of his thumb. Heady arousal bloomed in the small space, the scent making his mouth water and fingers tingle to touch her unblemished skin again. To trace every inch of her flesh with his tongue.

Stifling a groan, Lars let the bold move linger for a moment, before retreating with a wink to her chair, allowing her a moment to compose herself. He needed a moment himself as well. Lars willed his cock to soften, sending thin shadows to cover his groin.

Clearing her throat, Emelle finally spoke. "I've been thinking about this all day and I had an idea that might help us narrow down where to look," she started.

Allowing her obvious attempt at defusing the heated tension, Lars immediately became ravenous to learn how his little enchantress's brain worked.

He leaned forward, placing his forearms on her desk and clasped his hands, the picture of dutiful listening, and waited for her to continue. Pink crept onto her cheekbones, likely from the weight of his undivided attention, when she spoke next.

"If you know what his trial was, I may be able to cross-reference the specific challenge with fewer dates. It will probably still take a few days, but I think it could be faster than going through every page."

Surprise and desperate hope flashed through him. Lars thought how to carefully ask his questions without scaring her, but after her open generosity, he knew he wouldn't be able to lie to her for much longer. Something about the trust etched over her face compounded the crushing guilt he already felt. He needed to be quick about it, or risk damaging something irreparable.

He deliberately picked his words. "I don't know what his trial was. How would knowing help narrow down the dates?" His vision tunneled as he waited for her answer with bated breath. The room darkened imperceptibly as he lost hold of his shadows.

Her chin dipped, clearly not comfortable with sharing her hidden talents, gaze darting around the dimming room. "No one notices me, you know?" she whispered with a sad air of finality. Not giving him a chance to object, she continued. "I've worked in this tavern my whole life. Ever since I could remember, I've roamed these halls. I know where every squeaky step is. I know exactly how long it takes to scrub every square inch. I've heard every story you could ever imagine."

His ears perked as she spoke, sight now unfocused, staring blankly at the cracked wall behind him. Memories played behind her misty emeralds. He swore even the crickets stopped chirping, as though they were also waiting for what she was to say next.

"They used to fascinate me, you know? I'd head to bed before my parents even had to ask, always so eager for the next day because every dawn brought new Heroes sharing exciting tales of their adventures."

She smiled sadly as she took a moment to collect herself. "The appeal wears off after you realize the stories are all recycled. The Heroes are always the same self-absorbed men, and the only difference between them and the jesters and fools is that the Fates said so."

Lars couldn't help but agree. He was all too aware of how unbalanced the Fates left things.

"Anyways, I don't want to bore you with the details, but—"

"Who told you your details were boring?" he interrupted sharply, wanting a list of names.

Emelle visibly floundered.

Cocking his head, Lars continued: "Details are what make life so vivid. They are the distinction between emotions, the difference between a breath taken and a breath stolen. Do you look at a painting and dismiss the shadows creating contrast? Without details, everything would be so incredibly *boring*." Watching her closely, he dropped his voice barely above a whisper as his eyes dipped to her mouth.

"Show me your details, Emmy. I want to know them all." Snapping his gaze back to hers, he watched her pupils dilate in response.

Gulping, Emelle nodded. The low light of the dying candle flickered across her nerve-wracked face. Despite never having been known for his compassion, it was all Lars could do to keep his rough hands to himself, when he desperately wanted to reach across to offer his silent support.

"I hear everything," she admitted quietly. He'd suspected as much. "I think people have gotten so used to me floating around, or maybe I've just gotten used to being a ghost..." A careful pause as her head tilted. A lock of her strawberry hair fell forward, escaping from behind her ear. She didn't seem to notice it. He wanted to wrap those strands around his fist.

"As I got older, my teenage mind was too curious for my own good and I just *had* to know what my parents were always fighting about. Grandmother had been gone for a year or so at this point, and it was just me left with parents who seemed to forget I was still just a child."

A brief hesitation, before she scoffed, irritation laid bare at the years-old invisible injury. "Looking back, it's so comical how unoriginal the fights were: money and the tavern. So I learned where all the creaks were, *precisely* where to step to remain hidden, and I spied on my parents for so long that I knew they were separating before even they did."

His heart ached for the brave woman in front of him forced to watch her family crumble at such a vulnerable age.

"All I ever wanted was more siblings, a bigger family. They were so young when they had me that Mom wanted another child too, but my parents said she couldn't get pregnant again...Looking back, I think they realized that a baby wasn't going to fix things. But I had Greer, so it was going to be fine. *I* was going to be fine." Emelle's breath quivered as she paused and Lars couldn't take it any longer.

Reaching across the small desk, he plucked her hand from her lap and grasped it tightly. Her emerald eyes pleaded with him to hear her unspoken words. Tears shone, threatening to spill over.

She sniffled, using her free sleeve to wipe her cheeks. Red rimmed her lids and Lars hated the sight. "Anyways, I found comfort in listening to the adventures again. In the escape they offered me. I'd always tracked the trials and stories with little symbols I made up, a fun little game for me to play, but then I started to write down more. More detail, more of the adventure. That was how I realized just how similar each trial was.

"Much to my father's dismay, I used the booking ledger to scribble stories in the margins. A way to keep track of which Hero had which trial. Stories of the lives lived outside these village borders..." The faraway look on her face was like a dagger to his heart. "As a way to keep myself sane, to escape from this reality when all I felt was..." She stopped, eyes glazed over, lost in the past and Lars wasn't sure she'd continue. He couldn't help but feel like this was only a part of her story. That she'd left some crucial details out.

Realizing she was finished for the night, Lars cleared his throat and spoke for the first time in what seemed like hours. "Thank you. For trusting me." Lowering the veil he kept so tightly wound, he let her peer directly into his soul.

Earning people's trust was rare, having worked with so many deplorables for so long. To have trust so freely given was a breath of fresh air when he didn't even know he was drowning. A hand offered in salvation. The only absolution he'd ever seek out, despite being wholly and uncomfortably aware that he didn't deserve an ounce of mercy.

Her sight focused once again as she took in his open face. A timid grin, quirking the corners of her mouth, and he knew he never wanted to see this woman hurt again.

☽✲☾

Over the next several nights, Lars met Emelle after she closed The Finn to pore over her ledger. Even knowing he was running against an unforgiving clock, he found himself willing the Fates to slow the turning of the earth, so he could soak up as many moments with this curious enchantress as he could.

Lars could tell she was beginning to get frustrated as they searched endlessly for his "friend," who he knew wouldn't be in her ledger. Often, they got caught up in her retellings of each story. Late nights bled into early mornings as she answered all of his curious questions. She'd been right when she said they were practically all variations of each other. These Heroes raced after beasts of mythical proportions, slaying creatures they had no business fighting on their own. Crowns weren't the only trophy they earned after completing their trial; scars littered their bodies, too many close calls somehow dodged in time.

The lucky Heroes only had to find a piece of parchment, though many went mad searching for the scroll. They scoured the earth for the damn riddles only to wax poetry to the skies. And the missing women...Lars wasn't sure how that many could disappear without some concern from the public. Though most were found, he supposed.

And while the details varied, the bones remained the same. Many trials were found in the Wildlands, and the Heroes crossed into Eralyn from *Fates knew where,* passing through Mistwood in search of their quest. Lars wished he knew why trials were required before ascending a throne, but Emelle had no answer for him. It was simply what was done.

Lars was often drawn to her mouth as she spun each story, a lustful haze taking control of his mind as he fell captive to the lithe movements of her plush lips.

And Fates, he loved watching her mouth move.

Most evenings, Lars carefully angled his body so his hardened cock went without notice.

He was pretty sure she saw anyway.

With each sleepless night, he learned much more from her than he ever could from merely listening in the rowdy tavern on his own. Locations, hurdles, strategies...There was no end to the revelry the Heroes spun, jesters and fools hanging onto every word, but Emelle's knowledge and decade's worth of stories was invaluable.

"Are we sure he even had a destiny?" Lars asked incredulously. He didn't understand how the supposed Hero-to-be couldn't navigate the obvious traps around the sky-high tower that held his missing princess who'd been stolen away in the dead of night. By all accounts, the woman was better off without him if he couldn't do something as simple as scale the stone wall and dodge a few well-timed arrows.

Emelle sipped from her stein, a drop trickling down to her cleavage as if inviting Lars's eyes to follow it. Lars did as invited, his trousers growing uncomfortably tight. Jerking his gaze back to Emelle, she smirked. He'd been caught. He didn't care.

In fact...Lars took a long drink from his stein, spilling a little over his chin. Using his sleeve, Lars slowly wiped his arm across his face, never breaking eye contact. Emelle's pulse quickened as she flicked her tongue over her bottom lip, as if daring him to look at it, to imagine what it might taste like.

"Princess?" Lars asked innocently.

A beautiful blush crept over her cheekbones, and with the candlelight flickering against her smooth skin, Lars felt himself falling.

"Yes?" she asked, holding his gaze.

"Did he have a destiny?" he repeated, carefully enunciating each word.

Emelle shook herself and her elbow knocked onto the armrest of her new—to her—chair. She hissed an obscenity under her breath, rubbing at the joint as her eyes closed briefly. She'd brought the chair in a few nights ago after Lars had told her a simple stool was not fit for a princess. Emelle had just rolled her eyes, but the next day a dusty, though comfortable, armchair sat behind her desk. Her old office chair—which was still an upgrade from the weakened barstools—was now placed in front of her desk. She insisted on switching every other night, refusing to keep the comfortable chair to herself.

"I was shocked too, but yes, he had a destiny. And he'd better thank the Fates every day for how much they probably had to help him." Her adorable laugh wobbled out of her throat, making him wonder just how much she'd had to drink. He'd been too busy indulging in her thrall to keep track.

He knew it meant she trusted him. That she felt safe with him. It was something he wouldn't waste. He would protect her, no matter what it took.

"The Fates helped him?" he asked, curious to hear more.

She nodded, tucking her hair behind one ear. "Many Heroes claim they'd be nudged in a certain direction, claim they've been more clever, more savvy. Some even said they'd been saved from fatal wounds by ducking out of the way at the last second." Emelle didn't sound as if she believed the testimony. Lars couldn't blame her. He wasn't sure how much he believed it, either.

"How did he know where to find her?"

Emelle tilted her head in thought as she took another sip of her ale. "I don't know," she finally said. "They feel it in their gut, I suppose. Where to go, what to do…That must be the Fates as well…" She trailed off, lost in thought.

"If I listened to every gut feeling I had," Lars mused, "that first night I saw you would've ended *much* differently."

Emelle's eyes sparked with hunger. But she merely plucked a nut out of the bowl she'd been snacking and tossed it at his head. Lars caught it out of the air with a click of his teeth.

"So they *can* learn new tricks," she jested, falling into drunken laughter as mirth filled the space between them.

Lars rolled his eyes dramatically. "Princess, I have a whole bag of tricks I can't wait to share with you." He flashed his teeth in a bright smile, enjoying the way she reddened. "I also take requests." Tension crackled in the air.

"Requests, hm?" she hummed.

Lars just smirked, a raised brow his only response. Emelle laughed sharply, leaning forward ever so slightly, and Lars mimicked the motion without a second thought, as if anchored in her trance.

"I'll believe it when I see it." She winked and smiled coyly.

He lost it. Lars shook with laughter and Emelle joined in, the tension between them yielding to a different sort of intimacy. When was the last time he joked and laughed so freely? With someone who truly saw him, no less? Someone who peeled back the mask he donned as the Wraith and wasn't afraid by what they saw beneath?

Emelle smiled back at him, and he was sucked back in. Once again, Lars's gaze dropped to her mouth and he couldn't help but imagine how she tasted.

But a breath later, Emelle just shook herself, quickly returning to their earlier conversation.

"With only royals receiving a prophecy, it's been…difficult to get a clear understanding how they obtain them. They're not very forthcoming with that part of their story. They come far and wide from places I've never heard of, but from the bits and pieces I've gathered, it's like a vision they have sometime in their twenties. The Fates spin a story in their dreams, and they have to complete their quest. If they don't, they have to abdicate their crown to the next in line. And apparently"—Emelle hiccupped, the ale beginning to go to her head—"they nudge them towards their success. The Fates help them kill those awful beasts, solve impossible riddles, rescue a questionable number of missing women."

Lars chuckled, enjoying drunk Emelle. She was rather cute with her flushed skin and wet lips, and it was all too tempting to reach for her. He had to clench his hands into fists to hold himself back from gripping her neck, no matter how much he ached to pull her body against his.

"And?" Lars prodded, hoping she'd keep talking. He wasn't sure if he sought more information, or if he merely wanted to listen to her voice.

"Well." She straightened in her chair. "For example, the Cosmic Fates are the only ones who can slay the celestial beasts, so they offer a drop of their power to the Heroes to allow them to do so in their stead. But I also know the Heroes have to wash their blade with blessed water from a nearby grove, praying to the Fates to cleanse the weapon." She scoffed, as if the mere idea of praising the Fates was laughable. "The hardened, leathery skin of the celestial beasts are impenetrable without the Hero performing the cleansing rite. If you don't wait for the cleanse to take effect, you're as good as dead. You should hear how the Heroes talk about the creatures just in the Briars: taller than most men, drooling maw filled with razor-sharp teeth, claws that can tear through leathers like butter..." With a shudder, Emelle slouched over the desk, folding her arms under her head.

"Oh," she added around a yawn, "and they have to decapitate it and leave the head behind before burying the body in a sacred space. There's a whole ritual, I've gathered."

"What happens if they don't finish the ritual?" he asked, unable to help a smirk when Emelle peeked up from where she'd rested her head on her desk. Maybe he shouldn't have encouraged that last ale...

"Hm?" Another yawn. "Something about evil escaping, or something..."

When Emelle's voice trailed off, Lars's heart constricted at the sight of her falling asleep. Fates, she was so beautiful, cheeks flushed and lips wet. But it was her humor, her wit, her keen perception of those around her...Lars was drawn to her very soul. It bothered him that everyone seemed to turn away from her light when all he wanted to do was bask in her brilliance. He gently brushed a strand of hair behind her ears.

Sliding a bookmark in the ledger to mark where they'd left off for the night, he extinguished the scattered candles. Then he gingerly lifted a sleeping Emelle into his arms, carrying her to her room and tucking her into bed. She still wore her handkerchief, so he carefully removed it, placing it tenderly on the small bedside chest, before moving to her feet. Slipping her boots off, Lars eyed the worn leather. The seams appeared mended a few too many times. He needed to buy her a new pair.

Her cat—Evie, he'd learned one morning—hopped onto the bed, snuggling into Emelle's arms, and Emelle's grip tightened as if she'd known her cat was near, even in sleep. Lars's heart warmed at the sight, at the fierce woman cuddling her pet, before he tugged her blanket up to her waist and moved to the door.

With one last look at the most captivating woman he'd ever met, Lars shut the door, pausing for only the briefest of moments, before walking down the hall towards his room. All the while, he fought the urge to turn back and hold his sleeping princess. Soon, but not yet.

☽✶☾

As the nights passed, Lars had learned more than what he came for. Most interestingly, he learned his little barkeep was quick to blush but still hissed some of the filthiest words he'd ever heard under her breath when frustrated. Based on her lack of reaction to his stares, he was confident she didn't know his hearing was acute enough to pick up on her bawdy vocabulary. He learned that she fell into fits of surprisingly loud laughter with the most adorable snort if she really thought something was funny.

Apparently, he was hilarious. It was news to him.

Warmth bloomed in his usually cold chest. Emelle was single-handedly breathing life back into him. He was remembering there was a time when he laughed freely, back when he still lived with his mother. When he wasn't fighting for his life day after day, year after year. Lars saw how people lived when they didn't struggle under the weight of blood on their hands. Emelle may as well have taken a chisel to his soul, etching her name right into it. With each chip, she brought forth emotions he'd long since suppressed.

It was terrifying.

It was *enchanting*.

Lars knew he was slipping off an unavoidable cliff, but had no desire to save himself from the impending destruction.

He even swore the small office grew brighter with each night they spent huddled together over her ledger. Or was it Emelle who illuminated the space with her smile, her emerald eyes that sparkled with wonder?

"So, how did you know he was going to run?" she asked one night, when the laughter faded and she'd caught her breath.

Lars wiped away a tear. "It was all he ever did! The bastard has been running since he was a babe, but he only ever gets as far as his mother's house."

"His mother must be a terrifying woman." Emelle snorted and wiped at her own tears. "So he's a grown man"—more laughter—"who pretends to be a traveler to do...what?"

"*Everyone* knows Anders," he explained. "He tries to trick the travelers into investing in his entrepreneurial adventures." With his kingdom so close to the West Docks, the city saw its fair share of visitors. Whether nobility traveling to *Fates knows where* or men in search of work, Wellsmore was bustling year-round. "It almost always works until the next morning when the visitors realize they've been arrogantly swindled, and chase Anders through the streets until he returns their money."

"So this time you stopped him?" she asked, laughter in her voice. Lars could see the wheels turning in her mind, putting the pieces together.

"Of course I did—got a *priceless* future favor as payment, too. Knowing who the man was, I'm looking forward to collecting." He flashed a slick grin at her.

Emelle propped her head in her palm as she leaned an elbow on the desk. Her laughter quieted, though her gaze remained warm. His heart thundered, refusing to give a name to his feelings. Refusing...and yet failing. This enchantress of his was *incredible*.

He shifted forward until they shared the same breath. Sparks flashed between them, charging the air to cataclysmic proportions. Emelle froze, lost in the same haze he was succumbing to.

But a clamp deep inside had him pulling back, the reminder of his duty rearing its ugly head again. The shame of his deceit burned a hole in his chest.

He wasn't sure he was going to survive the eventual fall.

He fell anyway.

☽✶☾

After a particularly busy night a little over a week after Lars had become a semi-permanent fixture at The Finn, he followed Emelle into her office once more. Exhaustion rolled off her in waves and he stood behind her, desperate to touch her. Each night they huddled closer than the previous, but something acrid in his gut stopped him, forcing him to painfully extract himself before he could bridge that final distance. His mounting guilt over the ruse he played manifested physically, even invaded his dreams. He was no better rested than Emelle, but couldn't care about his state when she was so clearly drained.

Helpless but to reach out, Lars lightly massaged the tight muscles in her shoulders, deepening the pressure on a particularly stubborn knot. Emelle dropped her head forward, soft moans falling from her lips. The room was darker than usual, a stark difference from the familiar levity that filled the space.

"You need more rest." His voice was gentle, but firm. Unease gathered in his chest, since it was his fault she looked barely able to stand on her own two feet.

Shaking her head, Emelle disagreed, voice tired but unyielding.

"No, not until we've found your friend. If it were Greer, I can only hope someone would do the same for her."

His hands paused on her shoulders, guilt surging. Moving around the desk, Lars settled in for another night of lying to her. He swore the candles flickered in anger as his gaze fell, once again, upon the object of his ever-consuming desires. No matter how hard he tried to ignore it, his shame refused to let him be.

"So how'd he even find it?" he asked after Emelle shared a story about a Hero who'd found a riddle in the middle of the Wildlands.

"I'm not exactly sure," she said. "It seems like the Heroes are led to a place seemingly by chance—or their gut, I suppose. Maybe the Fates even guided them, whispering in their mind which direction to follow. But the Heroes' visions reveal they need to find a scroll, and are prodded towards a general direction in which to start, I think." She paused, head cocked, and drummed her fingers on the desk. "Well, I'm sure half the trial is just locating the damn thing. I've heard of some scrolls being found in the southeast towards the Burnes, but many are located in the Wildlands to the north of Silvermist. I'd say it's pure luck to be able to find one, but I think the Fates deal in more than just luck."

"And they find this scroll, and the riddle is inside?" Emelle hadn't shared many stories about the riddles yet. They were drier than the risk and challenge of hunting mythical beasts and navigating traps in hopes of rescuing a missing princess.

Emelle nodded, but she didn't elaborate.

"I bet there's a ritual that he has to do, too, huh?" he prodded, hoping he wasn't being too obvious.

She just rolled her eyes with a smirk. Of course there was.

☽✻☾

Lars could only watch dutifully, as Emelle's brightness dulled each day. It had been almost two weeks spent with this fascinating woman, and Lars couldn't be greedier with her time. But she was running herself ragged because of *him*. He knew he needed help in his search, but he wasn't sure he should accept it anymore from this woman whose will could crumble mountains. And while the deepest part of his soul craved to possess her, Lars knew his path only spelled misfortune should he bring her with him. The near-impossible pursuit of weaving his own destiny—of challenging the Fates themselves—was too dangerous for this precious woman.

And Fates, if anything happened to her, he'd rip the Cosmic Fates apart.

Chapter Ten
Emelle

"I can't believe you're taking the day off," Janie said. Emelle had brought her in early so she could surprise Lars with a picnic at the hot springs that afternoon. Janie's long brown hair was piled atop her head, a few tendrils slipping out to delicately frame her face. Her golden complexion tanned easily, and amber eyes shimmered back at Emelle with intelligence. She was effortlessly beautiful and had unquestionably grown into her toothy smile, though she was certainly slower to show any emotion than she was at ten. And when Emelle had apologized for how she'd reacted when she first saw Janie and Lars together, Janie just chuckled, telling her not to worry about it.

"It's not the *day*," Emelle insisted even as butterflies took flight in her belly. "Just an evening. Don't worry, I'll be back, hard at work, by the time the sun rises tomorrow."

The afternoon sun streamed into the tavern, and only a couple fools drank at one of the long tables. Their exceedingly disheveled appearance raised Emelle's hackles and she kept a wary eye on one who leered at them. But Janie just ignored him, polishing a few steins.

"I can take care of breakfast tomorrow, you know," Janie offered, waggling her brows and making Emelle smile, remembering

Greer doing the very same when she sought to tease Emelle. "There's not that many rooms filled tonight, I'm sure I could handle it."

With a sigh, she relented. "All right, deal. You can stay in one of the empty rooms tonight, if you want. You know where everything is?"

Janie rolled her eyes. "Yes, *mom*, I know where everything is. Don't worry, I've got this."

Emelle *was* worried. But she knew she needed to loosen the reins if she wanted any chance at finding a new partner in business. Janie just might have what it took. She was quick, sharp as a tack, and surprisingly good at handling the drunken leering of arrogant men. When Emelle had asked how she'd become so impassive, Janie's eyes shuttered and Emelle had left it alone. She suspected it might have something to do with her time at Meggie's Place.

"Janie..." she started, unsure how to ask. She was more than concerned about the young woman, and she knew from experience it wasn't smart to bottle everything inside.

Janie's levity dropped at the look on Emelle's face.

"Don't," she rasped. "I'm not ready."

Emelle just nodded, squeezing her friend's arm. "I'll be here...when you are," she whispered, earning a nod from Janie. She'd wait for her to be ready. She wasn't going to stop being there for her friend, whenever that day may come.

Leaving Janie to tend to The Finn, Emelle raced upstairs to change, beaming as she thought of the evening to come. Scooping Evie up to squeeze before plopping her back on the bed, Emelle ignored the disrupted cat's meows as she quickly rinsed off her body and wet her bangs.

Then she found one of her only dresses, a deep sapphire woolen masterpiece. Elaine, her grandmother, had hand-stitched delicate flowers from the collarbone and over the shoulders, dwindling as they reached the ends of each long sleeve, giving the illusion that she'd had a basket of flowers dumped over her head. It was high-necked and fit her curves perfectly. It was beautiful. When she wore it, she always felt like one of the princesses she'd only heard about in drunken stories. But she only put it on for special occasions. She was hoping tonight would be one of them. She was going to be *bold*.

Her heart clenched with a familiar pain, knowing her grandmother never got to see her in the dress. She'd been excellent at stitching her signature flowers—orchids—but that was the extent of her crafting abilities.

Her grandmother made the dress for Emelle's wedding. She still wasn't sure which magic she'd possessed to get the measurements just right. And over the years, Emelle had decided she couldn't wait, wearing it whenever she wanted to remember her grandmother on a particular day. It made Emelle treasure the gift even more, being able to remember all of the joyful moments she'd experienced in the gorgeous dress, knowing her fearsome grandmother was there with her in spirit. She didn't reach for it often, wanting to savor the feeling each time, but it made her smile nonetheless whenever her hands ghosted over the material in her drawer.

Hastily drying her bangs with a towel, Emelle pinched her cheeks and applied some tinted oil to her lips. The reflection in the age-worn mirror stared back at her, and Emelle wondered if the dark circles under her eyes were permanent at this point. With nothing she could do about it now, she left the bathroom and pulled on her longest socks before lacing up her boots. She was glad she'd cleaned most of the mud off and threw a few mending stitches along the seams earlier this morning.

Grabbing a shawl, Emelle quickly made her way downstairs and into the kitchen. Some hard cheese, two apples, and a hot loaf of bread she stole from a grumbling Janie made their way into a sack. She also grabbed a bottle of red wine and prayed it didn't taste horrible. The dusty bottle didn't bode well for her confidence, but it was all she had. Ready for her…picnic—it wasn't a date—Emelle waited with nerves simmering under her skin for Lars to return.

☽✷☾

"You see Emmy?" she heard Lars ask Janie.

Gathering her items, Emelle exited her office with the booking ledger, pulling the rickety door shut behind her. Turning at the noise, Lars's eyes almost popped out of their sockets, eating her up from head to toe. Hunger blazed as he took in her dress, her simple makeup.

Emelle gulped. She hadn't seen Lars this flustered since that first morning in her office. Sure, she'd seen the evidence of his attraction for her, but she'd always ignored it, opting to pretend she wasn't also burning each night she spent so close, yet so far away from him. She'd been too nervous to make the first move. She hoped that would change tonight.

"Do you have...plans?" Lars asked tentatively, alarm lacing his words and betraying his cool demeanor as he scanned the room filling with jesters and fools.

Shadows spilled around her feet and Emelle was, once again, stumped at the phenomenon.

"Yes, I do," she affirmed, matter-of-factly.

Acid-green sparked in his onyx eyes and Emelle fought a smirk. But before she had a chance to respond, one of the drunk fools from earlier crowded into her space.

"Yeah, the whore has plans with me." His rotten breath swirled in the air between them, choking her. The fool reached for her, as if to grab her arm, but Lars immediately stopped him with a grip that looked painful. The man had clearly misjudged the situation he'd just thrown himself into.

"Say that again. One more time." An inhuman Lars stared down at the man who gulped comically loud. "I want to make sure I heard you correctly."

Lars gripped him by the collar of his filthy tunic, his knuckles white. Sweat poured down the fool's forehead, who glanced at his friend, silently begging him to step in. But it turned out the jester had at least a shred of self-preservation. He stayed put.

"I—" he started.

But Lars cut him off, a menacing smile slashing onto his face.

"I don't care." A fist flashed and the fool was on the ground, knocked out cold, blood dripping from his nose down his splotchy cheeks. "Take him and leave. Now. Before I change my mind."

The man dashed forward and slung an arm around his friend, dragging him out of The Finn without a wasted breath.

Lars frowned, clearly upset with the unconscious fool who'd interrupted them.

Emelle cupped his jaw, bringing his attention back to her before dropping her hand. "It's all right," she said softly. "That was actually quite tame."

Darkness spilled from his body, shadows wrapping around them. "That doesn't make it all right, Emelle. Just because it's happened before doesn't mean you should ever have to hear the kind of names he had the audacity to think, let alone speak out loud."

Emelle was in shock. His words rang true, and yet...It had been a while since she had anyone to defend her. Greer had done a great job of it before, but Emelle just tried to keep the peace. To keep the chairs and walls intact. So she'd let their words roll off her back, she'd ignored the leers, the offers.

She stifled a grin and mumbled a quiet thank you.

Walking past him with her sack, she paused, looking over her shoulder at the delicious man. "You coming?" she teased, continuing towards the exit.

She'd never seen him move faster.

Emelle laughed as she was yanked back by the crook of her elbow. Lars winked. It was one that had her panties growing damp. *Damn him, he had to know what that did to her...*

Stepping around her, Lars opened the tavern door and held an arm out, waiting for her to pass through.

Emelle stepped over the threshold, curtsying in jest with a chuckle. "It's about a half-hour walk to where we're going, if you can handle it?"

"I can manage," he confirmed with a sly look she couldn't decipher.

Nodding, she turned left and led him out of the village. Before she could even get two steps in, he grabbed her sack, swinging it over his shoulder.

Emelle just rolled her eyes and boldly looped her arm through his.

☽✻☾

"Wow," Lars breathed, scanning the cave. She understood the sentiment. Her father took her here several times a year growing up. Emelle had always felt a strong connection to *life* here. It felt like she was transported away, to another place where she felt peace and wonder and joy.

Glow worms crawled over the ceiling of the cave, illuminating the natural space with an azure tint. Unique flora grew in the corners of the cave and Emelle always appreciated the chance to see something that wasn't the chickweed and bluegrass found in Silvermist. She was especially appreciative of the orchids that mysteriously grew in the damp space. Emelle always felt a little closer to her grandmother here.

Lars's gaze landed on the steaming spring in the middle of the cave, then seized hers.

"Wow," he repeated, voice breathy and raw.

"I know," she agreed, looking over her private sanctuary. "My father used to bring me here when I was a child. Not many people know about this place, even in Silvermist. I've always loved to come here, especially in the winter. It's been my safe space for as long as I can remember."

Lars's attention never left her as she spoke. Although the cave itself was small, the opening was actually quite large. Chilly winds rushed through the mystical space and Emelle shivered. Or maybe it was from the way Lars hadn't looked away from her yet. Burning under his undivided attention, Emelle's cheeks flamed.

"So anyways," she said, "I thought this could be our office

today. Plus, I brought dinner and wine." Blood rushed to her head, but Emelle held his gaze even as she went dizzy from the scrutiny.

Stalking right up to her, Lars's boots knocked into hers as he crowded her space. Emelle gazed up at him, wondering if he was going to finally kiss her.

Fates, please kiss her.

He lifted a large hand and swept her bangs behind her ear, and her heart sped in response, eyelids fluttering almost shut.

But after a moment, Lars just smiled softly and gracefully folded himself onto the ground, unpacking the contents of the bag.

Frozen, it took Emelle a moment before she joined him, shaking out her shawl to sit on, patting the space next to her. "I hope you like red," she teased, knowing how he felt about her ale.

"Who doesn't?" Lars joked, sliding over to where she sat.

Uncorking the bottle, Lars took a swig, eyes bulging as he drank straight from the bottle. He stilled, the bottle tipped against his lips as his sight darted to Emelle. Lars choked as he forced himself to swallow. Snatching the bottle from his hands, Emelle tasted the wine.

She had to force herself to swallow, too.

"Cosmic Fates, that is not very good," she laughed.

Lars joined in, until they both had tears streaming down their faces. Her heart swelled with the sound. He was much quicker to laugh than when she'd first met the broody man.

"Well, at least I know the food won't be as terrible," she conceded, passing him some of the cheese, fruit, and bread.

They ate and shared the bottle of wine, which tasted better with each sip, and somehow didn't reach for the ledger once. Instead, after a few prodding questions from Lars, they fell back into talking about her childhood.

"Soon after she moved out, I heard from Greer that she saw my mom out at the market with a little bump pushing her top out. I knew it wasn't my father's. A few months later, she was living with another man, who I hope was the father of her baby, but I wouldn't know. I haven't really spoken with her since. She stopped coming around after my father refused to let her see me. My half-sibling is probably almost a teenager by now." Emelle's voice quivered, remembering the years-old injury that burned as though it happened yesterday. Her parents had told her they couldn't get pregnant again. Knowing her mother had left so easily, started her new family so quickly...

"I could handle not knowing my sibling, because I had Greer. But then Prince Elwood was led to Silvermist and the Cosmic Fates declared them mates and..." She trailed off.

Lars reached over and squeezed her hand softly, offering comfort from his surprisingly tender touch. When he didn't pull away, she couldn't help but look down at their intertwined fingers. Crickets chirped around the cave, filling the silence.

"Anyways," Emelle continued, squeezing Lars's hand in return, "I lost Greer and just...retreated into myself. She had always been the one to bring me out of my shell, to see life through its beauty instead of its pain..." She shook herself, and chose to switch topics. His hand left hers to grab the bottle of wine again. She had to force herself not to pull his hand back.

Sharing a happier memory she held dear to her heart, Emelle had Lars near tears as she told him about the time when she was a young teen and had stolen the ugliest smock she'd ever come across in one of the stalls at the market.

"Greer took the fall. She told my mother that I wouldn't be caught dead wearing the hideous smock!"

"But you weren't going to be wearing it, were you?" he asked around his laughter, humor dancing in his eyes.

"I was going to cut it up, try to make my own handkerchief, you know?" she admitted, voice alight with the memory. She remembered the mutilated scrap of fabric that came from the poor smock. "I am apparently *not* destined to be a seamstress."

"What are you destined to be?" he asked, sincerity breaking through the warm levity. "What do you wish for your life, Emmy?"

Emelle's heart constricted, thinking of Greer being swept away by her prince. Thinking of all of the Heroes and jesters and fools who'd traveled through her tavern. How she was jealous but scared, all at the same time. How she *craved* adventure and excitement. And how she'd probably only experience the thrill of the journey through the stories told in her tavern.

She thought of how entirely *different* Lars was. How he consumed her thoughts. How he surprised her at every turn. As soon as she thought she had him figured out, he'd peel back yet another layer, sharing something so contrasting from her life in Silvermist as if it were just another day, like the time he'd saved a young woman from being abducted.

Her soul cracked. She also remembered he was temporary. That he, too, would leave her. Just like everyone else had.

He hadn't said it, but she felt the sand slipping faster through the hourglass. Their time was quickly coming to a close.

The heat from the springs choked her, or at least that's what she blamed the sudden difficulty to catch her breath on. She shifted on the hard ground, uncomfortable with the direction of her thoughts, but it did nothing to help.

It was bound to happen. A pin gleaming in the harsh sunlight as it rushed towards her blissfully ignorant bubble she'd been living in.

Voice meek and eyes downcast, Emelle finally spoke, breaking the quiet and her soul at the same time. "I think I am destined to live with eternal heartbreak. To die alone, with only my memories to hold me as I drift into the cosmos."

Tears slipping down her cheeks, Emelle didn't flinch when Lars's thumb caught them. All at once, Lars tugged her into a bone-crushing hug, and Emelle whimpered from how entirely *safe* she felt.

"I can't believe that," Lars whispered, voice barely audible. Emelle didn't bother to argue.

☽✳☾

They returned to The Finn a few hours after dark. All tension had fizzled from her bones after her confession. Heartache mounting over Greer, over Lars's impending departure, her eternal shackle to the tavern...

Emelle's soul was *tired*.

Waving a small hand to Lars at the top of the stairs, Emelle tucked herself in early and didn't wake up until noon the next day.

Chapter Eleven

Lars

Sitting across his little enchantress as she retold a harrowing tale of a prince who almost didn't succeed, a frown slowly leached away Lar's amusement, sound fading as his heart raced. It felt like the walls were closing in on him. The stain on his soul from lying to Emelle spread, oily tendrils coiling around his heart with each look. With each story she shared.

He had the information he needed. He knew where an active site was in the Briars, he knew what types of beast he could expect...He'd had the information for days now, he just hadn't been able to—

Guilt threatened to destroy him as he felt her trust in him growing with each day he stayed. Each late morning when he drifted down from his pitiful few hours of sleep, her eyes would light up when she saw him, before she schooled her lovely features into a meager smile.

His guilt ensured he wouldn't know peace, even in sleep. Visions of her death—body mangled and bloody, her unseeing eyes as she took her final breaths—plagued him each time he laid his head on his lumpy pillow. He thought that part of him, the part that would never—*could never*—fear again was long dead.

He was wrong.

After they spent yesterday afternoon in the cave, Lars had felt his soul already cracking as they'd made the trip back to The Finn in near silence.

The weight of his ulterior motives suddenly became suffocating as he sat with Emelle in her office, and he knew he had gathered enough information to—

"Are you listening?" Emelle said on a laugh, freeing him from his spiraling thoughts.

Snapping his sight back to hers as she sat in her chair on the other side of her desk, he noted her pinched brow and searching gaze. The placid evening air was surprisingly warm as humidity leaked through the cracked window.

"Sorry, I was...lost," he answered numbly, as if that was a sufficient excuse. A question formed in her gaze, one he knew he had to answer. Just not tonight. *Tomorrow.* Tomorrow he would cleave his heart in two. But tonight...

Tonight he was still Lars, friend of Denny, who was lost in his trial. Forcing his muscles to relax, Lars masked his tension, and nodded for Emelle to continue.

Chapter Twelve
Emelle

A sinking feeling in the pit of her stomach kept Emelle up most of the night. Well, what remained of the night. She needed to be up in a few hours to start her prep for breakfast, but sleep evaded her. Tossing in her cot, she eyed a sleeping Evie with jealousy, who'd grown tired of her mistress's futile attempts at sleep and curled up on some clean laundry Emelle had yet to put away. Evie's steady breaths and closed eyes taunted her.

Flopping onto her back with a sigh, Emelle closed her aching eyes and tried to think of *anything* other than the look on Lars's face tonight. Denial weighed heavy on her chest as she tried to dismiss the answer brewing in her gut.

As she had been in the middle of explaining how a Hero used a dull kitchen knife he'd fortuitously grabbed from his traveling cook's corpse—it had been impaled into his eye socket—to finally kill the beast he'd claimed to have fought for over an hour, she'd realized how silent the small office was.

Usually, the timber of Lars's deep chuckles or gasps of shock followed her stories, and she'd try to hide her blatant physical response to his voice. Since Lars arrived, she'd gone through more undergarments than usual as she replaced the sticky material ughout the day.

Noticing his lack of response, she'd found Lars lost in thought, unshaven jaw clenched as he stared unseeing at the papers on her desk. Twin smudges shadowed his eyes, and her heart hurt. She knew she'd been dragging her stories out, answering any silly question he had to keep him staying another night. Anything to keep him interested in what she had to say. Being the focus of anyone's undivided attention was new to her, and she was terrified for the moment he lost interest—for the moment she'd wake up from this fairytale and be forced to return to her monotonous life. Lars shook her world upside down and she could breathe again. But still, her dreams were filled with the heartbreak she knew was on the horizon. Were the sands of time finally settled at the bottom of their hourglass?

His dismissive answer and divided attention could only—

Fear seized her as panic threatened to overtake her. She'd realized what that look was. What it meant. Sweat tickled the nape of her neck.

She made a decision.

Determination fueled her as she flung the covers off and quickly dressed in a tunic and trousers from the bottom drawer of her chest. These particular clothes had been found in a case left behind by a traveler, but their loss was her gain.

Slipping out of the tavern, Emelle sent a rare thanks up to the Fates that the storm had yet to hit. Gravel crunched softly underfoot as she made her way to Janie's home.

☽✷☾

"You want me to do *what*?" Janie screeched.

Sporadic furniture was barely visible in the dark room and the Leon home was tidy. While they stood near the front door, the small space still echoed Janie's voice, and Emelle glanced around the quaint front room. Janie at least had the good sense to cringe in silent apology. She didn't want her parents waking up any more than Emelle did. Emelle had avoided the Leon matriarch after the incident all those years ago, too embarrassed over the whole ordeal.

"Janie, you can do this," Emelle insisted. "You'll stay in my room and—and use my office! I know you've only been working with me for two weeks, but *please,* I *know* you can handle this. We've both seen you behind that bar."

In the few minutes since Emelle rapped on the Leon's door, she'd hurriedly explained her plan and what she needed Janie to do. Bless the Cosmic Fates, at least she hadn't slammed the door in Emelle's face when Emelle told her that she didn't know when she would return.

"Look how well you did yesterday!" Emelle argued, desperate.

"Yes, for *one day!*" Janie volleyed.

Emelle shoved a hand through her unbrushed hair, hating that Janie had a point. But she was determined. "It's not much different. It's the same routine each day. I promise you can handle this. And Evie's easy, just give her food and let her out to roam and she'll love you."

"But you really won't know when you'll be back?" Janie's voice trembled as she tugged on the end of one braid. It, more than anything else, reminded Emelle just how young she was. Janie was only twenty, and Emelle was asking a great deal of her.

Closing the distance, Emelle grabbed the nervous woman's hands and squeezed them in hers, willing her to understand why Emelle needed to do this. Janie's eyes flicked back and forth between hers before she seemed to find her resolve.

Janie straightened, determination filling her bones as she nodded sharply. When she spoke, her voice was steady. "Go. I can handle The Finn." A laugh, and then she added, "And your baby," with a wink.

Emelle believed every word. And she knew Evie wouldn't mind having another friend to dote on her, either. The fluffy cat preferred to remain out of sight, so Emelle let her have the run of the tavern. sunup and sundown, she always knew where Evie would be:

eating from her dish in Emelle's room. Desperate hope blossomed in her chest as she realized *this might actually work.*

Pulling Janie in, Emelle hugged her tight, tears burning her eyes. Laughter broke out between them before they remembered it was still the middle of the night.

Attempting, but failing, to stifle their excitement, Emelle had to take several breaths before she was ready to make the fifteen-minute trip back to The Finn. The first rays of dawn slipped over Silvermist, and with a thankful nod to a woman most might dismiss at first glance, Emelle St. King set out on the adventure of a lifetime.

Chapter Thirteen
Lars

With every distracted step he took out of Silvermist, Lars felt the crack in his heart grow. He knew a piece of his soul remained in that tiny village.

Lars had deliberated all night, wearing a track into the floor of his room. He could stay until morning, saying goodbye to Emelle like a rational adult. Or, he could slink out on silent feet and let his absence speak for itself. Back and forth he'd paced, conflicted as warring emotions battled inside. He wasn't sure he'd be able to leave if he had to gaze into those twinkling emeralds while he told her he was leaving.

As the unforgiving morning sun began to creep above the horizon, Lars shattered his own heart as he came to a decision: a clean break.

He wasn't sure it was the right choice.

He continued anyway.

Leaving only a short note to thank Emelle for her hospitality—and a suspiciously large bag of coins he'd hoped would help repair the crumbling building—he skulked from The Finn on the whisper of a shadow.

Lars forced one unsteady foot in front of the other. He almost turned back as the phantom of her scent lingered on the unusually warm morning air. But he knew the truth: it was just his heart pleading with him to stay.

Rounding the corner, he paused on the gravel and looked back once more to the building that altered the course of his life, in more ways than one.

The slanted, weather-worn sign adorning the name of the tavern hung ominously above the damaged door. A shiver rolled down his back as he watched the wind slam the painted sign against the aged wall, as if raging at him for leaving.

He flinched at each clack, the dreadful noise echoing in his blood as he tore himself away from the woman he was certain was the other half of his ruined soul. If soulmates truly existed, he was sure she was his.

He left anyway.

Tarnished soul raging at him to turn around, Lars begged the cosmos to let him live through the impending bloodshed, so he could one day return for his mate.

He wasn't surprised to hear nothing in response.

Chapter Fourteen
Emelle

"Mother*FUCKER*!" Emelle grabbed at her foot, certain her pinky toe was about to fall off. Sweat dripping down her nose was the final straw. Planting her ass firmly onto the packed dirt of the footpath, Emelle cringed at the throb in her tailbone as well as her toe now. Face falling into her hands, Emelle groaned. Loudly.

"Fates, what was I *thinking?*" Emelle cried out to the empty forest all around her.

A crazed laugh escaped her as she recalled her "adventures" from the last ten days. After she had returned to The Finn from Janie's house, Emelle had ducked into her office to collect the ledger before rushing up the stairs to pack in a frenzy. Janie could start a new ledger: she'd seen Emelle's often enough to figure it out.

Smiling, Emelle had stuffed as many trousers, tunics, socks, and undergarments as she could fit around the large book in the traveling pack left behind by some traveler long ago. Evie had watched her lazily from the cot before falling back asleep, as if unconcerned by Emelle's urgency.

As she'd packed, Emelle considered how to enact her reckless plan: She'd go about her morning as usual while she waited for Lars to leave. Then she would follow him at a distance, waiting until they were a few hours away from Silvermist before approaching to insist he take her on his journey. She wouldn't give him a choice, or the chance to say no.

She was scared he would sneak out without saying goodbye. She was scared he *would* say goodbye, and what he might tell her. Or maybe he'd pretend all was well, then sneak out while her back was turned, leaving her forever wondering why the mysterious man with depthless eyes and heartbreaking beauty left her.

No, he wouldn't just leave. He couldn't.

He could.

Emelle's disappointment and heartache had threatened to topple her when he never appeared all morning. She had waited for hours, but not once did she spot his messy, inky waves. Needing to squash the final shred of hope, Emelle had calmly made her way up the stairs and to his door. All was silent behind it. A lone tear had escaped.

Emelle had grabbed her master key from her pocket, then unlocked the door, exhaled slowly, and pushed it open.

Golden afternoon light had streamed in through the window, illuminating a stripped bed which held only a folded note and a sack the size of her head. Approaching on shaky legs, Emelle had cracked as she'd slowly reached for the parchment.

Emmy,

Thank you.

Yours Always,

Lars

A muffled whimper escaped her as her hands curled, wrinkling the paper with his scratchy handwriting. She'd known this was coming every step to this room, yet for some foolish reason, she'd thought the anticipation of the ache would somehow lessen the pain when she was struck.

She always had been a fool.

After picking up the pieces of her heart, Emelle searched the room for any clue as to where Lars was headed. At least she knew he would be searching for active celestial trials in hopes of finding his friend. Remembering one of the last stories she'd told him, Emelle recalled the questions he'd asked. The growing gleam in his eye with each answer she provided.

And the answer unfolded.

But it had been nearing dusk, and Emelle had feared beginning her journey under the darkness of night. So the next morning, Emelle gathered her pack, kissed Evie several times on her sleek nose, and tumbled down the stairs. Seeing Janie duck behind the bartop, Emelle raised her hand in a silent goodbye. Janie just smirked and nodded her head to the door. Her way of saying goodbye, and to *get out of here*. Emelle blew her a kiss and left The Finn without a backwards glance.

In the ten days since she left the only home she'd ever known, Emelle had developed a new appreciation for indoor plumbing and access to fresh food. Gnawing on one of the last strips of jerky she'd purchased from the market in Silvermist, Emelle felt her body beg for something, *anything*, but dried meat.

She'd brought only half of the bag of the coins left by Lars, leaving the rest hidden under a floorboard in her room. She'd then purchased an aging horse and a frayed map from a neighbor, and was shocked when he produced two: One localized map that detailed Eralyn from the edges of a kingdom named Wellsmore in the west down to the Briars in the southeast, and one much larger that he had to unfurl. He'd pointed to a small space of land, barely noticeable on the map, and had told Emelle that was Eralyn. Her mind had spun, seeing just how tiny her life had been compared to the rest of the world. Suddenly, it made sense why there was always another Hero, always another princess. Her world was vast, and she couldn't wait to explore it.

After purchasing the localized map and the old horse—paying more than the horse was truly worth—she'd stopped by the market for the now-offensive dried meats, a wedge of cheese, and a loaf of bread. She'd hoped they would last until she reached Briarwood.

Not ten days, though, apparently. Not in this muggy southern heat.

Crossing the Esterian Channel, the shallow river that ran southwest from the Theston Gulf to the western edges of the Briars—splitting Eralyn almost in two—Emelle stepped into the South Forest on her third day. She alternated walking on foot and riding Selene, not wanting to exhaust the older horse, but also needing breaks herself. She had quickly lost her sense of direction, and where she was in relation to her map. She only knew she was no longer in the Woodlands by crossing the river.

Exhaustion left her tripping over tree roots and rocks near-constantly. Between the dirt and sweat and the blood from scraped hands and knees, Emelle was in a perpetual state of filth. She resembled the Heroes who stayed at The Finn more and more each day.

That first night in the South Forest, sleeping against a large oak tree was...odd but manageable, and Emelle had drifted off to the buzz of cicadas. Waking up with the sun, Emelle had stretched her arms to the sky and yawned. A pressure on her legs had her opening her eyes and *freezing* as a brown-spotted snake at least four feet long slithered over her shins.

Praying to the *miraculous* and *merciful* Fates, Emelle had closed her eyes and didn't dare take a breath. She only dared to peek one eye open, when the weight on her legs vanished. A breath of relief thundered out of her when she found the snake gone.

It was her last decent night of rest. Suddenly a light sleeper, Emelle had found herself taking *days* longer than she should have to reach Briarwood, the bustling village in whose outskirts sometimes dwelled mythical creatures occasionally found in celestial trials. The creatures were stealthy, expertly eluding the Heroes-to-be that hunted them. By all accounts, the beasts almost had a certain level of intelligence that regular animals didn't. It was extremely difficult to find one, let alone slay a celestial beast. Of course, no regular man could slay them...The Fates always had their rules.

Exhaustion forced her to retire earlier each night than the night before. She hadn't had any surprise snuggle buddies since, but she refused to let her guard down.

Crumpled and filthy clothes, sore feet, and stringy bangs were her constant companions and dirt became a familiar friend. She wasn't sure she'd ever feel clean again.

Eyeing the offensive meat, Emelle shoved the rest in her mouth before pulling herself onto Selene's back. She was scared to admit it, but she was fairly certain she was completely and utterly lost. The tree she'd spotted a half hour back looked suspiciously familiar.

Resigning herself to a lifetime spent wandering the South Forest, Emelle clicked her tongue against her teeth and Selene began walking, towards where she could only hope was the Briars.

Chapter Fifteen
Lars

Emelle—he still felt an ache at her name, but he buried it deep, in the same darkened box where he'd buried the person he'd become with her. Not the Wraith of Wells, but Lars. The box rattled, but he couldn't let his mind go there.

The Wraith had a mission, and it was he who crouched atop a sturdy branch, waiting for his prey to appear, and his first celestial trial to commence.

The creature he'd been tracking for a little over a week was one of brute force, hardened leathery skin requiring he get within close proximity to kill it with his cleansed blades. He waited in a tree high above a clearing, and his shadows snuffed his scent from the beast hiding below. They were about three hours northwest of Briarshire, and minutes from the Esterian Channel—he could hear its babbling waters on the occasional breeze. Warm evening air wrapped around his leathers, choking him as sweat dripped down his neck. But he could be patient. He'd had enough practice to last a lifetime during his time in Silvermist.

His little barkeep had said this particular beast was called a Babau and needed to be baited by a fresh rabbit carcass that had been "cleansed by the cosmos."

Interestingly, the cleansing was metaphorical, but somehow it softened the impenetrable skin of the Babau. All he needed to do was recite a prayer over the body of his offering before laying the trap. There was no joy to be found in sacrificing a defenseless animal, so he sent an extra prayer up to the Fates that it wasn't in vain.

Silently, Lars kept a watchful eye on the ground below. Any moment the beast would—

Lars tucked his shadows tighter around him, masking his large frame from view amongst the growing evening darkness. Willing his racing heart to slow, he watched the grotesque creature slink out of the darkness. He swore even the wildlife silenced, hiding from the predator now in their midst.

Its oddly shaped skull was oblong and held blazing red eyes fixated on the bait. The Babau stalked forward on quiet feet; its primarily bipedal gait coupled with the occasional use of its fists created a juxtaposition in Lars's mind as he tried to reconcile what he was seeing. He'd only encountered a similar animal once before, but the much smaller mammals swung from the vines in the tropics of Thoryn. A sort of primate, he theorized.

The beast stopped in front of the rabbit right below Lars's perch, sniffing the dead animal before unlocking its jaw and swallowing it whole. Lars shifted, and a stray leaf fluttered to the ground. Fiery red eyes snapped upward, and Lars swore he saw nothing but pure, celestial violence waiting for him, readying to attack. *Fuck.* Lars didn't know how long it took for the cleansing prayer to affect the beast. Emelle said it could take several minutes. Some Heroes died in those minutes. Lars wouldn't be one of them.

He jumped, dagger in hand.

Lars crashed into the rock-hard body, knocking the Babau to the ground, pain jarring through him. The Babau pushed off the ground with its thunderous legs, throwing Lars onto his back and knocking the dagger from his hand.

Rolling to his feet, Lars grabbed his dagger from the forest floor and feigned a strike. When the Babau lurched away, he swiped again in truth, but the Babau easily dodged it. Lars cursed. It was so much faster than Emelle had said.

The box in the recess of his mind thrashed and he stumbled, before forcing her from his mind. Now was not the time to be thinking about her.

But the Babau used his moment of distraction to its advantage, and Lars barely had a moment to dodge. His blood splattered onto the ground, pain slicing down his arm. The Babau's sharp claws sliced through his leathers as if they were cheesecloth. A cold focus settled as his training washed over him—he charged the creature, reaching behind his head to grab his claymore from its sheath.

Lars attacked, overhand swing after swing, forcing the Babau back and back and back. A flash of what he thought might've been fear eclipsed the soulless, blazing eyes as it retreated with every strike.

No. It took him *fourteen fucking days* just to get to this point, to get *here* in the clearing. He wasn't letting the beast escape.

Lars's stomach dropped as he realized the Babau's skin was still impenetrable. The beast seemed to realize the same a heartbeat later.

Opening its jaw in what might be a crazed laugh, the Babau went on the counterattack. It swiped its claws, swooping them dangerously close to Lars's face. The Babau lunged, thrusting both arms out in an attempt to grab him.

The beast screeched as Lars began dodging its attacks, frantically whispering the cleansing prayer all the while, over and over, in hopes the continued tribute would speed the effects of the cleanse. Emelle hadn't said one way or another if that would work, but he had to try.

The Babau swiped its claws at Lars's chest, but Lars raised his sword in the nick of time. As it screeched in pain, Lars swung his dagger at its belly—and gaped when his blade sank to the hilt in its flesh. The hilt glowed almost too quickly to see, making him wonder if he imagined the bluish light.

When he yanked his dagger free, the beast collapsed with a

pitiful whine. Panting as iridescent moonlight shined through the thatch of trees, Lars watched the celestial fire dim in the beast's eyes as it released a final breath.

"Heroes washed their blades in the nearest creeks, and thanked the Fates for their chance at fulfilling their destiny. It sounds silly until you remember just how pompous the Cosmic Fates are."

The ghost of Emelle's soft voice slipped through a crack in the box, and his soul raged at him, yet again, begging him to make the trek back to Silvermist.

The blades he'd washed in the Esterian Channel were now bloody, complicit. A pang of empathy struck Lars as he looked upon the corpse of the Babau. The Cosmic Fates bred them, like the other beasts Heroes could face, and set them free so that Heroes could slay them in their trials. Were these brutish creatures truly evil if they were betrayed by the very beings who created them? If they were created merely to die?

Lars steeled himself, knowing there were still two more steps in his trial, before raising his claymore. With newfound sympathy for the vicious creature, he brought down the sword and took its head clean off.

Hot, black blood sprayed his face, igniting the fire in his chest as he silently condemned the Fates for this fucking trial. A nearly imperceptible ball of energy from the beast's body *whooshed* past him and into the skies above.

Per Emelle's description, Lars left the head to the elements before he began the work of bringing the massive body of the Babau back to the nearest grove.

Good thing he stashed a cart back at the Channel.

Chapter Sixteen
Emelle

"Do you think she's dead?" a curiously young voice asked. Emelle's head *ferociously* ached and the sun blinded her, even through her closed eyelids. As she squinted into the daylight, something sharp poked her in the ribs. Emelle curled further into Selene's side, and opened her eyes to glare at the offenders, only to realize they were just young children.

"Where—" She cleared her dry throat and tried again. "Where am I?"

Exchanging a look, the taller of the two boys spoke. "This is Briarstone. You've been sleeping for a loooong time, Miss," he said, looking to the other boy as they laughed to themselves in secret mischief.

"Owen! Dawson!" shouted a new voice. "Get your asses over here right this minute! Your father did *not* dismiss you yet."

The boys went silent as a woman not much older than Emelle stormed into the clearing. Stopping short when she noticed Emelle, the woman reached her arm out to the boys, as if she truly feared Emelle despite the pitiful picture she must present. The boys quickly ran behind the safety of her arms. Their dark hair matched that of this woman, though hers was tightly wrapped in a neat chignon at the base of her neck.

"Who are you?" the woman asked.

Weighing the benefits, she took a chance on this woman's clearly protective instincts, speaking only the truth.

"My name is Emelle," she rasped through a parched throat and stayed where she was, so as not to frighten the woman further. "And I've been traveling for almost two weeks trying to get to Briarwood. I came from a small village in the North Forest of Mistwood. I must've passed out. I've been exhausted."

A shrewd gaze passed over Emelle and Selene as she waited for a response. Silence stretched thin. The forest had even hushed, as if sensing the weight of her judgment. Emelle didn't cower, but she certainly knew she was out of her depth and desperately needed help.

At last, the woman gave a sharp nod. "All right then. From Mistwood, you say?"

"Yes, I've been traveling for ten—no, *eleven* days." Looking around the quiet forest, Emelle added, "I was sure I was going in circles. It all looks the same, doesn't it?" The sun was nearing its peak in the sky, warming Emelle's skin and shining over the last of the yellow leaves still clinging to the oak trees. Small rustles in the surrounding brush and the bubbling from a nearby stream filled her with a sense of harmony she hadn't felt in a while, despite the unknown she faced.

"Eleven days?"

Emelle nodded.

"That journey should only take a week." Suspicion leaked into the air between them as the woman straightened. The olive-toned skin around her eyes tightened as she narrowed her gaze, waiting for a response.

"Yes," Emelle agreed, though she hadn't exactly known that. "Like I said, I've been hopelessly lost. I've never left my village before and my horse hasn't worked in years. I suppose I should've hired a traveling aid, but..." She trailed off.

Perhaps the pathetic figure Emelle made—covered in mud and blood, skin scraped raw and littered with cuts, leaves more than likely in her hair—had deemed her no immediate threat. Finally, the woman extended her hand in both offer to shake and to help Emelle off the ground.

Accepting the proffered hand, Emelle heaved herself up and thanked her on a light breath.

"I'm Emelle," she said again, introducing herself formally.

"Lorna," the woman replied with a raised brow, shaking Emelle's hand. "When's the last time you ate a proper meal, *Emelle from Mistwood*?"

☽✻☾

Shoveling the most incredible stew she'd ever tasted into her mouth, Emelle made an absolute fool out of herself as she seared her tongue. When Lorna asked when she'd last eaten, drool dribbled out of the corner of her mouth as she answered that she wasn't sure, only that her stomach twisted from hunger.

She didn't care how sloppy she looked.

Emelle had blindly followed Lorna and her boys into the nearby village of Briarstone, content to walk to her death so long as she was able to eat first. Evidently, when Lorna had found her, she had only been ten minutes away from Briarstone. *I almost made it,* her heart screamed. Not to Briarwood, which was her intended destination, but to *any* village in the Briars. She was only a day's ride from the bustling city. Pride swelled in her chest, the dirt covering her skin and clothes no longer itching under the realization.

She'd done it.

And at least she made it to Briarstone, rather than Briarshire. A small village to the northwest of Briarwood, Briarshire wasn't known for its kindness towards newcomers, or so she'd heard from Owen.

After leaving Selene with Lorna's husband, who had promised three times that she would be well taken care of, Emelle entered the quaint home where the family dwelled. Mismatching candles flickered at various lengths, casting a warm glow to the cozy entrance. But as soon as she caught the tantalizing aroma of seasoned stew and fresh bread, all thoughts left her.

And now here Emelle sat, eating her third bowl of rabbit stew and fourth slice of roasted-garlic bread. As the hunger pains eased, Emelle rubbed her soft belly, grateful for the body that had kept her alive for the past two weeks.

After guzzling what felt like an entire bucket of water, Emelle found herself sinking further into her chair, exhaustion pulling at her seams. Lorna sat opposite her at the table with a steaming cup of tea, sipping quietly as Emelle devoured her food. The boys had been sent back to their father, so the small room was quiet.

"What's in Briarwood?" Lorna asked, voice curious as she took a sip of tea.

Emelle smiled brightly, and for the first time in her life, she spoke to a stranger who hadn't stumbled into her tavern.

☽✻☾

It took three days for Emelle's feet to return to their normal size and for her wounds to begin to heal. Sleeping on the couch in the front room of Lorna and Sam's home, Emelle thanked the Fates for the distinct lack of snakes. She had to be shaken awake by Lorna's eldest son, Owen, that first morning. He took one look at her bedraggled face and disheveled bangs and burst into a fit of laughter, clutching his belly. Emelle joined in.

After spending that first day sprawled on their couch, Emelle spent the next two days of recovery helping Lorna cook a few meals. For once, Emelle didn't resent being in a kitchen. In fact, she realized she missed performing mindless prep work in idle chatter with a friend. An image of Greer and Emelle peeling endless potatoes until their fingers bled flashed in her mind. She smiled at the memory.

But once Lorna realized she only knew a handful of dishes, she sat Emelle down and taught her how to make one of the staples in

Briarstone: a flavorful dish with steaming root vegetables and roasted duck. Emelle had never paid more attention in her life, nor did she resent the ache in her fingers while they prepped the potatoes.

Lorna also told her about the thrum of magic that had been slowly growing noisier with each year. Crops took longer to sprout, livestock took longer to breed, the rate of stillbirths increasing by the year. Emelle was enraptured, having only ever known about trials and quests. Whispers of rumors had made their way to Silvermist, of course, but Emelle never put much stock towards them. Lorna explained briefly how the soil could never lie—and right now, the soil was dry. Too dry. Lorna hadn't outwardly expressed much concern over it, but Emelle saw through her darting eyes and the occasional *tap tap tap* of her finger pads on her mug. She wondered if it had anything to do with the steady increase of Heroes she'd seen pass through The Finn recently.

Despite Lorna only being a few years older than her, Emelle felt comfort from the maternal presence. The sting of how her own mother abandoned her surged to the front of her mind. She was glad Owen and Dawson had Lorna as a mother. Each night, Lorna and Sam huddled the children into their beds, tucking them in tightly and making up stories. Emelle had listened from outside the door, lip wobbling as the love they so clearly shared warmed the air.

On her last night, they gathered outside to watch the sun set. As the boys played in the copse of trees behind their cottage, Emelle glanced over to Lorna, who sipped her tea as her boys tumbled around. A thread wove around her soul, stitching together a fragment of her pain that she'd been carrying around for over thirteen years. She understood all too well the lingering effects of a parent who was always chasing the future. The one who missed what was right in front of them. Her world had been so small before, and with each step out on her own, Emelle let go of a little more of her pain. She felt almost at peace under the golden setting sun. Only one thing—or rather, one *person*—was missing.

The next morning, she gathered her weighty bag, tightly packed with the booking ledger, freshly laundered clothes, and replenished rations. Then Emelle hugged Lorna tight. "Thank you. For everything," she said, mournful to leave her new friend.

"Come back anytime," Lorna replied, glassy eyes shining. "I mean it, you're welcome here. Anytime."

With a nod, Emelle heaved herself atop Selene and followed her new guide she'd hired as they left Briarstone. By nightfall, they should reach Briarwood, her intended destination.

Settling in for the journey, Emelle could hardly contain her excitement, a grin curling the corner of her lips.

Lars, you bastard, you better be ready for me.

Chapter Seventeen
Emelle

Briarwood was nothing like Briarstone. A simmering village filled with vendors, foods, and creative architecture pulled her attention in every direction. She wasn't sure how people lived in such chaos, and yet...

The low hum in her bones grew louder, echoing with each step into the town. A fledgling thought formed as she passed the tall buildings with flat roofs, feeling insignificantly tiny compared to the towering structures. Unlike how she'd once felt inconsequential in Silvermist, here Emelle felt *free* amongst the bubbling crowd, as she became lost in the sea of faces. As she soaked in the vast difference in pace, in sheer volume as people crashed around her, she realized...

She...loved it.

Arriving just an hour or so after the sun set, Emelle admired the unique string lighting crisscrossing above her, lighting her path into the heart of the village. Around the corner, lively string music poured from the colorful instruments in musicians' skilled hands and threaded around her soul. She lost herself to the rhythm, ambling down the wide cobblestone in a trance as she passed by shops and a few restaurants. She stopped by one that had a menu posted on a window, and her eyes bugged at the variety. Duck prepared at least five different ways, vegetables she'd never tried, and something called *fudge*. Her mouth watered, but she moved on for the moment, eager to return.

Smiles worn easily, Emelle took in the eclectic people and found a matching grin overtaking her features. Not a Hero in sight. No jesters nor fools, just *people*. People who looked nothing alike, no common dress nor style. As though everyone here were visiting, either for a night or for a while.

She'd always understood why the Sable sisters wanted out of Silvermist. To be whisked away to somewhere, *anywhere*, with more excitement. To *see* more of Eralyn. And with the rolling hills she could see in the distance, Emelle realized she never would've understood unless she saw it for herself. The world around her had too much to offer for her to stay cooped up in Mistwood.

Emelle entered the marketplace, where vendors of all sorts lined a large clearing with bricks laid in an intricate design under her feet. In between all of the chaos was a spurting fountain and Emelle was, once again, stunned. In the center of the fountain stood a woman carved in stone, hair draped over her body and elbows tucked into her waist with water spouting out of her raised palms and into the basin. She'd never seen such a thing.

People milled about, haggling with merchants or munching on snacks...Some even spoke in languages she'd never heard. She listened to their conversations as she passed, not because she'd understand, but so she could appreciate the beautiful dialects that came from other parts of their world.

She grinned as she looked around the square. She'd bet the Sable sisters would like it here. It was fast-paced and lively. Hopefully they'd see it one day.

Overwhelmed by the many choices, Emelle dismissed her guide to deliver her belongings to the nearest inn, and set about the first stall to her left.

Walking along the bricks, Emelle's eyes jumped from vendor to vendor. The first stall held spices, and Emelle took her time smelling the samples. Some she recognized, like thyme and basil.

Others she didn't, their bright oranges and reds leaving a tang in the air, and it pained her to leave them behind. One day, she'd have time to appreciate them, to try something new.

The next stall sold oils, olive and avocado and more. After renewing her interest in cooking, Emelle had to pull herself away from this merchant as well, unable to bring the expensive bottles with her.

As she trailed away from his table, the tantalizing scent of seasoned meats wafted around Emelle, and her mouth watered. She floated along, led by her nose to the stall selling chicken skewers and Emelle promptly purchased two. She barely gave the meat a perfunctory blow before burning her mouth on each scorching bite. It was delicious though, and she couldn't bring herself to regret her impatience.

Emelle's eyes widened with each new wonder and she took her time making her way around the heart of the village. Many wares almost had her reaching for her coin bag, but she knew she needed to be careful with her remaining funds. It physically pained her to leave the generous stack of books one table had. She'd flipped through a few, and one held scenes that had blood rushing to her cheeks. She'd dropped it back onto the pile, and turned away, subtly darting her gaze around to see if anyone had noticed her reddened face. But as Emelle moved to the last stall, her greedy attention trailed back towards the small book collection more than once.

Silky handkerchiefs of countless different patterns and colors— some she had never seen before, or didn't even know existed—dared Emelle to touch as she stared slack jawed. Gently pinching the first that caught her eye, she brushed her fingers longingly over the exquisite material. She'd had no idea something could be so soft. It felt like water, pouring over her fingers.

After a moment spent noting every detail, Emelle gingerly tucked it back into place. Tears gathered as she carefully looked over the stunning pieces. She'd left all but one handkerchief at home, not willing to risk losing or damaging her precious possessions.

"Ten silvers, Miss," the merchant chimed, walking over to where Emelle stood.

Eyes bugging out of her skull, her head whipped around to the man. *"Ten silvers?"*

With a chuckle, he nodded. She had no idea how he could find any of this funny. Gulping, Emelle slipped away, ignoring how badly she wished to return.

Her grandmother had worn handkerchiefs in her hair until the day she died. She'd given Emelle her first handkerchief when she was six and they'd often stayed up late trying to sew their own. No matter how hard they tried, they could never *quite* get the pattern right. That's what Emelle had been trying to make with the stolen smock Greer took the fall for. Trying desperately to conjure her grandmother again, who'd been gone for only a few weeks.

Each morning when Emelle donned the fabric, she could have sworn she felt the ghost of a hand on her shoulder, offering her comfort and strength. Her grandmother had been a force to be reckoned with. The expensive cloth was certainly a luxury on its own, but the connection to her grandmother outweighed any monetary value.

Despite the late hour, the city square was still busy, people of all ages gathered around the fountain as a musician had set up a solo performance. His music spoke to passion, and pain, and she felt it resonate deep inside of her. Skin tingling, she looked up from the musician's fingers flying over the strings, and froze at the sight of eyes dark as night.

Stubble had grown into an unruly beard and a large cut on his cheekbone gave an air of danger, more so than he usually projected. *Wild*, even.

Frantic eyes searched her form, though she couldn't say for what. Perhaps to make sure she was all right. Dropping whatever he'd carried in his arms, Lars stalked across the square, forcing people to part around him or risk being bowled over. Emelle's heart raced faster and faster with each step he took toward her. And then, suddenly, he was here and close, so close that Emelle had to tilt her head back just to meet his gaze.

Being so close to him at least made her anxiety ease, peace settling over her bones. And with relief, Emelle threw her arms around Lars's neck, squeezing tight as she breathed in his cedarwood and cypress scent, familiar and welcome.

Cautious arms hugged her back, and when she didn't flinch, tightened their grip. The hustle and bustle carried on around them, people forced to veer away from their roadblock, but she couldn't care less.

Until she remembered: she was furious with him.

Pulling out of his arms, Emelle glared up at him and snapped, "You left me! You colossal brute, you left me! Without a word!" It took a moment for her to realize her vision had grown blurry with tears, and she moved to back away—only for Lars to take her hands in his and hold her close.

"Emmy—"

"You left me," she interrupted, lip quivering as she refused to look at his face. His chest would do just fine for her glare until she could swallow the tears.

"Why?" she asked.

He ducked his head, catching her gaze, midnight eyes searching hers. Emelle waited for an answer, desperate hope stealing her breath from her lungs.

Chapter Eighteen
Lars

Lars had scented her as soon as he entered the city square. Inhaling deeply, he had tried to rationalize the familiarity, tried to tell himself it was wishful thinking that conjured the memory of her.

Citrus and jasmine with a hint of smoky vanilla.

He'd never smelled the combination anywhere, on *anyone*, but his soulmate. The scents sang to him, overwhelming his senses.

Heart beating out of his chest, Lars paused with the arms of the wheelbarrow clutched in both hands to scan the space in front of him, searching with wild hope, and terrible, incredible fear.

If she'd followed him, he'd never be able to let her go again. His duty he tried so hard to remember, now faded away in her presence.

There, on the other side of the fountain stood a sinfully curvy woman wearing dusty trousers that stretched tight across her lush hips, and a disheveled tunic that begged him, even from across the square, to unlace it. His breath stuttered as he stared at the profile of the most enchanting woman he'd ever laid eyes on.

She blazed with passion, eyes alight with wonder as she perused the expensive fabrics in front of her. He recognized the cloth as similar to the handkerchiefs she wore in her hair most days, though not tonight. Tonight, her hair was wild, warm wind tugging at the strawberry strands in the evening air. Just as he had been in her tavern, Lars was wholly and completely in her thrall.

Several nights ago, Lars had visited that same vendor, picking out a handkerchief the exact shade of Emelle's emerald eyes. He'd resigned himself to carrying the cloth so he'd never forget his favorite shade of green, should he never have the fortune of seeing her again.

Not that he ever could.

But the weight of the fabric in his pocket grounded him, reminded him of what was at stake. *Who* was at stake. The path he was set on could only lead her to pain, and he shuddered at the thought of his father knowing she existed.

Emelle spoke briefly with the merchant, and Lars debated how to approach. He knew his abrupt departure must have caused his little enchantress pain and he owed her one enormous apology.

Cosmic Fates, he'd live on his knees if it meant she forgave him. Anguish shot through his chest as he recalled each forced step away from The Finn.

Fuck, he messed up.

Twinkling emerald eyes swung in his direction as she pulled herself away from the vendor. Crossing the busy square, Emelle stopped next to the burbling fountain as she finally noticed his presence. Her lips parted, drawing Lars's hungry gaze right to those plump lips. Sound faded from around them.

Fates, he wanted to bite those lips. Ached to find out if they were as soft as he'd imagined.

Striding over to his favorite enchantress, Lars crowded her space and confiscated her attention. He cataloged her features, inspecting her for injuries while she did the same. A few healing scratches along her hairline caught his attention.

Lars's sight tunneled at the thought of her getting injured. Which made him wholly unprepared for the little enchantress as she jumped into his arms. Just as quickly, she yanked herself away, tears in her eyes, fury shaking her voice.

"You left me! You colossal brute, you left me! Without a word!"

Phantom pain lanced through his chest as her tears finally escaped. "Emmy—"

"You left me," she interrupted, lip quivering as she refused to look at him.

He ducked his sight to catch hers, and her obvious pain broke his heart. He knew he couldn't lie to her. Not anymore. "I did."

"Why?" she demanded.

Lars searched for a reason that would justify his sneaking out as the sun rose, with only a pathetic note and some coin as farewell. As shimmering emerald focused on him, peace settled in his soul from finally being reunited with his mate.

The feelings he couldn't put a name to two weeks ago swirled in his chest, warming his bones. He never should have left without her. He knew she craved a life outside the borders of Silvermist, knew she longed to *see* Eralyn, and yet he left her anyway.

Lars didn't have regrets in his life, he'd never believed in the notion before. But searching her features, seeing the pain so clearly etched in every facet of her eyes, Lars regretted his decision to pretend he didn't know who she was to him—*what* she was to him. Regretted resigning himself to a life of blinding agony every day without his soulmate.

He knew the pain intimately, having felt the burn deep in his soul for each tortuous minute in the past fifteen days. His chest had tightened, as though a boulder sat atop him, forcing him to carry the weight of his transgression with each step he took away from Emelle.

Shame burrowed deep into his gut, its poisonous talons shredding any hope he'd harbored for forgiveness. Lars glanced around the square. They would need much more privacy for this conversation.

"I will explain everything. Just—Please just come with me. There are *ears* everywhere."

She must have heard the desperation bleed through his voice, for she nodded once. Grabbing her hand, Lars's heart lurched at the way she let him tug her forward, at the kernel of trust she must still feel for him. He practically dragged her towards the inn.

☽✻☾

"Wait here," he directed his mate as he entered the inn. The dim foyer was bustling, but Lars stalked straight up to the front desk, ignoring a few grumbling men as he cut in front of them. A single raised eyebrow silenced them. One openly shook with fear.

Addressing the innkeeper, he hurriedly instructed the worker. "You have *one room* available. Got it?" he said through clenched teeth, voice begging the man to disobey. It had been too long since he'd had an excuse to use his fists.

The innkeeper audibly gulped, nodding frantically.

"Did you actually think that was going to work?" Emelle questioned with a raised brow as she entered the inn on unhurried feet, approaching the men. The fools who waited behind Lars scanned her supple form as she crossed in front of them.

Lars saw red.

He took one singular step towards them, and an acrid smell wafted in the air. Emelle's nose crinkled, upper lip curled in distaste as the rest of the fools ran off.

Extending a hand, Lars waited for her to reach him. She slipped a warm hand into his, tiny in comparison, and he pulled her forward. She lost her balance, falling into his chest. She was only a breath away. It was surreal.

Flashing his teeth, Lars spoke confidently. "Not a chance. I look forward to punishing you for your disobedience." He grasped her shoulders, steadying her on her feet before bringing his attention back to the innkeeper. Lars felt the heat of Emelle's rising anger lick his eager flesh.

"Two rooms, please," he requested, false pretense dripping from each word.

Sweat dripped down the man's temple as he glanced nervously between Lars and his lovely enchantress. His gaze narrowed at the man, capturing his attention once again. The stranger didn't get to look at his mate. "I apologize, sir, but we only have one room available."

A barely audible scoff sounded behind him.

"With how many beds?" Lars feigned anger, single brow silently threatening the man to answer correctly.

"One?" He clearly hoped that was the correct response.

A subtle nod of approval from Lars and the man cleared his throat.

"One bed, sir," he said, this time with a little more confidence. It was enough for him.

Looking back at his steaming mate, Lars taunted her with a quirked brow. "That going to be a problem, princess?"

Anger snuffed from her face, a flirtatious smirk masking her earlier irritation.

"Of course not, sweetie," she responded, tone saccharine, before lightly tapping his cheek with her hand, the last pat carrying a little more force.

He caught her hand, and her eyes sparked with desire as he held her hand against his jaw, turning his head to lightly kiss her palm.

"These are her bags, I believe," the man interrupted with a gulp. Lars tensed, and the man visibly trembled before tacking on, "And your key."

On a wink, Lars grabbed the room key and pack from the innkeeper without breaking eye contact with his little enchantress. Color crept onto her cheekbones as he leaned over her soft form, speaking quietly so only she could hear.

"Are you ready for your punishment?"

Emelle's pulse visibly thrummed, lusty breaths falling from her. Neither broke their stare.

☽✷☾

Entering the too-small room, Lars locked the door behind them. Let someone try to interrupt them tonight. Emelle walked into the space and surveyed their lodgings, clearly trying to cut the tension from earlier by ignoring the imposing man. There was a mid-size bed—just big enough to fit the both of them—against the wall on the left. Two small tables on either side of the bed held candles, already burning. To his immediate left, a door to a washroom was propped open, and Lars peeked inside. A surprisingly large basin took up most of the space, but a latrine was tucked in the corner. It was clean, though aged, and his nose burned from the sharp lingering scent of soap. While he shouldn't have been surprised by the indoor plumbing, he was especially grateful. Dried blood and mud were still caked over his leathers after his late-night jaunt he'd just returned from.

Stepping back into the main room, a paltry excuse of a fireplace lay dormant on the right, and Lars moved to bring it to life. He struck the flint provided on a shelf, and the roar of the flames crackled in the otherwise quiet room.

"Come. Sit," he asked, nodding to the edge of the bed.

Emelle's head snapped around, her anger rekindling as she glared at his bold direction. All the same, she sat gingerly on the blanket.

Walking over, Lars settled next to her on the bed. The air cooled several degrees as he stared at the torn wallpaper in front of them. Seconds passed before he gathered the courage to start speaking. He knew he had to come clean, the guilt had been eating him alive and he needed her to know the truth.

Fates, please let her forgive him.

"I lied." He winced at the abruptness, but he didn't take it back. "To you, that is. I lied about why I was in Silvermist. I wasn't truthful about Denny. I mean, Denny *was* an old friend and he probably left for a trial recently, but I wouldn't know since I haven't spoken to him in over seven years. He's a young prince from a kingdom in Thoryn I'd helped when he was visiting my kingdom."

Emelle sat frozen at his side. Crickets chirped in time with his heart as he thrummed his fingers against his thigh. The crackles from the fireplace were notably sharp, warming the room and increasing his unease with each snap.

"My father is the King of Wellsmore. His concubine fell pregnant and made her excuses until it was too late; I was already on my way into the world when he ran into the birthing room." Lars paused, gathering his nerve. It was foreign, laying out the truth without knowing the outcome. He wasn't used to dealing in uncertainty.

With a deep breath, he continued. "He let me reside in the palace until my ninth birthday. I had to stay with my mother in her quarters, but I suppose after eight years he'd seen enough of me running around the place. His captain of the guard dropped me in the streets that same morning. I'd barely even been able to say goodbye to my mother. Another servant had to restrain her as they dragged me from our room. Her screams still haunt me." He sighed, the echo of his mother's cries resounding in his mind once again. "I heard she passed recently."

Unable to look at the quiet woman beside him, Lars's eyes burned with unshed tears. The outdated wallpaper blurred. "My father—" He cleared his throat. "King Winthorpe never had a legitimate heir and he's been ruling unchecked for over thirty years. He hasn't been sighted outside the palace walls in the past two decades. He hasn't seen—" His voice trembled, thoughts racing as he tried to find the words to describe the state of Wellsmore.

"He hasn't seen the hunger, the sickness, the fucking *cruelty*, that his subjects live with every day. It's deplorable." Shadows spilled from his fingers, curling around his hands in what he thought meant to be support. "His own guards are terrorizing the streets. It didn't used to be this awful, but over the last year—Fates, the last six months—I've watched too many bury loved ones."

"It's not your fault." Emelle spoke gently, as though not afraid of Lars's indignation, but in an attempt to quell his pain.

"It may not be my fault, but it's my fucking responsibility," he countered through clenched teeth. "One I will happily carry, except—" He stopped short, fear suddenly seizing his breath.

"Except..." Emelle lightly prodded him to continue, small hand landing on his thigh in comfort.

Another shaky breath. "Except when it keeps me from my destiny," he admitted.

"Your destiny?" Emelle's brows furrowed. She was rightfully confused. As a bastard, he had no destiny. Only those of recognized royal lineage received a prophecy from the Fates. Received a trial and the chance to claim the status of Hero and ascend their thrones—at least, he'd never heard of a bastard receiving a destiny before. No one knew why the trials were required—or if they did, they kept the knowledge a carefully guarded secret. It was simply how they transferred the crown.

A bastard had never challenged the Fates before. Lars would be the first.

"I am weaving my own destiny," he declared, the weight of the statement sounding out of place in the quiet room.

Emelle's eyes widened in apparent shock.

"One not handed out from the pompous *Cosmic Fates*. One that will save my kingdom. *I* will become a Hero." A mad smile split his face in two. "I look forward to dragging my father from his throne, and shucking his corpse into the River Hilt." Manic excitement bubbled from Lars as he gripped the edge of the bed, blanket rough on his palms.

"Lars..." She paused, voice hesitant, as if wary of ruining his delight. "You can't create your own destiny. Trust me, I've watched two women try for over a decade. They've danced around The Finn for years trying to fall into any destiny they could. It—it can't be done."

Lars dropped his veil once again. Let her see past his mask. A question formed in her gaze, brows furrowing as she searched his features.

"You're serious? You're weaving your own destiny?" she asked, voice timid and unbelieving. Her hand left his thigh to rest against her throat, the picture of disbelief.

"I slayed the Babau."

Emelle gasped. He didn't tell her to boast, but because it should have been impossible for someone without the Fates' blessing. And since only royals were given a prophecy, only *royals* were loaned a kernel of the Fates' powers, so only royals should be able to slay a celestial beast.

"It was close," he admitted. "That skin was even tougher than you described."

She threw her hands up. "They were *calculated guesses*! Based on years of listening to *idle gossip*! You weren't supposed to go running after a Babau—that's suicide!"

An involuntary chuckle fell from Lars as steam billowed from her ears. "I should probably also blame the swipe it got in on you. Its reaction was incredibly fast." He raised his forearm to show the almost-healed wound.

Surprisingly strong fingers grabbed his wrist and his body was wrenched towards hers as she inspected the injured appendage. Tears shone anew as she looked back up.

"I'm so sorry," she hiccupped. "I'm so, *so* sorry."

Grabbing her chin, Lars tilted her face towards his. "This is *not* your fault, do you understand me?" An emotion too quick to catch jumped in her emerald gaze. "*I* tracked the Babau. *I* entered a celestial trial without having a destiny. And the only reason I survived..." He paused, staring deeply into those shimmering eyes. "Was you," he finished. "Without you, I'd be dead twice over."

Humor broke through her tears as she allowed him to hold her still, a smile wobbling across her lips.

"So really," he said, "I should be thanking you."

Heat surged between them as Lars moved forward just so, invading Emelle's space.

"Do you want me to thank you?" he taunted, licking his lips. *Fates,* he needed to taste this woman.

The air heated between them as their earlier arousal returned in full force, lust pulling them closer together. Lars stared at her wet mouth, fantasies of everything he could do racing through her mind. Sharing her breath, Lars flicked his tongue over her bottom lip, teasing his little enchantress.

Slamming her lips to his, Emelle's arms twined around Lars's neck as she fervently kissed him. Returning her force, Lars slid his hand from her chin down to her neck, holding her in place as they kissed. A low moan escaped from Emelle as she pressed her soft body against Lars.

Fates, he needed to touch this exquisite enchantress.

Feeling her pulse thrum under his fingertips, Lars continued to gently grip her neck as her lips molded against his. They were even softer than he'd imagined, all those nights at The Finn, fucking his hand while pretending it was her mouth, her *heat*, instead of his rough palms. He couldn't wait for her to wrap those lips around his cock.

He was getting ahead of himself.

Breaking the kiss, he stared at her lust-filled gaze and swollen, pink lips. Their breaths fell heavy in the air between them and he dragged his hand down her chest, grazing over her pebbled nipple as he asked, "You wanted me to thank you, yes? For saving my life?"

A shallow nod as she bit her bruised bottom lip. Eyes hooded, Emelle was the picture of carnal lust. Lars's cock strained against his trousers, begging to be released. The heat in the room continued to rise as he smirked.

"It's too bad this is your punishment, then."

Chapter Nineteen
Emelle

Emelle's arousal dripped down into her panties as she processed what Lars had just said. Excitement danced in his face, the air now charged between them.

"Strip," he commanded, sending a tingle down Emelle's spine.

Standing slowly, Emelle gripped the hem of her tunic before lazily dragging it over her head. Shucking her shoes, her heart thundered in her chest. The ties at her waist were next, and she shimmied out of her dirty trousers, leaving her only in her underwear.

Reaching behind her back, Emelle cocked her head, hair falling over her bare shoulders, as she watched Lars. Emelle held the cloth against her chest for only a moment, unclasping the bind quickly before letting it fall unceremoniously to the floor.

Blazing with lust, Lars raked his gaze over Emelle's soft body, her heavy breasts, the dip in her waist leading to her plump hips...Lost to her passion, Emelle ran a hand over her still-clothed cunt and rubbed her fingers over her sensitive clit.

A low moan escaped before Lars was in front of her, grabbing her hand and bringing the offending digit to his mouth, biting gently in warning.

Pure, carnal desire threatened to take over Emelle as she felt him suckle on her finger.

"Now turn around, and run a bath," he ordered.

Confusion broke through her haze, but Lars just raised a brow in response. Doing as he said, Emelle yelped as a hand *smacked* her panty-clad ass.

Moving over to the large tub, Emelle twisted the handle for heated water, surprised when it worked. The floor was cold under her feet and it highlighted her need, her desire for this man that scorched through her blood. Leaving the tub to fill, Emelle spun around, eyes already undressing her stranger.

"Your turn," she challenged, daring Lars to play a little more.

Lars toed off his boots and carefully removed his belt, hands sliding along the leather sensually. A throb pulsed steadily in Emelle's core. Fingers twitching to rub her clit, Emelle gripped the edge of the tub to keep herself from touching herself as Lars undressed.

"I thought this was supposed to be your punishment," he chided, shucking his leathers before gripping his tunic by the back of the neck and dragging it off.

Emelle's lips parted at the seductive move. Kicking off his trousers, Lars stood naked in full glory, cock erect and bobbing against his tight abdomen. Steam billowed around her body and sucked the oxygen out of the too-hot room, stifling her labored breath.

Stalking towards his prey, Lars nestled in between Emelle's legs and tilted her face towards his, rigid cock pressed firmly against her belly. "I suppose it can wait until we're clean," he teased. Stepping around Emelle and into the half-full tub, Lars twisted the knob and settled into the steaming water, holding a hand out to Emelle.

Sliding her panties down slowly, Lars's eyes followed the movement, hunger sparking in his gaze as he caught a glimpse of the desire dripping down from her cunt. Emelle climbed in between his legs, leaning her back against his strong chest. She felt his stiff cock against her lower back and couldn't help but wiggle her ass. Water fell just below her chest, nipples lapped by the gentle waves their bodies created with each movement. It drove her mad.

A hand snaked around her front, grabbing her neck and squeezing softly just once. Tilting her head to the side, Lars ran his nose up the column of her damp neck and licked the soft spot behind her ear. She moaned.

"Are you trying to tease me, princess?" Lars whispered seductively. "I think you are, aren't you, my little enchantress?"

Chest heaving, Emelle was consumed by her lust as she fought to breathe normally. She hardly noticed the cracked tile on the walls of the washroom, her arousal overtaking every thought. There was no room for anything but Lars in this tub.

In the next second, Lars abandoned her neck, dragging his hand down her chest and lifting one heavy breast in his palm. Kneading the soft skin only once, Lars dipped his hand in the steaming water and dribbled the liquid at the top of her chest. The cool draft chilled the water as it rolled down her breast, over her nipple, tightening the buds to the point of pain.

"Look at those pretty nipples, just *begging* to be sucked."

Emelle panted at the thought of him suckling on her breast. Lars grabbed the soap from its dish and lathered a fresh cloth next to it, then ran the cloth all over Emelle's body, taking extra care to clean between her legs. All the extra attention had Emelle ready to burst as she ground her pussy against his cloth-covered fingers.

"Ah, ah, ah—we're just getting clean, princess. You filthy, wicked thing," Lars scolded as he moved on, scrubbing every inch of her skin except where she needed him most. Once finished, Lars directed her to tilt her head back so he could wash her hair. Emelle hadn't had someone wash her hair since her grandmother passed.

Mist pricked her eyes at the surprisingly tender gesture.

Rinsing her soapy hair, Lars planted a light kiss on the back of her head. "There. Done," he said softly.

Before he could speak again, Emelle turned around and took the cloth from his hand, then added more soap. Facing Lars, the tip of his length bobbed out of the water. Her eyes widened at the sight.

Fates, he was big.

A knowing chuckle fell from Lars as his hand reached up to tease Emelle's pointed nipple once again. When she didn't stop him, Lars took it as a sign to lean forward and latch onto the bud. Sucking gingerly, Lars coaxed Emelle's flames higher as he twisted the other nipple with skilled fingers.

Popping off her breast, Lars cleared his throat and Emelle shook herself from the haze, quickly washing his body while studiously avoiding his hard cock. Lars took every opportunity to lick and nibble as she leaned her breasts over his face while she washed his hair.

Desperate moans fell as she ground her empty pussy on nothing but cold air, the water barely touching her folds, driving her delirious. Rinsing his inky waves, Emelle sat back on her haunches and openly panted.

"Don't worry, princess. I'll clean it. Watch me." He lathered his hand with soap and reached under the water, pumping his length.

Emelle was his captive. His hand crested the water and his hips lifted with each stroke. Desperate groans of pleasure slipped through Lars's teeth and jealousy had Emelle smacking away his hand to replace his grip with her own.

Head falling back on the ledge of the tub, Lars's eyes fluttered shut as Emelle worked his length, leaning over his body. Zeroing in on the knot in his throat, Emelle knew he was getting close. He yielded nothing as she twisted and stroked his impressive length.

But after only a few moments, Lars stilled her hand, hissing through clenched teeth.

"The first time you make me cum, it will be in your cunt or your mouth, not a fucking bathtub."

Pleasure thrummed in her core at his filthy words.

Fates, she needed to be used.

"But what if I want to bathe in your cum?" she asked, wide, innocent eyes staring at his.

Lars cursed, and yanked Emelle out of the bathtub, dragging her to the bed. Emelle dripped onto the floor, her wet hair spilling over her shoulders.

Lars climbed onto the bed and Emelle took the brief moment to appreciate his firm body, especially his muscular ass. Her mouth watered at the sight.

Flipping onto his back, Lars propped up onto a strong elbow, ogling Emelle with obvious heat blazing in his eyes. He smirked, and his gaze licked her from her breasts to her sex. "Come here, princess," he ordered.

Emelle obeyed.

Crawling onto the bed, Emelle slid her body against his until she was face to face with him. They stared at each other for only a moment before she surged forward, capturing his lips with hers. Their wet bodies fused together as the heat in the room rose.

But all too soon, Lars pulled away, lust shining back at her. "That's not what I meant, sweetheart."

Confusion broke through the haze of her desire, her brows furrowing at her stranger. Licking her lips, she spoke, voice dripping with need.

"I don't understand."

Mirth filled his gaze, and Emelle blinked once, twice.

"Have a seat," he said salaciously.

Emelle floundered, his words stirring a deep need in her. A need she hadn't even realized she had.

Lars saw her hesitation, and slid his strong hand between their heated bodies to grasp her chin. His grip was firm and Emelle panted at the gesture. At the ownership. Lars's attention flitted to her parted mouth and his pupils dilated. His tongue darted out to wet his lips while his thumb swiped across her bottom lip. His gaze didn't leave her mouth as he spoke.

"I said," he began, voice leaving no room for argument, "take a seat, Emelle." A heartbeat later and his onyx eyes crashed into hers.

Emelle fell into his depths, wholly and willingly. That is, until Lars slapped a sharp hand on her ass, spurring her into motion.

Emelle placed one shaky hand on his firm chest before sliding her right leg up. She held his gaze as she climbed onto his face, his wild beard tickling the inside of her thighs. Strong fingers gripped the flesh where her hips met her legs, indenting his claim over her body.

Lowering herself only slightly, she held his gaze as he breathed her scent in. His eyes darkened even further, if that was even possible, before he nuzzled his nose and lips into her apex.

The old bed creaked below them, but Emelle couldn't bring herself to care. She dragged her right hand through the inky waves that had haunted her dreams for the past several weeks. The silky strands were soft as she curled them between her fingers, securing her hold on his head as he started to lick her in earnest.

Emelle moaned, the feeling of his tongue in her cunt too pleasurable after the weeks of desire building in her. All the heated looks, the lingering touches...It was finally happening. Her wet hair continued to drip, cooling her quickly overheating body. The contrast was maddening.

But far too soon, Lars pulled his mouth away, and Emelle gaped at him. His fingers tightened on her hips. She hoped he left bruises.

"I said sit," he growled.

Emelle's eyes widened right before he slammed her down onto his mouth. Doubling his efforts, Lars fucked her with his tongue as he rolled her hips back and forth. Her body was his to manipulate.

Her eyelids fluttered shut, heat curling in her abdomen as he ate her sex like the sweetest ambrosia. She groaned, losing herself to her desire as she took over riding his face. Lars smothered himself with her, only the waves of his dark hair visible under her soft belly. He removed one hand from her hips to reach around her body, sliding two fingers over her wet hole from behind. He teased her entrance and used his tongue on her clit to drag her higher and higher.

No other man had ever made her feel such intense pleasure, and she was quickly racing towards that euphoric peak.

The room darkened imperceptibly as Lars's other hand left her hip and grabbed one of her cheeks, spreading it open so her holes were on display. The air against her pussy was chilly and she clenched around his fingers as her eyelids dropped closed, the pleasure too great.

A breath later and she lost her balance, slapping her hand onto the wall above the shoddy headboard. Her eyes snapped open and she groaned, the stimulation quickly becoming too much. Lars took the opportunity to release her ass, but only for a moment. His palm crashed down on her cheek with a *smack*, and heat bloomed in its wake.

Delicious, *addicting* heat.

Moans fell coarsely from her as she rolled her hips over his lips, chasing her release. She was so close. Her movements stuttered, about to be launched into the cosm—

Lars lifted her off his face, stopping all motion. Emelle's heart thundered, her fingers curling against the wall in frustration. The scratch of the old wallpaper was a harsh contrast to the fires licking along her spine.

"What the *fuck*, Lars?"

He just smirked and licked his drenched lips, groaning softly at the taste of her desire. He blew a hot breath onto her sex and she shuddered.

"I'm sorry, were you about to come on my face, princess?"

Emelle wanted to throttle him. He knew damn well what he did.

"Didn't I say this was your punishment?" Lars leisurely leaned his head forward, licking one long stripe up her seam before kissing her mound lightly.

Emelle saw stars, from both the fire that lingered in her bones and from the need to sit down and smother him to death. He must've seen the threat, and chuckled darkly.

"But what a way to go, dearest."

Her gaze narrowed.

Another chuckle, and then—

"But fortunately for you, it's not my time," he quipped before slamming her back down on his face. His tongue went back to flicking and sucking, dragging her right back up to the edge.

Emelle ground her sex onto his mouth, chasing her release before he could change his mind. Lars stared into her eyes, heat blazing in the dark depths as she rode him. His tongue, no matter how it infuriated her sometimes, was devilishly talented.

Emelle placed both hands on the wall again, grinding her hips and building herself higher and higher. Stars flashed behind her lids, *no—*

Lars lifted her again, labored from the breath he'd sacrificed, a smirk quirking the corners of his swollen lips.

Emelle screamed.

"Lars, what the *fuck!*" She banged a frustrated fist on the wall.

"Have you learned your lesson?" he asked.

Her mind raced back to when they first arrived at the inn, how he said he was looking forward to punishing her. For her disobedience. As much as she wanted, *needed*, her release, she always did love playing games. It made the win that much sweeter. She supposed she could play this game with him. She raised a brow.

"My obedience is earned. Have you earned it?"

Lars leaned forward and slowly licked her again, sliding his tongue between her dripping folds and circling her clit. Emelle groaned, her lips parting as he continued his ministrations.

"I don't need your obedience." His dark eyes sparked with an emotion too quick for her to catch. "But I crave your willingness all the same."

With that, he dove forward, fucking her cunt with his tongue and reaching around to slip a finger into her from behind. Emelle rolled her hips, sliding a hand down into his dark hair and coiling her fingers around the strands. She pushed his face into her sex, not giving him an option to stop again.

His tongue paused, but his lips remained a hairbreadth away from her apex.

"Beg the Fates for forgiveness, princess. Beg them to forgive your wickedness." He spoke directly against her dripping cunt, his breath swirling around his words and tickling her sensitive flesh.

A gasp fell before she could stop it. She'd been riding the edge for so long, she was aching for her release. She only needed a touch, a *whisper* of a touch, and she'd be launched into the cosmos.

"Please, Fates, please forgive me," she moaned, her hips twitching above his waiting lips.

A dark chuckle, and then—

"I forgive you, princess," Lars said irreverently, before sucking directly on her clit.

It was enough.

She was the cosmos and the cosmos were her. Stars flew behind her lids, whiteness overtaking her vision. Her orgasm went on for what felt like eons, as her legs seized under her. Lars licked her through her waves, savoring every last drop of her release.

"Look at me."

Emelle's eyes shot open, her sight glazed over as she tried to focus on him.

"There you are," he murmured, warmth from another emotion flickering back at her.

Slowly, Lars shifted her off his face, and gingerly laid her over his chest. His wild beard glistened with her release.

Emelle fought to catch her breath, her cunt still pulsing from the explosive orgasm. Lars kissed the crown of her head delicately, and the tender move curled around her heart. The quilt they laid on was scratchy against her sensitive skin, but Emelle was intimately familiar with the cheap, but effective, soaps used to clean them. Emelle relaxed into his hold, delicious pleasure still sparking where his fingers gently skimmed across her curves.

After another moment, once she had fully returned to their plane, Emelle became aware of the sharp prodding in her side. Lars's chest heaved under her, and she peered up at him. His pupils were still blown as his gaze bored into hers. Flames rushed back to life, and Emelle slid down to where a rigid cock jutted into the air.

Leaning over his legs, Emelle stared at the hardness in front of her, saliva gathering in her mouth. Her damp hair fell over her face, and Lars reached a hand down to flip it over her shoulder. She tilted her head ever so, looking at him from the corner of her eye. Licking her lips, she winked before reaching for the delicious treat.

But Lars stopped her with a gentle touch on her shoulder. His other hand gripped the base of his hard cock, his hand on her shoulder shifting to the crown of her hair to guide her mouth down to his shaft.

"Suck," he commanded.

Emelle obeyed.

Lars kept a hold on the top of her head as she licked and bobbed on the inhuman length. Fates, she wanted him to choke her on that cock.

But one, two more pumps and Lars exploded with a groan in her mouth. Emelle waited but Lars kept spurting down her throat. Before she could swallow, a hand wrapped around her neck. She gazed up at him, still hovering over his cock, ass lifted in the air.

"Don't." Depthless eyes commanded her body, a puppet under his total control. "Open," Lars said, still blazing with residual heat.

Emelle parted her lips and stuck out her tongue, evidence of his release pooling in her mouth. Sitting up, Lars pushed her over until she was the one laying in the bed and he was laying over her, firm body pressing hers into the mattress. She opened her lips once more and his pupils flashed with hunger. He slid a hand down to her neck, pulling her chin down with his thumb. A heartbeat later, he *spat* on her tongue.

Before she could react, Lars ducked down and kissed her sloppily. He fucked her mouth with his tongue like he'd just fucked her pussy with it, sharing his salty cum and saliva.

Pulling back, satisfaction gleamed in his eyes.

"Swallow," he commanded as he pushed his thumb up, closing her mouth for her. Darkness gathered in the room as Emelle followed his instruction, his hold remaining on her throat, feeling her swallow.

Tingles shivered down her spine as they stared into each other's souls, seeming to understand at the same time: if they were to go up in flames, they would burn together.

Chapter Twenty
Emelle

Curling into a ball, Emelle groaned as bright morning sunlight streamed into the room. A soft chuckle rumbled in the hard chest her cheek rested on, bringing memories of last night rushing back. Heat flushed her cheeks and Emelle buried her face in Lars's bare flesh.

"Oh, no you don't," Lars said, grabbing her hair and tugging gently, forcing her to meet his gaze. His eyes sparked with laughter. "You don't get to hide this bird's nest from me."

Shit, she fell asleep with wet hair.

Emelle tried, and failed, to escape his strong arms. Gathering her close, Lars just kissed her forehead before pulling her in to nuzzle into her neck, inhaling deeply. His beard tickled her bare flesh and Emelle prayed her heady arousal from the night before was now diluted. She wasn't sure she was ready for round two.

"Why did you say you'd be dead twice over without me?" Emelle asked, voice still raspy from sleep. Her head bounced on his chest as Lars laughed. "Whoa, settle down."

"Well, obviously you saved me from dying of a chill that night in the rain," he said, dark eyes twinkling with mischief.

Emelle groaned, burying herself further into his hold.

"I *was* worried! I just...didn't want you to leave," she admitted, embarrassment heating her cheeks. Deciding to tell her full truth, she continued, mumbling into the pillow she wanted to suffocate in. "I'd wanted you to stay with me that night, in my room. But your *enormous* frame cornered me in my office and I got flustered. I couldn't spin a lie quick enough that I didn't have room for you anywhere else."

Lars lost it, bursting into laughter.

Emelle's cheeks flamed.

"Don't—" Another laugh. "Don't be embarrassed, princess. If we're laying our truths out..." He paused, wiping his tears with the back of his hand. "I threatened the innkeeper last night to only give us one room. That's why I ran ahead."

Emelle's jaw dropped, eyes alight with mirth as she stared at the hulking man, still gorgeous even with bedhead. The curl above his brow was perfectly coiffed, and it frustrated her as much as it aroused her. Why couldn't her bangs look that sexy in the morning?

But she just laughed.

After a few moments, Emelle swallowed her amusement and wiped away her matching tears, snuggling into his arms once again. "I forgive you. I understand—" She paused, emotion suddenly choking her. "I understand why you did it. You didn't know me, you didn't owe me anything. But—I wish you would've trusted me."

Lars untangled himself from her body, searching her face for something, but she wasn't sure what.

"I should've told you," Lars said, brushing her bangs behind her ear with a trembling hand. "But you panicked when you saw me in your office, and I rushed to find the simplest reason why I needed to be rifling through your ledger. I didn't know about the notes you made, but I hoped there was *some* sort of clue towards any recent celestial trials written somewhere in that office.

"That first night I entered The Finn, I couldn't focus. I tried to listen to the Hero, but all I could see was this luscious little barkeep flitting about. I spent seven days drowning in the pouring rain in the Wildlands, chasing down half-leads and mixing the details from his tale and another I'd heard from a fool a few tables away." A sigh escaped, frustration bleeding through his tone. "I finally made it back to The Finn and realized I needed to change my strategy. I saw you, darting around the tavern, somehow hearing everyone all at once." Lars's rough fingers traced the shell of Emelle's ear.

Emelle waited with bated breath, hoping her silence would yield more answers from the enigma in front of her.

"I knew if anyone would have information on the celestial trials, it would be you. The barkeep who moved on silent feet, always listening to the tales being told in her tavern. I knew I needed your help. It's been tearing me apart knowing how I used you. That I only saw you as a strategy." He gulped, his eyes shutting in apparent shame. "I am so sorry, Emelle."

Emelle cupped his cheek. Eyes fluttering open, Lars leaned gently into her amnesty.

"I forgive you," she repeated, voice barely audible. "You had no reason to trust me, I was just a stranger."

Onyx eyes snapped open, and Emelle inhaled sharply at the emotion she saw in them.

"You are not just a stranger, you're—" A jagged breath and Lars stopped, eyes wide. Whatever he was about to say would change her forever, she just knew it.

Waiting for him to continue, Emelle deflated once he spoke. "How did you get to Briarwood, princess?" he mused, deftly changing the subject.

Understanding they both needed a reprieve, Emelle shared the details of the tortuous past two weeks. Lars laughed unabashedly when she got to the part of waking to a slithery friend. Smacking his chest lightly in admonishment, Emelle's heart filled to the point of bursting as she mooned at this stranger, *her* stranger.

Rowdy noise filtered through their wooden door, patrons making their way down for breakfast. She and Lars ignored the call, choosing to remain in their private bubble for just a while longer.

Emelle smiled as Lars pulled away from their light kiss. She already missed the wild beard he'd shaved while she tamed her bird's nest just before heading downstairs. They hadn't come down until the sun was well into the sky, haggling with the kitchen for some breakfast leftovers. Emelle didn't get very far until Lars mysteriously appeared over her shoulder. Suddenly, the kitchen staff were more than happy to plate some leftovers. Eating the day-old bread and hard cheese, they both left the suspicious-looking gruel untouched.

Heart in her throat, Emelle debated how to ask the question she'd been too afraid to put into words upstairs. She hadn't wanted to ruin the moment. Afraid of his response, she needed to have that memory untouched by heartbreak, in case he wanted to send her away.

"So, where are we headed next?" she said, infusing each word with confidence. Fates, even she believed her false bravado. Maybe she was getting better at spinning charades.

"What makes you think you'll be coming with me?" Lars asked with a blank expression before breaking into an easy smile.

Emelle tossed a piece of cheese at his delighted face, scoffing to stifle her own grin. It still seemed foreign for him to crack a smile rather than a frown, but Emelle hoarded each one, burning them into her memory.

"I'm not sure how many trials I'll need to complete since I don't have a destiny of my own to fall into." Calculating eyes scanned the quiet room. Most guests had emptied onto the streets or back upstairs, so they had the space almost to themselves.

Still, he continued in a hushed voice. "I don't feel any different after slaying the Babau, other than some lingering guilt. I found it in the outskirts of Briarshire and tracked it for well over a week before I could lure it into the trap. I buried the headless body that same night in the nearest grove, placing a few stones to mark its grave. It took damn near all night to dig it deep enough," Lars sighed, dark circles shadowing his eyes despite the heavy rest they had the night before.

"I followed your instructions down to the most *minute* detail, and it *worked*. I had just gotten back to Briarwood when I saw you drooling over the vendor with all those handkerchiefs," Lars teased.

"They weren't *instructions*, you fool!" she scolded. "You weren't supposed to go chasing after mythical beasts! You shouldn't have even been able to trap it, let alone kill it. And I wasn't *drooling*."

Smiling brightly, Lars just tossed another piece of bread in his mouth.

"They were instructions, you just didn't realize it. And I know I saw some drool right there," he said, lifting a callused hand to playfully wipe the corner of her mouth.

Huffing, Emelle slowly matched his smile. Sight drawn to the healing pink scar peeking out from Lars's sleeve, Emelle softened, grateful that he came out *mostly* unscathed.

How did he heal so fast?

"Here," he murmured, pulling out a deep jewel-toned green fabric.

Emelle gingerly accepted the expensive cloth with wide eyes.

"I bought it last week from that wildly expensive merchant you visited last night. I figured..." He paused, his voice catching on the emotion bleeding through. "If I never found my way back to you, at least I'd never forget the exact shade of the only color that would surely break the last of my ruined soul if I never saw it again."

Emelle's gaze snapped back down to the cloth. It was the exact shade she saw reflecting in the mirror each morning. A rogue tear slipped over her cheek and she smiled at Lars.

"I think I'll keep it. You aren't getting rid of me so easily," she whispered, blindly fixing the handkerchief to her head, pulling out two wispy pieces in habit. She wouldn't let him have it back, if she had any say about it.

Lars searched her face, a grin pulling at his lips as he watched her. Then he said, "We need to find another trial," steering them back to safer territory. "Maybe if I complete a handful of different trials, it will force the Fates to grant me Hero status."

Emelle was skeptical, to say the least. "Most come to the Briars to slay the Babaus and a few other celestial beasts, but that's about all you'll find in the South Forest. The sites also cycle, so they're not always active. You got really lucky," she added. "If you don't feel any different, perhaps we should try our hands at one of the other trials?"

"I think you're right. And now that I have the brightest barkeep in all of Eralyn on my side, I say we go solve ourselves a celestial puzzle."

"First, we'd have to *find* a celestial puzzle. I've heard of some found in the Burnes to the east, but usually Heroes have the Fates helping them locate the scroll. If we travel there, we may not find anything at all."

Lars just waited, an eyebrow raised in challenge.

She nodded, a coy smile quirking the corner of her mouth. "What is your gut telling you to go? Which direction should we start?"

"Let's head east," he responded without hesitation. "We'll start in the Burnes and pray we find one." His jaw ticked, and Emelle knew he was anxious. She felt the same. Challenging the Fates right to their faces was dangerous, and she prayed they weren't heading down a path of no return.

She nodded once again, before clearing the emotion from her features. He needed to know she was serious. "Don't lie to me again. Understand?"

Lars visibly gulped. "I won't. You have my word."

She searched his remorseful face and saw only the truth staring back at her. Accepting his promise, Emelle nodded, breaking the rising tension.

Lars's shoulders dropped with relief as he reached into his bag and flipped a few coins onto the table. Emelle raised an eyebrow and Lars just chuckled, tossing a few more onto the wooden surface.

Standing, Lars extended a hand to Emelle, guiding her out of the chair and back to their room. It was time to plan.

Chapter Twenty-One
Lars

"You're going to hurt yourself, princess," Lars warned.

Emelle ignored him, stretching for the scroll just out of reach. She refused his help and he took the chance to ogle his little mate. Studying her from across the cave, Lars felt his cock swell, tightening in his trousers to the point of pain. Even with the dirt that covered them from head to toe and the mud that caked their knees, she was a sight to behold.

In the eight days since they left Briarwood, they'd barely touched other than to innocently warm each other at night. Six days of hard travel to Thorneburne and two days of incessant searching for scrolls exhausted both of them.

Despite the heat during the day, the nights chilled their bones and left them shivering the further southeast they traveled. Lingering looks and bashful touches left him steadily boiling.

He needed another taste of his little enchantress.

Now they were deep in an enormous cave filled with stalagmites and crevices, which they'd been searching for over twenty minutes. It was the third they'd found along the tunnel so far. If not for the fact he knew with certainty which turns they had made, he would have otherwise started to worry how far they traversed.

THE FOOL'S ERRAND

"Almost...got...i—" Emelle's voice cut into a scream as she lost her balance, slipping backwards.

Having prepared for the fall, Lars caught his mate on a chuckle. Emelle blew her bangs out of her eyes. She had wiped the sweat from her brow at some point, leaving behind an adorable smudge of dirt.

"Not a word," she chided, humor breaking their earlier tension.

Lars sobered as he eyed the unassuming case clutched in her hands and set her onto her feet. "If this isn't the right scroll, I'm going to curse the Fates." They'd found two so far, but neither held a celestial riddle. Emelle had glanced at him sheepishly before explaining that not every scroll held one. Or at least, one they could read.

She'd said the right riddle would appear on the right scroll at the right moment. Because of course it would. Why would the Fates make this easy for him?

"Lars, we've only been at this for a few days. We will find one, I promise. You've got the brightest barkeep in all of Eralyn helping, remember?" Emelle teased.

"The people of Wellsmore are *suffering*, Emelle. They're starving and they're broken, and no one is doing anything about it!" Lars cried, the injustice tearing at his seams. "The king remains sequestered in his castle, letting his subjects suffer and die to keep his coffers full."

Anger rolled off him in furious waves, and he swore it heated the damp cave they were in. Dense shadows seeped from his body and dimmed the already dark space. He pinched the bridge of his nose, eyes shut. This duty, this *obligation* of his was pulling him under, when all he wanted was to run away with Emelle, to take her anywhere but down this path.

"We're going to find it, Lars," Emelle said, voice unyielding. She gingerly rested her palm against his cheek.

Opening his eyes, Lars searched her face. Yes. They were in this together now. She was here to help him. It was strange, to have someone volunteering to help rather than awaiting orders.

There was no choice but to succeed.

With a firm nod, Lars inspected the case holding the parchment, releasing the shadows that had slipped from his control. It was worn by age, one end forming a sharp point that curved into a notch, while the other end was blunt. His heart thundered, hoping for any clue about where they needed to go next.

"Here." Emelle pointed, noting a small symbol that he missed at first glance.

Bringing the case closer, Lars eyed the marking.

"It looks like..." He paused, searching his memory. "The mountain we passed a little while back," he whispered softly, afraid to disturb the air. It seemed as if the cave itself absorbed the sound.

"Mountain!" Emelle rushed back to her pack to find her ledger. She'd taken to reading it before bed, trying to find any detail that might help find the celestial trial. Echoes of her steps sounded down the long cave, an unsettling side effect of being so deep in the tunnel.

Flipping to a page, Emelle scanned the words hastily, and then flashed a blinding smile to Lars. She pointed a finger to an image drawn in the margins. "*Look,*" she said.

Lars rapidly read the words under the symbol, a triumphant grin slowly forming.

"'Climbing a two-pointed mountain, the Hero dodged trappings—psychedelic plants and quicksand—and wildlife, before cresting the western point,'" Lars read aloud. Desperate hope lanced through his chest. "'Finding the scroll he'd discovered in a nearby cave, the Hero read the riddle aloud to the iridescent moon. After a moment of silence, the Hero whispered his answer to the skies. Answering correctly, the Hero felt the air heat and steam began to rise from the water. Hearing the Fates' booming voices in the quiet, they accepted his answer, and the Hero knew his trial was complete.'" Lars's eyes widened as he smiled broadly at Emelle, his heart thundering in his chest.

Her laughter filled the small cave and Lars couldn't help but join in. Twisting the casing open from the blunt end, Lars tapped the scroll into his waiting hand. Emelle pressed her cheek against his arm as he unraveled the scroll. They scanned the parchment, reading the riddle in tandem.

What is lost to time,
Rejected by history,
Remembered by dust,
Welcomed by few.

"What?" Emelle said finally, breaking the silence. He read the riddle thrice over.

"I—I don't know. It makes no sense," he whispered, hope dimming by the second. He read over the page again before he turned desperately to his mate.

"All right, it's all right," Emelle soothed. "We'll head back towards the mountain. We know we'll need to climb to the western peak, so we'll head back that way. We can stay in that small village we passed through, about a days ride back."

Lars couldn't admit it at the moment, but he was so incredibly grateful for Emelle's steady logic, that she took charge.

Nodding, Lars took the heavy ledger from Emelle and shoved it into her bag. Swinging both packs onto his shoulders, Lars took Emelle's hand as they navigated back through the tunnel to their horses. Lars helped her onto Selene before mounting Helios, and led the way back to the small village of Cloudburne.

☽✷☾

Emelle and Lars dragged their feet up to their room for the night. Lars had to stifle laughter as Emelle almost tripped. When she glared back at him, Lars wiped any trace of amusement from his face but couldn't resist lightly smacking her on the ass.

Entering their room, they had laughed about how it was a near mirror image to the room they stayed in Briarwood—a large bed against the right wall and a small washroom to the right of the entrance. Lars and Emelle then bathed promptly before Lars left to collect hot stew and bread from the kitchen. Eating quickly, they didn't care how it tasted, so long as it filled them. Lars's pulse hammered as Emelle suckled on her spoon, oblivious to the way he watched her finish her supper. Discarding his empty bowl, Lars reached across and plucked Emelle's from her grip.

"Hey!" she said, spoon still hanging from her delectable mouth.

Pulling her by the hanging spoon, Lars crushed Emelle to his body and flicked the offending metal off to *Fates knew where*. He captured Emelle's soft lips, pouring his unspoken emotions into his kiss.

Teeth clacking, Lars and Emelle tumbled onto the bed. He dragged her thigh up to hitch above his hip, her shift riding up to her waist. Lars ground his rigid length into her panty-covered pussy and Emelle moaned directly into his mouth.

Fates, that was music to his ears.

Sliding one hand down to her hip, Lars ground Emelle on each upward stroke of his hips. Frenzied panting fell from Emelle's lips as her desire leaked through her underwear. Lars stared at her hooded eyes, unable to resist licking the bead of sweat gathered at the column of her neck.

"Fates, you're so beautiful," he whispered against her neck, nipping at her pulse. "I'm not even inside you and you feel so good."

When she moaned, he caught the sound with his lips. He was embarrassingly close to ruining his trousers right now.

"*Fates*, I'm so close," she cried, humping her cunt on his hard cock. He could feel her heat beckoning him like a siren but he held himself back, ignoring the desperate need to hitch her panties to the side and plunge in to the hilt.

"Fuck, princess, just like that." Lars was breathless, resting his forehead against hers as she worked herself into a frenzy. Her desire coated him and the air, an ambrosia he could easily be addicted to for the rest of his life.

Emelle moaned and—

Bang! Bang! Bang!

Someone pounded on their door. Emelle rolled aside and Lars

sprang off the bed. Grabbing his dagger, he quietly approached the door, motioning to Emelle with a finger to his mouth to remain quiet, waving for her to stay calm as she tried to control her breathing.

Then Lars turned back to the door, opening it just enough to poke his head out. Looking down both hallways, Lars scanned the area for anything out of the ordinary. Down one end stood a parent scolding their young daughter. A prank, then.

Climbing back into the bed, Lars crumbled at Emelle's face, at the pure terror that had replaced her lust, twisting her features. Scooping her into his arms, Lars petted her hair and whispered soothing words.

"Shh, princess. I'm here. Nothing's going to happen to you," he quietly reassured. "I'm here, you're safe."

Irate tears filled twinkling emerald eyes as she snapped her gaze to his. "I'm not worried about *me*, you idiot! You didn't know who was on the other side of the door. You could've been seriously hurt, or even ki—" She hiccupped, tears spilling over.

Lars cupped her cheeks, wiping the hot tears with his thumbs.

"No, sweetheart. It was just a little girl playing a prank. I would've been fine," he promised, and when she tried to shake her head, he tightened his hold on her chin to stop the movement. He searched his mate's face as he finally told her the last of his truths. "I told you my father sent me to live on the streets when I was a boy. What I haven't told you is that I spent the next two decades learning every secret those streets had to hide. I learned to—to survive. I learned what true sacrifice meant. I watched men gamble their souls away to provide for their families. I bore witness to horrible, *horrific* things..."

He trailed off, staring over her head and into the aged wall. "And I realized it could change with me, if I overthrew my father and ascended the throne. I've never wanted to be king, but for the people I will be. For over twenty years I've trained, I've manipulated...I've wrestled control of a terrifying group of men—" He paused, thinking of the state The Den was in right now. "I...I don't think my hands will ever be clean of the blood I've spilt along the streets of my kingdom."

Lars stopped, emotion choking the rest of his words. Fates, he couldn't bear to look at his mate. To see her repulsion.

A soft hand slid over his cheek, turning his face towards her. He closed his eyes, unable to witness the disgust he feared might be on her face.

But cautious lips gently pressed against his own, for just the briefest moment. Lars gambled with his heart, opening his eyes to see the most enthralling woman he'd ever found, gazing at him with nothing but mercy.

"Hold me?" she whispered, voice sleepy and low.

He audibly swallowed, then nodded fiercely before he tucked her into his chest, circling his arms around the little enchantress.

"Forever," he rasped, kissing the crown of her head. Minutes later, Lars listened to the soft snores of his mate, succumbing entirely to the overwhelming weight of her forgiveness.

Chapter Twenty-Two
Emelle

"We need to find a historian," Emelle said, eyes scanning the scroll for what felt like the hundredth time. It made no sense. They'd been turning the riddle over for two days, and they were nowhere near close to finding an answer. They hadn't even left their quarters, opting to take each meal in the privacy of their messy room.

Much to her dismay, every waking minute was spent trying to unravel the riddle. She wasn't sure if he could feel the rising heat in each look she sent him, but she was ready to burst from the weeks of back and forth. Especially after that near-explosive evening a few nights ago.

"It says *rejected by history*. How would a historian be able to help?" Lars countered, frustration settling in his muscles as his jaw ticked. The dim light of the small fireplace barely lit the room and flickered against his skin. A fleeting image of the blond Hero who'd caught her eye at The Finn a few weeks ago surged to the front of her memory, and Emelle knew what she'd felt then was nothing compared to what she felt now for Lars.

He gave her a knowing glint as she focused back on the conversation. Ignoring the unspoken tease, she turned her attention back to the riddle. That *was* what it said...Emelle swiped a finger under her ear, certain her brain was melting. But alas, there was nothing there. So much for being the brightest barkeep.

Emelle fell back onto the bed, exasperation and pure exhaustion weighing her down. She could fall asleep right now if she wanted.

What is lost to time?
What is lost to time?
What is lost to time?

It clicked.

She sat up in a flash—startling Lars—but she just said, "What is lost to time?"

Lars was silent, waiting for her to explain.

"What is *lost* to *time?*" she emphasized, waiting for Lars to catch on. "Ha! I was right! We need to find a historian." Slipping into her shoes, Emelle grabbed Lars's strong hands and pulled him towards their door.

"Emmy. Whoa, slow down, if it's lost it can't be found," he insisted gently, as if afraid she'd finally cracked.

"That's what it *wants* you to think, Lars. But if it's been lost to time, we just need to search further back, *before* time erased it. A historian might be able to tell us about old legends, and we can see if any fit the rest of the riddle!" Emelle's enthusiasm began to rub off on her brooding man as a matching smile slid onto his face.

"All right, all right, *breathe*, princess. Where are you going? It's not like we're going to be able to find a historian at this time of night."

"No, we aren't. But I know someone who can."

She dragged him down the silent stairs, entering the quiet taproom of the inn. Scattered tables had chairs flipped onto their surfaces, and only one older man sat at the bar, sipping from a half-full stein. A dying fire across the quaint room crackled, filling the near-silence. The sight was achingly familiar and, for once, she didn't mind the sea of brown wood.

Emelle and Lars crossed the room in a few strides, sidling up to the bar in front of the server, currently drying a stack of glassware.

"Hi there," she began, settling onto a rickety stool and feeling right at home. "My friend and I have some questions that we're hoping you can help with." Emelle propped her elbows atop the bartop.

The barkeep merely raised an eyebrow at her as they continued to polish a stein.

Realizing what they were waiting for, Emelle looked to Lars and gestured towards the barkeep. Lars sighed but plopped a few coins on the wooden bar. The barkeep snorted. Lars set a silver coin on the bar next and, satisfied, the barkeep nodded and poured them each a stein.

The familiarity wrapped around her, a balm over a wound she hadn't realized she'd been carrying. So eager to leave The Finn, Emelle couldn't have known she'd miss her routine—at least, that the tiniest part of her would. She glanced around the taproom and back to the barkeep—Kai, she'd learned after introducing herself. Lars remained silent, allowing Emelle to lead. Kai's brows had lifted as though surprised, and Emelle had an inkling why. No one ever asked for the barkeep's name. Emelle smiled, feeling a kindred spirit in Kai.

"Where can we find the closest historian?" Emelle asked, a whisper of nostalgia warming her soul as she sipped the glass filled with shit ale.

☽✹☾

After checking out early, Emelle and Lars made the half-day journey to the northeast village of Windburne in search of the local historian. After plying Kai with a few more coins, they'd finally opened up, sharing an unsurprising amount of knowledge. Emelle was all too familiar with the kind of information you heard working behind the bar, where everyone assumed you to be nobody special. Lips were especially loose when someone thought you were under their station.

Lars had grumbled about his dwindling funds, but Emelle had

seen his secret pouch in his pack. At this rate, they would be fine for at least a couple more weeks. Besides, Emelle was used to not having much in the way of money. She was sure he was, too.

"Kai said he lived in a cream-colored home with a purple door and red roses planted around the yard. That shouldn't be too hard to find, right?" Emelle mused, wholly unprepared for the number of homes with one feature or the other. After about three hours of searching, it was growing dark, and Emelle was worried they'd never find the historian in this sea of cream.

"Look, over there." Lars pointed, surprise coating his words.

There—a two-story cottage with a rose garden and a purple door. Emelle nearly wept.

The historian's home sat at the base of a large, grassy hill. A few oak trees stood tall around the cottage, leaves rustling from a balmy breeze as the evening sun cast shadows over the roving hills, blanketing them in shade. In the distance, birds chirped gracefully. Windburne was decidedly idyllic.

Approaching the home, Lars helped Emelle out of her saddle and tied their horses to the nearest oak tree. Emelle knocked on the front door and peeked at Lars, hope shining brightly up at him.

A few moments later the door cracked open, a weather-worn face peeking out. "Yes?" an old voice croaked. He sounded horribly frail, and Emelle was worried he might not even be able to answer their questions.

"I'm sorry for bothering you so late, but are you the historian of the Burnes?" Emelle asked.

"Yes, I was," the old man answered. "Though it has been many years since someone here has needed a historian."

He opened the door a little further and Emelle took in his appearance. His tanned olive skin was leathery from age and sun, and long white hair adorned both his scalp and his chin. Wobbly legs supported a waif-thin body, and knobby hands rested atop an ordinary cane. Wearing a long purple cloak tied around his neck over a knee-length, thin, cream night shirt, he looked more like a kooky wizard than a historian.

"We have a few questions about some old legends, if you might be able to help us?" Emelle said.

The historian glanced between Emelle and Lars, and then paused on Lars's attire—specifically, the lack of emblem on his chest.

"We'd be eternally grateful," she said, pulling his attention back to her.

With a nod, the old man opened his door the rest of the way. After stepping inside, the historian directed them to sit on his worn couch, leaving the room as he muttered something about tea.

Emelle glanced around the space, though nothing quite stood out. The walls of the small front room were painted a creamy orange and white rustic furniture lined the space. A few square windows were open, and a breeze ruffled gauzy curtains. As Emelle sank into the soft fabric of the well-loved couch, an ache formed in her heart.

While she was undoubtedly excited to finally be out on her grand adventure, she felt a surprising pang of homesickness hit her. She missed her parents—the kind they were before the separation—her grandmother...She missed the family they used to be, one that took the time to sit on couches when she was younger. To connect with each other after a long day of running The Finn. When had they stopped reaching out to each other?

At her silence, Lars glanced towards her, as if sensing the shift in her mood. She wasn't sure how to explain, nor did she think she could, so she just shook her head.

The historian returned a few moments later and set two cups of steaming tea onto the low table in front of Emelle and Lars. They both picked up the mugs, warming their hands on the ceramic.

Sitting across from them in a rather comfy looking chair, the historian raised his brows, as if waiting for them to start.

"Thank you," Emelle said softly, taking a sip. It burned her tongue, so she placed it on the table to cool. "My name is Emelle, and this is Lars." She motioned to the brooding man sitting next to her. The historian didn't offer his name in return, so she continued. "I know it's late, so I'll get right to it, if you'd like?"

A nod was all she got. She hoped he'd be able to give them more of an answer when she asked the important questions...

"We're researching old legends," Emelle began, deciding to keep it as vague as possible, "and hoping to find the beginnings of the celestial trials and how the Cosmic Fates started weaving destinies."

Clouds cleared from the historian's eyes as his head snapped to Lars with an alarming quickness. But he said nothing as he studied Lars's form once again.

"Do you...know anything about such legends?" Emelle asked, once again pulling his attention back to her. They'd agreed Lars would speak only when needed, his gruff attitude with anyone who wasn't her not boding well for gleaning answers from strangers.

"Yes, I remember some of the legends," the historian answered, voice crackly but resolute.

Blind hope stole the air from her lungs as the historian rose from his chair and shuffled over to another room. It took everything in Emelle to remain seated as they waited. Lars reached over and grabbed her hand, squeezing once, twice. Emelle squeezed back. Hard.

As the historian wobbled back into the room, Lars leapt up from his seat to take the large stack of books the frail man carried. When he set the stack on a low table meant for tea and flowers, Emelle's jaw dropped at the sheer amount of knowledge that sat before her. Cosmic Fates, the *stories* that were at her fingertips. Lars waved a hand in front of her face, breaking her focus. Teeth clacking as they slammed shut, she looked at the historian.

"May I?" Emelle asked with a hand paused over the stack, waiting for permission. Hunched over the aged cover, Emelle met the historian's gaze. A nod, and she plucked the first from the stack. Opening the book, she began to read.

Lars gingerly grabbed his own, and they set to finding their answers.

☽✷☾

"Emmy." A soft voice whispered in Emelle's ear, and she snuggled further into her folded arms. *Wait*—her eyes snapped open and met Lars's dark gaze.

"How long was I out?" she asked, stretching her arms up, her shoulders aching from the overstuffed wingback chair she'd moved to.

"Only about an hour, not too long. But it's late, and we need to find a place to stay tonight," Lars said.

Nodding, Emelle stood, knees cracking.

"You can stay here for the night," the weathered man offered, entering the room from Fates knew where. "It is a bit dusty, but I wouldn't mind the company."

Emelle turned to Lars, letting him make the decision. She wouldn't mind staying, and it would certainly be less of a hassle than finding a room at this hour. Lars seemed grateful, too.

"That would be lovely, thank you," Emelle said. Placing a bookmark in her tome, she followed the historian upstairs to a guest room while Lars tended to the horses. She quickly used the facilities and rinsed her face and mouth.

As she stared at her reflection, Emelle noted the light behind her eyes. It was pouring out from her soul, overflowing from her heart with each gust of balmy wind, with each crunch of dirt under her sore feet. She was proud of the woman she saw in the mirror.

A few breaths later, Lars entered the room, softly shutting the door. He placed both their packs on the floor before rustling through hers to grab her night shift. Handing it to her, Emelle gaped at the familiarity of the gesture. When had she gotten so used to a nighttime routine with Lars?

Climbing into the large bed, Emelle's bones melted into the shockingly comfortable mattress. It was certainly more comfortable than any she was used to. She smiled to herself as she felt a presence behind her, Lars pulling her into his near naked body.

"Better," he murmured, quiet voice breaking the silence.

"What do you think?" After hours of poring over at least two of the thick books, she didn't feel any closer to answers.

"I think—" He paused, kissing the crown of her head. "That we need sleep. And that we'll be able to *think* once we're not dead on our feet."

Emelle agreed, and wiggled deeper into his hold, blushing into the darkness as Lars grumbled sleepily.

"Princess, if you don't stop grinding your perfect ass over my cock, I might just think sleep is the last thing on your mind."

Rolling over, Emelle studied Lars in the dark room. She wasn't sure if he could read her as easily in the cover of night, but she didn't mask the emotions that she usually kept a tight hold on. The emotions that had a name she wasn't quite ready to face.

Leaning forward, Emelle gently kissed him, hands resting on his bare chest. When he kissed her back, her heart swelled, and she knew she'd follow Lars wherever.

"Goodnight, stranger," she whispered.

"Goodnight, princess," he replied in kind.

Emelle rolled back over and snuggled into his hold, lulled to sleep by the beating heart holding her.

☽✷☾

Someone smacked her in the face. Emelle woke in an instant, eyes snapping open as a low groan crawled out of Lars's chest. When she turned over, Lars's arm smacked her again as he twitched.

"No...Fates, no!" Lars cried, eyes still closed in sleep, body jerking in the bed. Sweat beaded along his furrowed brow, and Emelle's heart lurched, seeing the pain etched on his beautiful face.

"Lars," she whispered, carefully hovering over the trembling man. "Lars, wake up. Please, *please* wake up."

He didn't.

His head continued to twitch, tears slipping from the corners of his eyes and onto his pillow. She tentatively reached a hand out, wiping the salty tracks from his overheated skin. Matching tears slipped from her, racing over her cheeks as her heart broke for the invisible monsters Lars was fighting.

At the touch of her palm, Lars snapped awake, hazy clouds clearing by the second as he fought his way past the pain. He scanned her eyes, her arms and hands, her *fingers*, before the fear drained from his face.

"Emmy, thank the Fates," he whispered, pulling her close, hot breaths shuddering against her neck. His strong arms circled her frame, squeezing tightly.

Emelle gave herself over to his embrace. She felt his heart pounding, echoing in her chest with each beat. Whispering calm assurances into his inky waves, Emelle felt his body relax. A few minutes later, he was asleep again.

That night she fought the tempting tendrils of sleep, opting instead to hold Lars. To assure both him, and herself, that he was safe. That *they* were safe.

She finally drifted off as the sun began to rise.

It was the worst sleep she'd had since the snake. She didn't begrudge a second of it.

Chapter Twenty-Three
Emelle

Groaning, Emelle shut the tome with a little too much force, earning a sharp glare from the historian—Ozram, they'd learned that first morning. But two days after arriving, Emelle and Lars had almost finished every single one of the books Ozram had brought them.

Emelle dropped her head into her hands with a curse. So far, they'd learned about the forming of kingdom boundaries on the southern continent, the history of royal bloodlines, the unusual legends of soulmates, the magic of sun-blessed crops, and a brief mention of something called *The Reckoning*.

Despite its intimidating name, *The Reckoning* only referred to a period of time, *long ago*, when craters mysteriously formed in the wilds, disrupting the wildlife and neighboring kingdoms. Flora suffered and the sun dimmed, night falling earlier than usual, shadows covering the lands in a near-constant darkness. But after a couple decades, the earth began to grow over the cracks, and the flowers blossomed again, life returning to normal. Not much of a reckoning, in Emelle's opinion, though she didn't understand how craters had affected the earth so greatly.

"None of this helps," Emelle lamented to Lars. "I'm sorry, I think I was wrong."

Tender understanding shone back at her and she was grateful he didn't say *I told you so*.

"*What is lost to time?*" Emelle repeated the words seared into her memory. She'd forget her own name before she forgot that question. Even her sleep was consumed by the riddle, with dreams of her tumbling into the recesses of her mind ensuring she woke feeling uneasy and panicked.

"*Rejected by history, remembered by dust, welcomed by few,*" Lars finished, voice contemplative as he rubbed his temples.

Ozram glanced up from his book, the fog clearing from his aging brown eyes.

"You are...solving a riddle?" he asked hesitantly.

Lars raised a skeptical brow at Ozram. "Yes. Do you know what the answer is?"

A wry chuckle fell from the historian until laughter broke from his chest. It looked like it should've been painful, the force of his laughs on his frail body. Gathering himself, Ozram finally responded. "I do. As do you," he said cryptically and stood, taking the books still open on their laps. "You don't need these anymore; you have the answer you've been searching for."

"We don't, Ozram," Emelle said, voice thick with frustration. "Have the answer, that is. We've been trying to crack this for days and we're no closer than we were when we found the scroll. We're stuck. Can't you give us a clue? Or better yet, the answer?"

"This is a trial, yes?"

Emelle nodded.

Oz chuckled, shaking his head. "You'll figure it out," he said, walking away. Pausing, he glanced back and spoke one final time. "What did you come here for?" When Lars opened his mouth to speak, Ozram cut him off. "Think about it."

With that, Ozram took his books back to wherever he'd grabbed them from, and didn't return, effectively dismissing them.

"I guess we've been kicked out," Lars snickered, somehow knowing she needed one of them to not freak out and that it wasn't going to be her.

She was freaking out. How were they supposed to solve an impossible riddle?

☽✻☾

Several hours later, they arrived back in Cloudburne and settled in early for the evening. Bathing hastily and sending out their clothes to be laundered, Emelle and Lars spent the evening relaxing in the privacy of their room. Well, as much as they could having not yet solved the riddle that had been plaguing them for almost a week.

"What if—"

"No more, Emmy. Not tonight. Let's just—leave it for tomorrow. We'll figure it out."

Searching the eyes she loved so much, Emelle saw the exhaustion he tried valiantly to hide. They had matching dark circles under their eyes. Emelle couldn't help but laugh.

"What's so funny?" Lars questioned, a lilt curling the corner of his perfect mouth.

"I was just thinking how tired we look. We both could probably use a year's worth of sleep."

Lars smirked, brushing her wild hair behind her ears. "*I* look tired. You look beautiful. You always do."

Emelle snorted, slapping his shoulder. "Stop, I thought I told you not to lie to me anymore." She buried her head in his bare chest.

"It's a damn good thing I'm not lying to you, then."

There was no hint of deception in his depthless onyx eyes. Emelle snuggled deeper into his hold, hiding her blush.

When he spoke next, it was low and quiet in the minute space between them.

"How could I lie when every time I close my eyes, my heart crumbles because I can no longer gaze upon the most radiant light I've ever had the chance to behold? How could I lie to *you*, Emelle, when leaving you shredded the last of my very soul with each step out of Silvermist? Knowing I was making the greatest mistake of my life while simultaneously hurting the one person who's come to mean more to me than the cosmos."

When fingers brushed her chin, she looked up to meet his gaze.

"You *consume* me," he beseeched her. "Body, mind, and soul, you hold every jagged piece of me in the palms of your hands. You are all that I see, all that I hear, all that I *know*. I would happily suffer a thousand deaths if it meant I had the chance to spend even a single day with you. Do you understand me? I am *yours*."

Emelle's heart thundered. She'd never imagined someone could look at her like this, let alone feel what he felt for her. That she could consume someone so entirely and equally as she was consumed by him.

"And I am yours," she said, just as fiercely.

The air in the room settled and Emelle knew whatever they just spoke into the cosmos was heard.

She was his. Just as he was hers.

☽✷☾

The next morning, Emelle remade their traveling packs with their fresh clothes, the scroll and ledger, and replenished rations as Lars tended to the horses. She eyed some jerky as she packed it, not looking forward to having to eat it any time soon. Securing the handkerchief from home onto her head, Emelle folded the expensive emerald cloth into her pack. She didn't want to risk losing it during the ride, or getting it dirty.

After breakfast, they mounted their steeds and set off for the half-day ride to Mount Haleburne. They reached the base in the early afternoon, and settled in for the night; it was too late to start the climb now. The transformation to the desert-like landscape was a stark difference from the grassy fields of Cloudburne and Windburne. Cacti were scattered around the sides and base of the mountain, and she swore she even saw a tumbleweed roll by. She shifted on the unforgiving packed dirt. She doubted she'd sleep well under the stars that twinkled above them, as sounds of animals baying in the distance sent shivers down her spine. Emelle eyed the ground and Lars chuckled at her obvious dismay.

"Not a fan of sleeping under the stars, princess?"

Head jerking towards Lars, Emelle flipped him her middle finger. "I'm fine with the ground. I'm *not* fine with the possibility of waking up to a slithery not-so-little cuddle buddy. Or worse." As if on cue, another creature howled in the distance.

"Well, as long as you know it's big," Lars joked.

Emelle just scoffed and threw her blanket at his head. At least his jokes seemed to be improving. Somewhat.

"Don't worry, princess, the only slithery cuddle buddy you'll wake up to is attached to a very intimidating man who will scare all the other wild snakes away." A beat, and then laughter broke out in tandem.

Fates, she loved this man.

Emelle stopped short, eyes widening at the realization. She was...in love with Lars. She wasn't sure exactly when it had happened, but she knew by the warmth in her heart that it had been a while.

Lars seemed oblivious to her life-altering revelation, having moved to start a fire and lay the blanket down. Settling down, Lars held out a hand, helping a dazed Emelle to the ground. They shared a measly dinner of dried venison and a few apples they'd snagged from the kitchens back in Cloudburne, falling into distracted chatter.

That night, Emelle fell asleep in Lars's arms, and as she stared up at the cosmos, she wondered if the Fates were on to something.

Chapter Twenty-Four
Lars

The next morning, Lars tied their horses to a towering ash tree. He was fairly confident they'd spend their time eating the grass and basking in the shade.

"Ready!" Emelle announced after shouldering her pack. He wished he could take her bag, but he needed his arms free to dispatch any of the traps. Emelle had reviewed the ledger and saw that most Heroes only had to dodge a few sections of quicksand, but a few had mentioned avoiding patches of psychedelic plants. That and the local wildlife meant he needed easy access to his claymore.

Lars extended his hand to Emelle, then pulled her toward him so she collided with his chest. Her twinkling laughter burrowed into his soul. Hazy images of possible futures flashed in his mind, ones where Emelle and Lars lived long and happy together. Her compassion he'd once thought innocent naivety, instead was a genuine desire to help others, despite the masks she donned. The hardened wall she clung to so tightly in the face of uncertainty was one born of necessity, and he couldn't fault her for it. It had been a joy to dismantle her wall, brick by solid brick, and join her on the other side. Once again, he silently prayed to the Fates to make it out of the impending bloodshed, so he could spend the rest of his hopefully long—and safe—life with her.

Emelle just huffed and slapped his chest in false annoyance, oblivious to his inner musings.

"Stay behind me, Emmy. I'm serious. If anything goes wrong on this mountain, I need you and your beautiful brain to stay out of danger. I need you safe."

"Wow, just using me for my beautiful brain then, huh? Make a woman feel great about herself," Emelle grumbled, a sly lilt quirking up the corner of her mouth.

Bending down, Lars planted an abrupt but fierce kiss on his mate.

"Of course I am. Are you just now figuring that out?" He kissed her once more. She wore one of his favorite smiles, a shy one that had his stomach flipping before rolling her eyes at his antics.

Turning, Lars began the trek up the mountain, his heart and soul following close behind.

☽✻☾

"This doesn't seem very dangerous," Emelle observed, kicking a small rock over the ledge of the cliff they sat on.

"Sure, why don't you invite the Fates to throw some obstacles our way? That sounds like a great idea," Lars teased.

Emelle stuck her tongue out at him. Heat flashed through his body.

"Careful flaunting that thing, someone might get the wrong idea."

"Oh, I have an idea all right." Emelle closed the distance to kiss him. Her lips were quickly becoming one of his favorite things about her.

Deepening the kiss, Lars swept his tongue over hers—but a rustling sound behind them had Lars whirling, one hand reaching for his dagger.

Foolish, he'd left his claymore resting with their packs a few feet away. Rising slowly, Lars carefully made his way over and slowly grabbed his sword. The rustling continued and Lars held his claymore at the ready.

Moments later, a rabbit hopped out of the brush to munch on a patch of grass. Lars laughed, lowering his sword as Emelle fought laughter, lips pressed tight.

"Hey, you would've been grateful if it were a—" Something slammed into Lars, throwing him to the ground. Enormous paws scrabbled at him as he threw himself onto his back, hauling his claymore between himself and the wolf.

Teeth closed on his forearm, splicing the skin as damp, rotten breath washed over him, claws tearing over his leathers. Trapping a shout behind his teeth, Lars shoved upward with his sword, the blade sinking into the wolf's belly and making it roar as it tore itself free. Lars scrambled to his feet, struggling to breathe, the bitten arm stinging with pain.

Bleeding and sporting several new wounds, Lars straightened to his full height. The snarling creature seemed to sense the change in him and retreated, never giving Lars its back. Dark gold eyes held his as it took each step backwards, leaving a trail of blood in its wake.

As quickly as it appeared, it vanished, and a guttural cry sounded, before Emelle rushed to his side.

"Hey, *hey*, I'm all right. Princess, I'm all right, see?"

Hiccupping, Emelle searched him over from head to toe, tears slipping with each cut she found. Lars rubbed her arms, and repeated, "Emmy, I'm all right. Just a little bit of blood." His heart broke watching the fear and despair linger on her face. Wiping her tears from her cheeks, Lars pressed his lips to hers once, twice.

"I'm not going anywhere except home with you."

Emelle threw her arms around him, squeezing tightly. Lars grunted, and the pressure immediately released.

"Shit, I'm sorry," she apologized and reached for their packs for their medical supplies.

"I'm fine. Are you ready to get out of here? I want to keep moving."

Finding a bandage, she glared at him. "Keep moving? You were just *attacked*."

Lars rolled up his sleeve and assessed his arm, which was still bleeding, but slowing. He wiped the wound against his trousers, and inspected the bite again. It oozed a few more drops but nothing he would be concerned about.

"And I'm fine, just some scratches. I can handle it. What I don't want to handle," he emphasized with a raised brow, "is if the giant wolf comes back, this time with its pack. So let's load up and head on. I think we're getting close to the peak."

All the same, he held still while she cleaned the wound with water before wrapping the bandage around it. It seemed to calm something in her, and he wouldn't begrudge her that.

☽✻☾

"Look," Lars said after another hour and pointed at a narrow break in the steep mountain, only a slight peak rising above. "That might be the peak right there." So far, all they'd passed were more cacti and massive boulders that made navigating the mountain difficult. Lars kept a watchful eye on Emelle.

"Lars, I think you're right. Do you see that?" she asked, hand shielding the afternoon sun from her eyes. Lars followed her line of sight to some shimmer that could be water if he squinted.

"I'm not sure if that's water, Emmy. It could just be a mirage. Let's go check it out, we might be as high as we can be," he said.

Emelle grumbled, and walked towards the peak, up and over the next ledge. He followed only a few steps behind.

But one moment she was there, and the next she was slipping, shrieking, *gone*—

"Emmy!" Lars shouted, racing up to the edge where his mate last stood. The quicksand was unmoving, as if hardly disturbed by swallowing Emelle whole. Flipping his sword to the hilt, Lars shoved the handle deep into the sand, palm and fingertips slicing on the sharp blade. Extending it as far as he could, Lars tried to find her, but his blood wetted the blade, and it slipped out of his grasp. Lars's world went dark. He didn't think—he simply dove in.

Bearing down, Lars willed the sand to give way. He was wholly unprepared to be dropped onto a hard cave floor. Heaving himself to his side, he coughed up wet sand, pawing at his eyes to clear them. It didn't seem to make a difference but he forced his eyes open all the same, desperate to find Emelle. He seemed to have dropped into a cramped cave filled with an odd azure light from a tunnel to his right, just bright enough to see by. It revealed the drop hadn't been far, but it was unexpected. Lars knew Emelle could've been easily hurt if she hadn't been prepared.

At last, he spotted her sitting against a wall across the cave, turning over her wrist. He raced over, inspecting her for injury. Emelle groaned and he zeroed in on her wrist, which was swelling by the second. He gingerly lifted her arm to assess the damage.

"Emmy, princess, how bad does it hurt?"

She winced with a hiss between her teeth and the sound slashed through his soul. His gaze snapped up to her face in time to watch a trickle of blood drip down her temple. Panic lanced through his heart—blood on her, any blood, was far too reminiscent of the nightmare plaguing him lately.

"It hurts," she answered plainly, gingerly testing the range and unaware of the blood on her face. "What the *fuck* happened?"

"You fell through quicksand. I jumped in after." He had little on him that wasn't covered in sand, but he tore off a strip of his tunic to press to the cut all the same.

Emelle saw his bloody palm and snatched his hand closer to inspect. She carefully turned his hand over, inhaling shakily. "This didn't come from jumping," she choked.

Lars winced, the pain finally hitting him. "I used my sword to reach into the quicksand. I'd hoped I could've pulled you up, but I didn't realize it was going to drop you into this cave."

"You—you put the..." Emelle's eyes widened. "You held onto the blade?" she screeched, jerking her gaze to his.

Lars flinched from the shout, not feeling the need to answer.

"You fucking idiot," she snarked, and tore off a strip of her own tunic to wrap his wound. Though her touch was gentle, her scoff of "Men" was clearly meant to scold.

While he held one bandage to her head and she held one to his palm, they were close enough to share breath. Emelle fought a wobbly smile. Lars found it difficult to return the sentiment, even when she said, "That sand was fucking quick," on a laugh.

Lars didn't join in. "Next time, I'd appreciate if you *didn't* go traipsing into quicksand, all right, princess?"

Emelle just shrugged.

His palm tingled. Lars flipped his hand over again and his eyes widened. They watched in awe as the skin stitched back together. Emelle gasped, grabbing his hand to inspect. It was as though he'd never sliced it open. Only a shiny silver slash remained on his palm and fingertips.

Lars went still, glancing to the wound on his arm from the wolf. His black sleeve was still rolled above the bandage and he slowly untied the bloody cloth, not sure what he'd find beneath. He was unsettled as the wounds faded away, only the deepest puncture settling into a silver scar.

"It's gone," he blurted. "How are they gone?"

His gaze snapped to Emelle, searching her scalp. Only a few traces of blood stuck to the strawberry strands. He looked at her wrist, which had returned to its normal size.

Emelle audibly swallowed as she passed a scrutinizing eye over the cave. "I'm not sure, but I don't think we should linger here."

With a nod, Lars stood up and reached a hand out to help Emelle. Dusting off as much of the sand as they could, Lars fixed his pack before helping Emelle with hers. He couldn't help but look everywhere he remembered seeing a wound, awestruck as he found nothing but the faintest of scars. Shaking his head in disbelief, Lars found his claymore and led the way through the high arch in the wall leading into a long tunnel. Their only exit.

THE FOOL'S ERRAND

Azure light illuminated their path in the dirt, the ceiling, leading them through the simple—though lengthy—tunnel. He kept his sword at the ready as they walked, his eyes glued to the ground in case they came across yet another pit of quicksand. He refused to let Emelle get hurt again. Magic healing cave or not, she wasn't going to be spilling another drop of blood.

"There," Emelle said, making him raise his eyes to find an even larger archway some ten meters ahead. The edges were smooth, as if carved by man or mystic. Lars remained on high alert as they approached the new opening.

Dim light flickered in the larger cave, and Lars motioned for Emelle to stay behind him as he poked his head inside. Torches sporadically lined the cave walls, seemingly lit by magic. In the middle of the cave was a large hot spring, steam rising from the intensely blue waters, but the room was seemingly empty of any immediate threat. The temperature rose as they entered.

"It's an orchid," Emelle whispered, pointing to the patch of flowers near the spring. "My grandmother loved stitching orchids, and not just because they were the only thing she could stitch. She put them on the dress I wore to the hot springs back in Silvermist."

Lars followed her gaze to the flowers, heart aching. She hadn't shared much about her grandmother, but he could only assume that her mother leaving only a few years after her grandmother passed would've compounded the grief even further. It was unfortunate they both had an intensely selfish parent.

"She was the one, you know, who wore handkerchiefs." Her hand drifted to her hair, though she wore no handkerchief in it today. "She gave me my first one as soon as she saw how much I hated my hair in my face. We loved when travelers visited because we'd trade and bargain to add more and more to our collection. Not that we really ended up getting that many. Not many people wanted to trade such expensive fabric for a hot meal and laundry service. But most of the fun was in the chase." Emelle paused, taking a moment. "It was something that was just *ours*. She left all but her favorite handkerchief to me."

"What did she do with her favorite?" he asked.

Emelle smiled softly, continuing with a somber voice. "She was buried in her favorite. It was this gorgeous deep green. Almost exactly like the one you bought. She looked...beautiful. Peaceful."

Lars couldn't take it anymore. He pulled Emelle into his arms, hugging her tightly.

A few breaths later, her face lifted, her chin propped up on his chest. "She would've liked you. She'd admire any man who could handle my sass."

His heart swelled at the compliment. Leaning forward, Lars kissed his mate. "I'd have liked to meet her."

"There's always stories," she mused, and kissed him on the cheek. Then she ducked away from him. "Come on, let's check this place out. I, for one, don't want to die in here."

Chapter Twenty-Five
Emelle

Emelle walked along the cave's walls, searching for something, *anything*, that would let them out. As far as she knew, they were just at the dead end of a long tunnel. Trying to quell her rising panic, Emelle focused only on the details.

Details. Lars had once told her that details made up the most interesting parts of life. Scanning the stone walls, Emelle searched for any clue, even the smallest. And then something caught her eye.

She tilted her head to find faded colors stained on the wall, too difficult to see in the dim lighting. Humming, she strode over to a torch and pulled on it—only to nearly fall on her ass when it came free without fuss.

Waving off Lars's concern, she lifted the torch to the cave wall. Sure enough, it looked like there was art on the walls. Emelle cataloged each detail, trying to decipher the paintings.

Near the top, there was what appeared to be a field, with what might be flowers sprouting from the ground. A bright sun shone down on them. The wind was gentle, lilting through the long stems of grass. It looked...tranquil. Or as tranquil as cave art could look.

Emelle shuffled over to the right, her steps near silent along the dirt floor. Here, it appeared the ground had cracked in two, the flowers wilting, sun running from the darkness.

This made no sense.

"Lars, are you seeing this?" Emelle called over her shoulder. She jumped when she felt hands on her waist.

"I'm right here, princess," Lars whispered in her ear.

"What do you think they mean?" she asked, determined to ignore what his deep voice did to her, and took in the next painting. This one was near the dirt floor, directly under the first painting. The haunting art chilled the air in the room. Or maybe it was from the sudden grip of unease that seized her. The third painting showed humans fighting creatures, hordes of both dying on the ground, blood soaking into the spliced earth.

The final painting depicted life again. It was level with the painting on the right, though it was on the left. Water rushed into dried canyons. Flowers blossomed from fresh rain. Sunlight shone, and there was no darkness to be found. They were aligned in an abstract circle, like a compass, with the first drawing starting over.

"A cycle, then," she mused, inspecting the wall for any clue as to *when* this cycle happened.

"I wonder when the last time anyone was in this cave," Lars murmured. "Surely we would've heard about a legend of this caliber."

Emelle was inclined to agree, a half-formed thought slipping away on the edge of her memory.

Walking back around the walls of the cave, Emelle tripped on a rock. A hand caught her around her waist and Emelle thanked her stranger, who just squeezed her once in response before letting go. Leaning forward, she inspected what stumbled her: a long, white stone about the length of her forearm. When she picked it up to hold it up to the light, she shrieked and dropped it. It shattered.

"It's a bone," she cried. "It's a fucking *bone*." Shivers rolled down her back, bile gathering in the back of her throat as she waved away the bone dust in the air.

Lars stepped around her and picked up a shard of the remaining bone, only for it to crumble in his hand.

Emelle gagged.

"These are old." He sifted through the dust. "Possibly from the person who marked these walls?" He searched the small area and found a pile of what might have been a skeleton at some point.

"I really hope they *chose* to die here, rather than finding themselves trapped," Emelle muttered, arms wrapping around her body.

"There's no markings, nothing to tell us who this was," Lars mused with a frown, seeming to share her remorse for the person who died by themselves in this hidden cave where no one would find them for centuries upon centuries.

"They must've been so scared," Emelle whispered. She vowed she would never forget the person who laid down in this cave, never to rise again. They would be remembered by at least two people in this world.

Stepping away from the skeleton, Emelle walked over to the hot spring. It gave her the same sense of peace that the spring in Silvermist gave her. She needed some peace right about now.

All the same, she had recently resolved to be careful and knelt by the pool's edge. It looked clean, the water clear despite its strange blue hue, so she picked up a rock and dropped it in. The water didn't bubble angrily. The rock didn't disintegrate as it sank below the surface. Setting aside her pack, Emelle dipped her fingers into the steaming waters. She groaned at the refreshing feel. She felt filthy after tumbling through all that sand. Reaching both hands into the spring, she began to clean under her nails and scrub her skin.

"You know better than to make those kinds of noises, princess," Lars said, joining her by the pool. A hand gripped her jaw, turning her face towards him. "Do you know what those noises do to me?"

"Yes." Emelle's voice was quiet, barely above a whisper, but she held his gaze unashamedly. Boldly, even.

Lars bit back a laugh. "Are you doing this to me on purpose? When we're trapped with nowhere to go?" Equally as boldly, he took her hand and brought it to his stiff cock, straining through his trousers.

Desire curled in her abdomen as she squeezed his hardening length.

"Use your words, princess."

"I need you," Emelle whispered.

A breath hissed through his teeth as she rubbed him over his trousers. Heat flashed through his onyx eyes and Emelle gulped at the throb in her core, the quickening of her pulse. The steam was steadily rising, curling around their bodies, turning the air sticky and warm. Shadows coiled around them, cocooning them in their hunger.

"Stand," Lars commanded, offering a hand to help her up. Once on her feet, Lars grabbed the hem of her tunic and began to undress her, driving her wild with each whisper of a touch—caressing her dips and curves, as though he'd perish if he didn't.

"Get in the water, Emelle," he ordered.

She rushed to obey.

Emelle was enraptured as Lars stripped and slid in beside her. Glow worms crawling along the ceiling cast a glow against their naked bodies. And Fates, he was devilishly handsome. Emelle wrapped her legs around him as soon as he found a ledge to sit on. His body was hard under her touch, and she shamelessly dragged her wet fingers over his shoulders, his chest.

"Fates, how do you get more devastating with each day?" Lars breathed, more to himself. Steam rose between them, sweat licking down their heated skin. Emelle felt herself flush, from both the heat of the water and the desire burning her from the inside out.

Surging forward, he captured her lips with his. Emelle ground herself on his firm body, aching for him to finally slip inside her. After all these weeks, Emelle was desperate for him. Dragging her clit against his length, Emelle worked herself into a frenzy. She lost herself to the rhythm, panting as she climbed higher and higher.

"Oh, no you don't. Not until I say so, princess," Lars admonished. Grabbing her damp hair, Lars tilted her head back, running his tongue along the column of her neck. Her heart beat wildly against its cage. Bringing his lips to her ear, he whispered, "Not until I've had my taste."

Emelle's eyelids drooped as she looked at Lars. Fates, she needed that, too. His face in her sex, licking and touching her until she saw the cosmos.

"Sit on the ledge, princess."

"What about the bones?" she asked, glancing over to where the skeleton lay. The haze of arousal lifted, and she thought it might be disrespectful to fuck her here in their final resting place.

"I'm sure this is going to be the most excitement they've seen in a while." All the same, he encircled the spring with shadows.

Clambering back onto the ledge, Emelle was already panting as Lars dropped between her legs, spreading them wide. Greedy eyes memorized her dripping cunt, but Emelle felt no shame. How could she when he looked at her like that? There was nothing but carnal, wanton need.

With a quickness she was sure he wasn't prepared for, Emelle grabbed Lars's head and shoved his face into her sex. Lars chuckled, sound reverberating against her folds, before he did as she bid. He licked and suckled on her sensitive flesh, lifting a hand to slip two fingers inside of her. Emelle ground her cunt against his face, chasing her release. She'd been needy for days now, the desire building in her from weeks of foreplay.

"Oh, Fates, *fuck*, don't stop!" she cried, delicious friction sending her higher with each stroke.

"The Fates aren't here right now. But I am," he rumbled right into her as he continued to work her with his fingers. "Give it to me, princess. Let it out. *Come. For. Me.*"

Emelle saw stars. Light burst behind her eyes as pleasure hurled her into the cosmos. It took several moments for her to return to this cave, this pool, this man. Hand still gripping Lars's hair, she slowed the roll of her hips, heart pounding as she came down from her orgasm.

"Fuck, that was hot," Lars groaned, cleaning her thighs where her release had dripped with his tongue. "Come here," he demanded before dragging her back into the pool.

Emelle straddled him as he sat back on the ledge.

"You're perfect, you know that?" he asked, and her heart lurched. She'd never felt perfect before, and in a way, she knew she wasn't. But with Lars, she'd found perfection wasn't achieved from being flawless. It was embracing the flaws and loving yourself because of them, not in spite of. And Lars loved her flaws, and so did she. Dark eyes searched hers, private emotions playing behind them. Soon. Soon, they would talk.

But for now, she wasn't done yet. Lifting her hips, Emelle grabbed Lars's rigid cock and angled it toward her cunt. With a grin, Emelle slowly impaled herself on his length. As soon as he was as deep as he could go, they groaned in unison. She rolled her hips, getting used to the feeling of being stretched, enjoying the way each little movement made Lars's hips twitch.

"Ready?" he murmured softly.

Her response was to simply loop her hands behind his neck.

He smirked, rolling his hips up into her, drilling into her from below. "Oh, fuck," he gritted out, then captured her lips. There was little finesse to the kiss, but it hardly mattered.

Emelle met him thrust for thrust as she built towards that impossible high again. Her peaked nipples dragged against his bare chest, sending tingles straight to her clit.

Hands flying to her hips, Lars gripped her as he thrust up into her, and *Fates,* she hoped he left bruises. Moaning, Emelle ground her clit into his pubic bone, the delicious pressure almost sending her over the edge.

"Are you close?" she asked, trying to hold on. "I need to be filled. *Please.*"

"Yeah, princess, I'm so close." He groaned loudly, and the sound reverberated in her core. "You feel so good, Emmy. *Too good.*" His voice was gravelly against her skin as he bit into her shoulder. She prayed he left marks.

Leaning back, Emelle grabbed his chin, like he'd done so many times to her, and rode him hard.

THE FOOL'S ERRAND

"Come inside me, Lars," she demanded as her own orgasm washed over her, cunt pulsing on his length. She rode his cock through each wave, moaning loud enough she was sure even the cosmos heard her.

Lars groaned and his hips stuttered, pumping her full of his hot cum. It took several long moments for it to end, and several long moments for her to stop rolling her hips, eager for everything he had to give her. Heart racing, Emelle leaned her forehead against Lars as they caught their breaths.

"Mine," Lars whispered, voice quiet enough she wondered if he meant for her to hear.

Emelle opened her eyes—she wasn't sure when she even closed them—and smiled.

"Mine," she repeated, and kissed him. When they parted, she suddenly became aware of the cave around them as the shadows dissipated. "I can't believe we might die in a cave in the Burnes."

Lars pulled her head back gently by her hair, and stared deeply into her eyes. The movement shifted her weight, grinding her body on top of his, reminding her that he was still inside her. Lars leisurely began to thrust inside her again, making her head drop back.

How was he already hard again?

She realized she didn't care. She rolled her hips, matching his agonizingly slow pace.

"You are not going to die in here, you understand? I will get you out of this cave if I have to dig through the rock... with... my... bare... fingers." He accentuated each of the last words with a sharp thrust.

Falling into his rhythm, Emelle gave herself over to his fire. Lars wrapped an arm around her waist, pulling her back to him. Capturing her mouth, he kissed her sloppily, fucking her slowly. Pulling back only slightly, his lips barely touched hers as he breathed in her air, groaning into her mouth.

Fuck, that was so hot.

Several strokes later, they raced towards that peak together, twin shouts echoing through the cave. Emelle fought to catch her breath, resting her forehead against his as her heart rate finally returned to normal.

A few minutes later, Emelle glanced around the cave. "So I guess we're camping in here tonight, with some old bones for company?" she asked. She wasn't looking forward to sleeping next to a skeleton.

"At least there won't be any snakes," Lars mused with a smirk.

Emelle lightly smacked his chest. Searching the cave for any missed clue, Lars wrapped his arms around her waist and froze. Emelle paused, head turning to follow his line of sight.

"Do you see that?" he asked, squinting as he looked across the dark cave.

Climbing out of the hot spring, they quickly dried off with a spare cloth and dressed in their lighter clothes and boots, making their way to the wall. Lifting a torch, Emelle gasped as Lars's fingers traced a crack in the wall. It was so subtle, she wasn't sure how he'd even noticed it.

Hesitantly, Lars pushed on the cave wall, waiting for something, *anything*, to happen. After a moment, air hissed and the cave wall shifted backwards and off to the side. The same glow worms flickered along ascending steps carved into the rock itself.

"Grab your pack. We don't know if we're going to be able to get back down here," Lars instructed, heading for his own bag and sword.

Emelle followed suit, casting one last glance towards the pile of bones that was destined to stand sentry over this cave, these paintings.

Following Lars, Emelle grabbed the torch and climbed the stairs, flinching as the cave door slammed shut behind them.

Chapter Twenty-Six

Lars

As he climbed the stairs, Lars kept a watchful eye on their new surroundings, claymore at the ready. Glow worms provided extra light, illuminating just enough to make out each step but little else.

"Where do you think this leads?" Emelle whispered, voice curious with only a slight twinge of fear.

Lars only shook his head as he crested the top step, a wall of solid rock only a few steps in front of them. Reaching behind him for the torch, Emelle silently passed it to him. It wasn't as bright as he'd like, but he searched the stone for any indication of a crack. At first glance, there was none. They were effectively trapped.

"Look, right there." Emelle traced one finger along the slightest crevice and landed on the faintest marking. "Do you see that?"

Bending down, Lars examined the symbol just off to the right of the crack.

"The mountain," he breathed, tilting his head at where she pointed. "It's the same symbol from the scroll." Turning towards a grinning Emelle, Lars broke out in a matching smile. "There's a gap, like it needs a key to open."

Emelle beamed, whipping her pack around and rustling around

until she pulled out the scroll. Understanding washed over Lars, but he let Emelle fit the notched end they'd originally dismissed into the slot. The symbol lit up briefly, the same azure glow as the worms, before a loud groan had them stumbling backward a few steps.

Slowly, an opening appeared as rock slid away, fresh air filling their lungs. Handing the torch back to Emelle, Lars grabbed the scroll and exited the tunnel.

As Lars reached the top, he scanned their new surroundings. They were at the peak of the western point of the mountain they'd been climbing. The tip on the west point blocked most of the setting sun, a shadow falling over the space. A medium-sized pond sparkled near the northern edge of the plateau, and Lars looked over the ledge, barely making out the horses they'd left at the base of the mountain. Luscious green grass covered the ground and small flowers sprouted, a stark difference from the desert landscape of the mountainside.

Little blue glowing bugs floated around in the air, one landing on Emelle's crown. Lars stifled a chuckle as Emelle remained unaware of her newest friend.

"This is...breathtaking," Emelle murmured.

Lars tried to agree, but his sight returned to the most enchanting woman he'd ever had the grace of knowing, gilded in the setting sunlight.

"Yes, breathtaking," he agreed.

Blue light glowed around her hair, and she flashed him one of those blinding smiles, oblivious to the true emotion behind his words.

Lars kissed her lightly once, twice. Then he set his sword against a large rock and pulled out the ledger, flipping to the bookmarked trial to reread Emelle's notes aloud.

"'Finding the scroll he'd discovered in a nearby cave, the Hero read the riddle aloud to the iridescent moon. After a moment of pure silence, the Hero whispered his answer to the skies. Answering correctly, the Hero felt the air heat and steam began to rise from the water. Hearing the Fates' booming voice in the quiet, accepting his answer, the Hero knew his trial was complete.'"

"Have you figured it out yet?" Lars asked.

Emelle shook her head. "No, but I feel like it's on the tip of my tongue..." Plopping onto the grass, Emelle laid down, staring up at the pastel pink and orange sky as if it held all of the answers.

Without a better idea, Lars laid down beside her. "I kept thinking it would just come to me," he murmured, finally giving voice to his secret fears.

"Me too," she whispered. "'Why did you come here?'" Emelle repeated Ozram's words to the dusky sky. Lars didn't have an answer to that cryptic question either.

Reaching over, Lars entwined their fingers together, closing his eyes for just a moment.

☽✷☾

"Lars, wake up," said a voice next to him.

Lars snapped his eyes open, searching the darkness for any danger.

"It's all right, we just fell asleep. For a few hours, I think," Emelle said, looking even more beautiful as the moon shone on her unblemished skin.

But something felt...off. He rubbed his eyes, in hopes it might clear away the blue hue that had settled over the mountain peak.

Calculating eyes swept over the peak and the sky, and Lars realized—

"Look at the stars," he gasped, seeing the iridescent moon swarmed by blue stars in the sky.

"That's odd." Emelle's face was adorably scrunched, though he could see the wheels turning in her head, putting together invisible puzzle pieces. He knew she thought he'd been joking, but Emelle truly was one of the smartest people he'd ever met. It was captivating to watch her work through puzzles.

"I guess now is as good of a time as any," she said, though uncertainty bled through each word.

Still praying to the Fates the answer would come to him, he stood up and offered a hand to Emelle. She scooped up the scroll before following Lars over to the rippling pond. Glowing water lilies floated peacefully.

"Ready?" he asked his mate, knowing the tension he felt must be obvious. But she smiled at him, squeezing his hand in quiet reassurance, and it eased. A sense of peace washed over him and he knew no matter what lay ahead, he had her. His mate. His Emelle.

Fates, he loved this woman.

He froze at the realization, though he wasn't sure why. He'd known for a while how he'd felt, had known since their time at The Finn. He'd just never given his feelings a name. Her light sang to his darkness, and maybe it was selfish, but each day he basked in her warmth, each morning he woke to those twinkling emerald eyes, Lars wanted to abandon his duty just a little more.

But a nod from Emelle, and Lars unfurled the scroll. Reading aloud, he lifted his face to the skies.

What is lost to time,
Rejected by history,
Remembered by dust,
Welcomed by few.

Silence fell, the crickets abruptly going quiet, the burbling of the pond pausing. The very world seemed to slow as it awaited his answer.

In the deafening silence, Lars began to panic. He'd thought the answer would come to him in the moment he needed it.

Fuck, this was bad.

Lars looked to Emelle, whose brows were furrowed before she whispered, "The truth," and looked to the grass.

"What?" he croaked.

"*The truth* is lost to time...rejected by history...remembered by dust...welcomed by few..." Emelle's voice was hushed, her gaze darting to Lars as they waited. A beat, and then—

Sound returned and the pond began to bubble, steam rising from its water. Warmth surrounded them, and Lars knew she was right.

On a laugh, Lars picked Emelle up, swinging her around. She joined in, and it was the most incredible sound he'd ever heard.

"Drink, and remember the Truth," a voice thundered in his head.

Lars whirled, sending shadows to cover Emelle as he scanned their surroundings again.

"I think that was the Fates," Emelle said, voice low but unafraid. "I heard it, too. The Hero said someone spoke to him, though it didn't tell him to drink anything."

After a long, tense, silent moment, Lars freed her from the shadows and turned to his mate. Her gaze searched his, as they both realized what they needed to do.

"I'll do it," they both spoke at the same time.

Lars glowered at her. "I will drink the water. You stay here."

"Like hell you're drinking that by yourself." Irritation bled through her words. "I deserve to know the truth, too."

"Of course you do, Emmy. But I don't know what's going to happen. I can't risk it hurting you. I'd sooner throw myself over the cliffside right now than let you put yourself in danger."

"Let *me* put *myself* in danger? What makes you think I want to let you risk yourself, either?" she asked with a raised brow. But after a breath, she must've seen the fear on his face. With a sigh, she cupped his jaw and rested their foreheads together. "I know. You're an overprotective man, but we're walking this path together. And we're going to finish this together. The Fates wouldn't let us get all the way here just to hurt us. And besides, if you get injured, then how the hell am I supposed to get us back down that mountain? We may as well go out together."

Lars sighed, a frown pulling down the corner of his mouth, and kissed her. "Fine. We'll drink it together. But I'd like it noted that I was against the idea."

Emelle smirked but nodded in agreement, eyes twinkling with excitement. Kneeling, they both cupped their hands to gather some of the tepid water before lifting their hands to their lips.

"I—" he started, the one syllable thick with emotion, before Emelle interrupted.

"Tell me after," she whispered. Emelle closed her eyes as she tilted her palms to her lips.

Following close behind, Lars drank deeply. Nothing happened, and they looked to each other.

"I don't feel—" he started, before tipping over on his side, blacking out entirely. His last thought was of his precious mate.

Chapter Twenty-Seven
Emelle

Emelle stood in a meadow she didn't recognize. *How did she get there?* It felt like something vital was missing. Confused, she began to walk in the field of wildflowers, basking in the peaceful warmth of the shining sun. Some of the flowers she passed were tall enough that she could brush her fingers over their soft petals as she walked. Red flowers faded to orange to yellow and so on. Shiny leaves on a massive tree in the distance ruffled in the idyllic breeze.

A few minutes of ambling along the meadow, she realized the large tree in the distance hadn't gotten any closer. Looking down, she saw the flowers were once again red.

She supposed she was where she was meant to be, then. Laying down in the grass, Emelle closed her eyes, content to just *be*. She felt a comforting presence settle beside her, and let herself relax into the welcoming earth. The sun shone even brighter, balmy light washing over her.

Intrigued by the presence to her left, Emelle tilted her head to find a golden female beside her, radiating warm light in the mystical grove. Pearly skin glowed as soft brown eyes welcomed her. Emelle grinned, feeling only tranquility.

This female was a friend.

A soft halo of honey waves fell over her shoulders, covering her breasts, but the rest of her naked body remained somewhat obscured, almost fuzzy, as if Emelle looked at her through blurry eyes. Golden cuffs adorned her biceps and wrists, and rings glittered on her slender fingers.

"Lovely, isn't it?" the female asked, turning to all the beauty this world offered.

Emelle watched as birds flew around each other and small creatures hopped through the brush. Nodding, she agreed as the wind caressed her skin. She never wanted to leave.

But she sat up, and death began to crawl up the stems of the flowers, the sunlight soon replaced by night. A starry sky twinkled back at her as she gaped at the sudden change.

"What's happening?" she gasped, voice quaking as fear settled into her bones.

The ground shook with her, and a crack formed in the earth, splitting the clearing in two. Emelle's eyes bulged, though she was frozen with terror. Destruction spewed forth from the crevasse, horrible beasts climbing out into the meadow, flowers and grass and animals dying under each step of their feet.

Death incarnate.

Light suddenly guttered, drawing Emelle's gaze back to the female in time to watch the iridescence fade, her features twisting in pain. Thunder crashed, echoed by the screams of dying animals.

Emelle could do nothing but watch in horror as the female decayed right before her eyes. Her skin was *leached* of moisture, bones protruding as flesh withered away, her luster dulling and dulling and dulling. The female gasped in pain, mouth moving, as if she wished to speak to Emelle.

No sound emerged.

"I don't know what you're saying," Emelle cried, reaching out with one hand to offer some kind of connection as the female died right before her eyes. She fell still, eyes closed, before Emelle could reach her.

She didn't open them again.

In the distance, a warrior cry bellowed and Emelle whipped around to watch a man slay the horrible beasts in his path. A woman laid over his shoulder as he fought the creatures, slicing them in half. A familiar bluish tint glowed from his dark brown skin, his sword...

As the blood of the beasts spilled into the earth, so, too, did some of the azure light. Emelle watched, bewildered, as the earth slowly stitched itself back together.

The warrior gently lay the unconscious woman on the ground, whispering hushed words to the sky. The last of the glow left his skin, rushing skyward into the blackness of night. Suddenly, the woman sat up, jumping into his arms.

They disappeared on a phantom wind.

In a blink, blinding sunlight replaced the darkness, and Emelle cringed, shielding her eyes with her hand. A groan sounded from beside her, and she watched the female rise, faintly glowing, her skin supple once again. Tears burned Emelle's eyes as she thanked the Fates she was alive.

"Do you see now?" the female asked, her voice soft and patient. "Do you understand?"

Emelle surveyed the land, still repairing itself. The flowers were starting to regrow, before flopping over as if too weak to fully stand back up. The breeze was still cold, slapping against her skin. The earth was...*healing*, but not yet healed.

Where was she? And where was Lars?

She wasn't sure she was supposed to be here.

But the female just walked away, leaving her alone in the meadow. A glow captured Emelle's attention, and she glanced down. The same azure tint now flowed from her own palms and into the earth. Where she sat, flowers blossomed, standing erect and healthy against the wind. When she raised her illuminated palm, the flower flopped over.

In a daze, Emelle stood, slowly walking towards the long fissure still bisecting the meadow. Flowers bloomed around each cautious step. When she rested her palm over one of the jagged edges of the crack, light flowed into the ground, before leaving her entirely. The ground grumbled, knocking Emelle over. Her head hit something solid, and everything went black.

Chapter Twenty-Eight
Emelle

Emelle's eyes snapped open right as the sun began to peek over the horizon. She was surprised to find she still lay on the grass next to the pond atop the plateau. Groaning, she lifted a palm to her forehead, rubbing the residual ache.

What just happened?

Remembering she wasn't alone, she turned her head, looking for her hulking stranger. A few feet away, Lars began to stir as well. Crawling over to him, Emelle leaned over his body to shield him from the approaching dawn.

Somehow, they'd been out the entire night.

Lars finally opened his eyes, only to flinch and rub at his head, as if he too felt an ache. "What—" He paused. "The fuck *was that*?"

"Some sort of vision, I suppose?" Emelle answered. "Were you in a peaceful meadow that was torn to shreds by literal beasts?"

A nod, and Emelle turned the vision over in her head. "Was there a beautiful naked female sitting next to you, too?" There was something *other* about the female, something inherently nurturing.

"No, he was a powerful male. He...he glowed brightly as if he held the sun inside him, before dying on the ground next to me."

"That's what happened in mine, too. Then a warrior came and slayed most of the beasts that had escaped. He disappeared with the woman he'd been carrying."

Emelle looked at her hands, which were painfully dull. Not a glow to be seen. Her brows furrowed as she flipped them over. "Do you feel any different?"

Lars sat up and peered down at his body, flexing his hands before visibly deflating.

"I think we need to pay Ozram another visit," she said in his silence.

Lars agreed.

☽✻☾

"Did you find it?" Ozram asked when he opened the door for Lars and Emelle. He left them at the threshold and hobbled over to the sitting area where they'd pored over the legends. Emelle saw he already had three teacups prepared.

Cautiously, she entered the home, Lars close behind.

"Sit, sit," Ozram muttered, picking up a warm cup and settling into his favorite wingback chair.

Emelle rounded the cozy room, settling into the couch and picking up a mug.

"How did you know we were coming?" Lars asked, suspicious, even as he sat beside Emelle. Perhaps he, too, was tired.

"The winds whisper here in the Burnes." A knowing glint shone in Ozram's eyes, as he sipped the steaming tea. "So, you figured it out, yes?"

Emelle smiled meekly. "Yes, we saw the truth, but we're not sure how to understand it." Eyes darting to Lars, she continued: "We were shown a vision, one where a tranquil meadow turned dark, the ground splitting with a large crack that had creatures from the pits of the earth escaping. A warrior appeared, slaying many of the beasts, and light spilled from him into the ground." The sounds of the dying animals would ring in her ears for a long while. She shuddered.

Ozram nodded for her to continue.

THE FOOL'S ERRAND

"The ground started to heal from the light he gave, but it wasn't enough. Flowers still wilted; animals were hunted by the few creatures that escaped. The ground felt icy, death disturbing the once-peaceful earth."

"It looked like the art in the caves, Emmy," Lars chimed.

Chuckling, Ozram stood, and shuffled into his secret room, then returned with a smaller book. This one appeared more preserved than the earlier books they'd searched through.

"*The Reckoning*," Emelle breathed, the air glimmering as if the name itself was magic. "I read about this...In one of the other tomes *The Reckoning* is mentioned, but I thought it only said something about craters forming and the sun growing darker for a few years..." Her eyes widened with each word as she realized the resemblance it held to the vision they'd seen on the mountain.

Ozram nodded, and Emelle swore the air went still as he spoke. "Not many remember a time before the Celestial beings roamed this earth. The few who did guarded the information in secret locations, having been shunned from the kingdoms by the new kings. They sacrificed their lives to safeguard the history." The riddle flashed in her mind, connections forming quicker than she could keep up.

What is lost to time?

"The truth was terrifying," Ozram continued. "They called it *The Reckoning,* causing mass panic across the lands. Kings ordered the truth to be buried, for they did not want their subjects to remember. Eventually, the kings forgot as well. The Fates let them, but I'll get to that in a moment."

Rejected by history.

Emelle's heart broke as she realized the lone skeleton they'd stumbled upon had given their life to conserve the truth. Had been burdened with protecting a history that most wanted to forget.

Remembered by dust.

Belatedly, she realized what—or rather, *who*—the dust was. Only the people in this room and possibly a few others would remember him. Would know what he sacrificed.

How terrifying a thought that such a significant piece of history had been washed away, forgotten throughout the generations. To the point where only a small handful would know the truth.
Welcomed by few.
Ozram sighed, and set his cup of tea back on the table. "The earth's power was once supplemented wholly by the Cosmos, or the Cosmic Fates as you know them. I'm sure you met them up on that mountain; they usually present as a singular being but whenever you have the fortune to meet the Fates, you're meeting them all. The combined consciousness of their power..." He trailed off, before inhaling deeply. "Anyhow, the earth's raw magic could be found in hidden nexuses, often forming hot springs in secluded caves, as you have now seen yourself. The one in Mount Haleburne is quite the vision, yes?" Emelle nodded automatically, and Ozram just continued. "The Cosmic energy channeled the crude earth magic into something tangible. I may be ancient, but even I have not seen what the earth's magic originated as." He chuckled at his own expense. "Their combined power helped feed the flowers, grow the crops, fill the streams...It was all things beauty and peace. Life was tranquil for a long while.

"But darkness fell, Celestial beings gaining power across time and space as they grew closer to our earth, drawn to the *life* that teemed in the soil. They came down in shadows, burrowing into the earth and splitting open the core of our planet. Releasing fragments of their powers into the mythical beasts they had bred in the darkened depths of the earth, they created the ancestors of the creatures you hunt down today. The Celestials couldn't leave the core of the earth, too sensitive to the light, but they could send slivers of their powers—their *will*—to the surface. Later, they learned how to trick and abduct the humans, each devastating act poisoning our world with more Celestial energy. They suck the very essence of life from the earth, fueling their energy from below."

Emelle sank into the couch, clasping her hands in her lap at the information.

"Unprepared for such an attack, the Celestial beings forced the Cosmos from the earth. For many years, the kingdoms lived in darkness, beasts roaming free. This is what we refer to as *The Reckoning*, the period of darkness the earth fell into. The Cosmos underestimated the force of the Celestial attack and we all paid dearly for it.

"Finally, the Cosmos were able to make their way back, but they did not possess the same strength anymore. They no longer had the same connection to the world, for the Celestial energy had burrowed too deeply. They could only lend their powers to the humans and hoped they would give it back to the earth. But the humans didn't do anything with it. Instead, they drew new borders and created kingdoms with leaders who ruled with total control. The first humans they lent their power to became the first kings of the new earth. With the power remaining in their bodies, their lineages became some of the strongest, most lethal to ever exist. They were the only people who could handle such raw power, and thus, they became the only ones the Cosmos chanced."

Emelle suddenly froze, gaze darting to Ozram as something occurred to her.

Just how old was he?

"So the Cosmos made the trials," Ozram continued, seemingly oblivious to her sudden realization. "They played on the pride of men, creating accolades meant to stroke their egos. They figured if there was a prize, the men would use the power for good. And it worked. Though most do not know there is a difference between the evil Celestial energy decaying the earth and the peaceful Cosmic power that brings life. If they knew...most would not risk their wellbeing, no matter the prize offered.

"With each trial, the Fates were able to imbue their power into the men to help eradicate the oily shadows of Celestial power. They had discovered three main quests that were the most effective, and those are the trials you hear about today. By completing each test, the Hero released the Cosmic power back into the earth, pushing the Celestial energy *out* and effectively bringing a little more Cosmic force back. In exchange, the Fates granted them fortune and fame, to thank them for their sacrifice.

"They also nudged them towards their soulmate, so they would never know a night of solitude, like they had, drifting in space during the Dark Years. Very few know that the natural magic of the earth also weaves bonds between souls that are cleaved upon birth, splitting one soul into two bodies. Over the millennia, the knowledge of such mates faded into legends, and the Cosmic Fates have used that to their advantage. Most ignore the innate knowledge, the *pull* of their soul recognizing its other half, and dismiss it as purely attraction or lust. That is, if they ever even meet their mate. But by bringing the two halves of the soul together, the bond helps strengthen the natural magic in this earth, thus strengthening the Cosmos' ties once again, so it is mutually beneficial for them and the inhabitants they care for."

Everything Emelle knew about the trials and the Cosmic Fates was shifting, tilting her world upside down. The Cosmic Fates were *fighting* the Celestial infestation. Through the Heroes, of course, but they were trying to save this earth. They weren't sending royalty off on silly quests...They'd found the only way to save humanity. When she peeked at Lars, she saw he was clearly working through the same implications.

And then his gaze suddenly snapped to hers, awe shining in his depthless eyes. She frowned, not sure what he'd realized, but Ozram's voice drew her back before she could ask.

"For the last few centuries," he said, gaze distant, "we have been at a rather unprecedented balance. After a little over a millennia, this earth was effectively the Celestials' home as well, providing an...unfortunate sort of balance to the earth. A push and pull. But recently, the Celestials have been pushing out more destructive power, decaying the earth from the ground out. Crops are yielding less each year, livestock having stillbirths...The world is suffering and the Cosmos have remembered there was a time when the earth was tranquil, a time before the Celestials invaded."

Ozram grew quiet under the weight of what he'd just shared, and Emelle was grateful. She felt as though her brain was about to melt from her ears.

"That's..." Lars trailed off, unable to find the words.

"How do you know all of this?" Emelle asked, still wondering just how old Ozram was.

Ozram chuckled, wry, as he ran his thin fingers through his long beard. "Like I said, the winds whisper here," he replied simply.

Emelle supposed that might be the most she would get out of him.

"What are we supposed to do with this?" Lars asked.

"Nothing," Ozram said. "Unless the Fates ask something of you."

Yeah, that wasn't cryptic at all.

Chapter Twenty-Nine
Emelle

In the early afternoon light, Lars and Emelle mounted their horses, leaving Ozram behind to return to Cloudburne for the night. Emelle felt a pang of sadness. Another person they were leaving behind. First Lorna and her family, then the skeleton in the caves, and now Ozram.

Shifting, she settled onto Selene, turning over the events of the past few days in her head, all of the new information weighing her down. Everything she knew about the Cosmic Fates was wrong. Where she thought they were pompous, they were selfless. Where she thought they favored, they sacrificed. To think she'd judged them so harshly, for so many years.

The entire ride to Cloudburne, Emelle remained lost in thought as she worked to rewrite what she had believed to be the truth for over twenty-eight years.

When they finally reached the inn, Emelle sighed with relief at the prospect of a hot bath and long night of sleep. They checked into a room, and Emelle let Lars handle the horses as she ordered some supper in the taproom.

Steam billowed in front of her as a server carried out her bowl. As soon as Lars joined her, they almost seared their tongues on the soup as they inhaled it. They didn't care.

They just ordered some ale to soothe the burn, and a hulking man who couldn't meet their eyes plopped the steins in front of them, ducking back to the bar without a word. Kai was nowhere to be seen tonight.

Despite the growing volume, they sat in near silence, each vowing to *not think* for the evening. Making their way upstairs, they bathed quickly, and fell into a deep sleep.

☽✹☾

Jostling rolled Emelle awake and she groaned as she struggled to open her eyes. Something threw her into the air, and with a start, she realized she was *moving*.

Cosmic Fates, *what was happening?*

When Emelle raised her hands to feel around the dark space she was trapped in, she realized her wrists were bound together, and when she tried to shout for help, her voice came out muffled. It took her a minute to feel the gag in her mouth, her tongue was so dry. Panting, Emelle forced herself to slow down, to not panic.

What would Lars do?

He'd be focused, calculating. He'd find any clue, any detail that would give him an advantage. Breathing deeply, Emelle forced her pulse to slow, counting in and out.

She searched the cart she was in, but it was empty, save for her. The sides of the cart were narrow with a domed leather-hide, effectively sealing her in. Bumps from their quick travel tossed her around, throwing her into the wood, and she knocked her head against the sidewall. Shaking off the injury, she resumed her search but found nothing distinct, no emblems or crates—or, most importantly, something she could use to cut her binds and escape. Sun peeked through the slats of the wood, so she knew it had been at least several hours since she'd been taken.

Emelle tried to remember what exactly occurred the night before. They'd gotten to the inn, and she went to grab supper while

Lars tended to the horses...They ate a too-hot soup and drank a bitter ale.

On a gasp, Emelle realized—the ale hadn't been flat. It had been drugged. *They* had been drugged. That's why they fell asleep after their baths, not a heated look to be found.

Emelle tried to quell her rising panic. It had to mean Lars was drugged, too, which had to mean he was probably just waking up, like she was. She could be hours away, in any direction, and he wouldn't know.

She was on her own.

Her panic surged and seemed to choke the air from her lungs. Emelle welcomed the blackness as she passed out.

Chapter Thirty

Lars

Pain lanced through Lars's head. Groaning, he lifted a hand to rub at his temple. Light filtered into the room, burning his eyelids as he struggled to open them.

"What the *fuck*?" Lars ground out, sitting up against the headboard. Squinting, he hoped Emelle wasn't feeling as bad as he was.

Why did he feel like shit?

Lars's eyes cleared as he felt the bed next to him. Cold blankets met his fingers.

"Emmy?" he asked, searching the too-still room. The air was still, the only noise filtering in from the other patrons through the wooden door.

"Emmy?" he repeated. Scrambling out of bed, Lars ripped open the washroom door, only to find it painfully empty. He whipped around, scanning the empty room once more, and bolted through the exit.

"EMMY!" he bellowed, the door slamming into the wall as he sprinted through the hallway and down the stairs. Lars searched the tavern, desperately hoping that she had just gone in search of food.

"Sir?" a quiet voice said.

Whipping his head around, he belatedly realized the voice came from below. Lars took in the small girl, who couldn't be older than seven or eight. Glancing around the room again, he didn't see anyone keeping an eye on her.

"I think I know what happened," she whispered.

Lars's stomach plummeted.

The young girl grabbed his hand, leading him over to a small alcove, giving them the illusion of privacy.

"I heard these men talking...the last time you were here. They were saying something about the woman you were with. They didn't sound very nice." Her tiny voice shook with residual fear.

"What do you mean, when we were last here?" Lars questioned, suspicion rising.

The girl looked around, but no one was paying them any mind, all too busy mumbling sleepily into their coffee. A stark difference to the storm brewing in Lars.

"I tried to warn you," the girl said. "I banged on your door, but my guardian dragged me away before I could talk to you. They were upset I'd disturbed a guest."

Lars leaned down, speaking softly as he tried to calm down the girl. "Hey, it's all right, sweetie. I'm going to get her back, but I need your help. Can you do that? Can you help me?"

A timid nod, and Lars continued: "I need you to tell me everything you know."

☽✲☾

Thirty minutes later, Lars was leaving Cloudburne and headed back to his home. Back to *Wellsmore*. It was an easy decision to sell Selene to a farmer, purchasing an extra saddle bag to carry Emelle's pack on Helios, who was powerful enough to handle the brutal ride. He knew she'd want her things if he found her.

When he found her.

The swatch of emerald green silk in his hand stared up at him, and Lars's heart hardened. He stuffed the handkerchief in his pocket, and lifted his gaze to the horizon.

Riding harder than he ever had before, Lars cut the twelve-day journey down to nine days.

He promised the Fates he'd rip the cosmos apart if anything happened to his mate.

Chapter Thirty-One
Emelle

Emelle sat in the back of a covered cart for over four days. Stopping only for a few hours of rest each night, Emelle was exhausted despite doing nothing but sitting here, and her bones *ached*. Her captors didn't let her see their faces, wearing dark masks to cover any distinguishable features every time they let her out to relieve herself. All she could see were flashes of their uniquely maroon eyes. Eyes like she'd never seen before.

Yellow and purple bruises covered her arms from their repeated manhandling, fresh bruises replacing the faded with each day. Each shift of the cart sent ripples of pain through her body. The skin of her bound wrists was raw and bleeding, and they only removed the gag when they fed her, one spoonful of gruel at a time.

She stayed awake as often as she could, trying to gather any information, but they were moving so quickly, and spoke so rarely. She didn't even know which direction they were headed in, the slats barely allowing any sunlight to spill in—certainly not enough to gauge anything by. It was all she could do to count the passing of days.

Her bare feet were raw and bleeding in some spots from being dragged and the several days she'd gone without her boots. She supposed they must've broken into their room in Cloudburne once she and Lars had fully succumbed to the effects of the drug. Emelle doubted grabbing her footwear made it on their list of priorities.

At one point, she felt the air change, and it was suddenly familiar. She swore the shadows seeped into the wooden slats of her cart, curling around her weak body to offer any comfort they could give.

But like everything in the past several days, it was temporary. They kept moving.

☽✻☾

"Wake up," a gruff voice ordered, an equally gruff hand grabbing Emelle by her arm and yanking her out of the cart. The sudden glare burned her eyes after so long in a darkened cart and she stumbled, barely catching herself with a wince as a bag was thrust over her head. She hardly had her wits about her before they hauled her forward, forcing her to stumble as she tried to keep up with their brisk pace.

All she had seen in the brief moments before the sack blinded her was an intensely regal castle. Intricate pearly spires speared towards the skies with sharp points that gleamed menacingly against the golden light, appearing more daunting than majestic. A beat later, she tripped, her bare foot slicing open on something sharp, as her captor wrenched at her shoulder to keep her from falling. Several steps later, she was tossed to the floor, her knees crunching under the weight of the fall.

The sack was ripped from her head. One of the men who'd taken her untied her gag, and she greedily gulped in the fresh air as she scanned the courtyard, disoriented.

Ferns arranged in a decorative square created a secondary enclave in the center of the courtyard, making her feel as though the space were smaller than it was, pressing in on her. She'd been deposited on a square of patterned stone in the center, the harsh floor bruising her bones. Jesters and fools masquerading as guards lined the walls, staring blankly ahead as though a near-naked woman hadn't just been shoved to the ground in front of them.

Goosebumps rippled over her arms as the wind chilled her exposed skin. She was still in her night shift, now filthy and torn and practically transparent. Her breasts strained against the material, her nipples hardened from the icy air. But she refused to outwardly show her fear, remaining stark still while on display. Her hands were still bound, and blood from the wounded skin dripped onto the stone, drop after drop after drop, almost as fast as her heartbeat.

She either needed to stay alive until Lars found her, or she had to save herself. But she was no Hero. She wasn't sure she could do it alone. Fates, she wished Greer were here, she'd have given these bastards a piece of her mind.

A swaggering man exited from the ornate door ahead of her, which she assumed was the entrance to the palace. He leisurely prowled towards her as though he held the sands of time in his clasped hands. His dark auburn hair was thick and appeared silky, and his golden skin was lush against the sunlight. But his obvious beauty was tarnished by the sinister glint behind his fiery eyes. He looked her over, and whatever he saw sent a shiver down her spine. Her heart pounded in echo of each casual step he took towards her.

"Welcome to Wellsmore, Emelle St. King," the man boomed, arms spreading wide as though she were an honored guest.

Silent, Emelle refused to respond. How did she get to Lars's kingdom? And in only *four days*?

And more importantly, how did he know her name?

A dark chuckle fell from the man as he stepped right up to her. She would have to tilt her head back to look at him, and she refused to, choosing instead to stare at the stone beneath his feet. Strong fingers pressed under her chin, forcing her head up. Her neck ached at the angle.

"I hope you enjoyed your journey. I pray my men did not hurt you too much." A chuckle, and then he added, "Though I suppose you have yet to feel true pain. We haven't even begun."

Emelle bit down on her tongue, hard, to fight back her fear. Something rueful sparked in the man's eyes, gone too quick for her to discern. Whatever it was, she wasn't sure she'd survive it.

"Take her to the dungeons," he ordered, flicking her chin to the side in clear dismissal. He strolled away as though she were but an afterthought, only to pause. The man turned back to Emelle, a wicked smirk quirking the corner of his mouth.

"Do not worry, sweet girl, you will be seeing the Wraith of Wells very, *very* soon. He would not let a slight like this go unpunished." At a wink from one of those smoldering eyes, Emelle knew.

Lars was headed straight into a trap.

And she was the bait.

Chapter Thirty-Two

Lars

Lars snuck past the guards who stood sentry over the borders of the Kingdom of Wellsmore. The walls were impenetrable, built from cinder blocks and over ten meters tall. But Lars was no ordinary traveler. He covered himself in his shadows and snuck around to the eastern wall. Using a secret passageway he'd discovered in his youth, Lars ensured his entrance into the kingdom would remain unnoticed.

Slinking through the cobblestone streets he'd grown up on, Lars felt uncomfortable in his too-tight skin. He didn't feel like the Wraith of Wells anymore, not since he'd found such a beautiful soul in his mate. She'd shown him how much more there was to life than secrets and isolation.

Crossing the street, Lars entered The Den, the discreet establishment that he used for Sceptre business.

"Well then, welcome back, Wraith!" boomed a boisterous voice from across the dimly lit room, triggering an automatic smile from Lars. He may have outgrown the Wraith, but these men were his family. Or the closest thing he'd ever get aside from Emelle and his mother.

"You couldn't get rid of me that easily," he replied gruffly, crossing the room to clap Willam on the shoulder, who froze for only a moment before a grin curled the corner of his mouth.

Lars was thankful for the slightly older man, who'd taken over running The Den and the Sceptre business while he'd been gone. Lars had always thought of the man as a mentor, and knew that just under his hardened exterior was a tooth-achingly sweet spirit. His dark brown skin was rippled with muscles, and his stature demanded attention. His eyes, however, always seemed to give away the kind nature he tried to hide.

In their business, it didn't pay to be kind.

Together, the two of them managed to slip under the crown's attention, instituting small changes that shifted the Sceptres' trajectory throughout Lars's time as the Wraith. He credited Willam for orchestrating several of the trade routes they'd set up through the Heron Sea, using Willam's keen eye and swift judgements to form deals to their advantage. It was because of him that Lars was even able to become the Wraith of Wells. His ability to command the shadows secured the position, but Willam's name was just as feared throughout Wellsmore.

His mood soured. If he couldn't rescue Emelle, he didn't deserve the title.

"How'd the trip go?" Willam asked, voice curious but with a hint of unease. After almost fifteen years of working together, Lars knew Willam trusted him implicitly, but he wasn't sure he was ready to face the truth.

Instead, he chose to scan the dim room, taking in the space he'd spent so much time in. A few of his men sat at the bar in the back, drinking in near silence. Most Sceptres were here for coin, not conversation. The roaring hearth on the left of the large room provided light, illuminating both the fresh—and years-old—stains from blood. The wood slats beneath their feet were steeped in the lifeforce, and he gave up years ago having the Sceptres give more than a cursory wipe when more was shed.

The majority of his life was spent in this infernal space, either suffering the orders of his predecessors or lashing his own at the Sceptres. He was broken and rebuilt in this darkened corner of Wellsmore.

Lars wasn't sure if it was the room that had changed, or if he was the one who'd outgrown it.

At the reminder of his current circumstances, shadows spilled into the room, choking the light from the candles momentarily. He vowed to rip the seams of the earth and cosmos apart to get Emelle back.

He dared the Fates to make him their enemy.

Sight catching again on the bar, Lars froze. Sitting on a stool was a familiar woman, but from where? As she turned her face, it slammed into him. The woman he helped at the docks all those months ago.

What was she doing here?

As though she'd heard his thoughts, the woman spun around. She lit up and whispered to the man she was next to before she rushed over to Lars.

"You're here! When we got in last night, Mr. Archer told me you were gone and he wasn't sure when you'd be back. We said we'd wait at least a few days, before we made our way east," the woman spilled, enthusiasm filling the usually gloomy room.

Lars looked to Willam, who suddenly found the floor incredibly interesting.

What had happened while he was gone?

He turned back to the woman, hiding his confusion. Lars wondered why she was in Wellsmore. Last he saw her, she was boarding a ship at the West Docks, declaring that she never wanted to return to the south again.

"What brought you back to Eralyn?" he asked, finally noticing the not-so-small roundness to her belly that hadn't been there a few months ago. At least he knew he had saved her before the men had the chance to violate her, so this must have been someone else's child.

She rubbed her belly. "*Well,* I got back to my mate once the ship arrived in Thoryn, but we had to work out some legal issues with the wedding. Once the dust settled, everything caught up to me and I finally broke down and told him what happened. How you saved me from being...*abducted* by those men."

A sniffle, and then she continued, a knowing smile lifting the corners of her mouth. "You helped my mate, too, you know."

With that, the man finally made his way over from the bar. Two burly men shadowed the woman's mate at a distance, but matched each step he took. Recognition at the man's closely cropped dark hair and rich brown skin reminded Lars of where he'd met her mate.

"Elix," he said, offering Lars a calloused hand. The man he'd recovered swindled funds from Anders stood in front of him. *What are the chances?*

Shaking the proffered hand, Lars introduced *himself,* not the Wraith as he'd done when they first met. Willam arched a brow.

"I know I already owe you a favor," Elix said, "but I also owe you a lift debt." And then he dropped to a knee and bowed his head as he held onto Lars's hand. "You saved my mate and unborn child, though we did not know she was pregnant at the time. I will forever be in your debt." Elix looked up, tears glimmering and threatening to spill over.

"You may regret offering the debt," Lars whispered, to which the man shot him a confused look.

But Elix shook it off, bringing his wife forward. "And this is my mate, Greer," he said, rosy smile plastered on his face as he lovingly stared at his bride.

Lars's world tilted.

"Greer?" he asked, voice shaky.

Willam eyed Lars in suspicion. Very few things on this earth could rattle Lars.

"Yes, I know, it's an older name, but I happen to like it," Greer joked with a wink and a firm elbow in her mate's side.

"You're Greer..." He paused. "From Silvermist?"

Silence fell, as Greer and Elix both looked at him with the same suspicion.

"How would you know that?" Elix questioned, taking a small step to shield his pregnant mate.

"Because Emelle is *my* mate," he declared for the first time aloud. A shimmer in the air and it was as though the cosmos were weighing the statement.

Greer beamed, pushing past Elix to throw her arms around Lars. After a belated moment, Lars just closed his arms awkwardly around the woman, patting her a few times on the shoulder.

"Where is she?" Greer asked, peeking past Lars as though Emelle would pop out of thin air, bright smile lighting the room as it usually would.

His heart cracked.

"Where's Ellie?" she repeated, eyes snapping to Lars.

"She's been taken," he admitted as he dropped his gaze to the floor, not able to look Greer in the eye. "By the King of Wellsmore."

He refused to acknowledge his parentage.

"I've returned to get her back. And to end the king's reign, once and for all."

Greer gasped, a hand falling to her swollen belly as she stepped into the comfort of her mate's chest. Wrapping a strong arm around Greer's shoulders, Elix became a mask of resolution. "How can we help?"

☽✳☾

Lars and Elix planned well into the late hours of the night. Having escorted Greer to their accommodations, Elix left one of his men behind to guard her, while Lars ordered two of his Sceptres to be stationed outside her door.

Stepping into his spacious office, Lars fell into the crumpled cot under the window, moonlight illuminating the tidy room as he resigned himself to a few lousy hours of sleep. The space somehow felt smaller, as though he'd physically outgrown the office, outgrown the neat desk filled with orders and plans. This room no longer felt big enough to contain the man he'd become with Emelle.

So he grounded himself, his breathing, for fear of the walls closing in on him, as irrational as it may be.

His soul screamed at him to *go*, to slip in undetected and get Emelle *right now*, never to return to Wellsmore again. To keep her protected, no matter the cost.

Even at the cost of Wellsmore.

But his head screamed at him to grab Emelle, kill his father, reduce the palace to rubble, and save the kingdom.

The depth of his duty to his mate slated against the duty he'd burdened himself with, only one of which he'd begun to resent. The other...he cherished. He'd never wanted to rule the kingdom, but he would do it if he needed to.

But that was before.

The more time he spent with Emelle, the less he desired a future stuck in a castle. He craved to see her face light up as she saw all the sights their world offered. His shadows filled the room as he released his control on them, no longer wishing to see these cursed brown walls.

Hours later, as Lars finally drifted off to sleep, the only thing he was sure of, the only thing he knew for certain, was that he was going to save Emelle.

He'd made his decision.

He didn't care if his kingdom burned if it meant she was safe.

He could live with the blood of Wellsmore on his hands. What was a few more thousand souls? He wouldn't, *couldn't* live with a single drop of hers.

He'd sooner follow her into the cosmos.

Once again, his dreams were plagued with terrifying images of Emelle, and Lars woke with tears burning down his cheeks. Somehow, the fear burrowed deeper without Emelle by his side to quell it. The dreams always felt so real. And now, more painful than ever.

When the sun was nearing its peak in the sky, Lars left The Den without a backward glance. Elix remained to keep Greer safe and to stay ready to help Emelle once he brought her back. The Den's location had been a secret kept safe for over four decades, and Lars had agreed it was the best location to bring her should she need any healers. Elix was to have the men he'd brought in on standby, should this turn into an all-out war. He was sure the man would've done so regardless, but Lars couldn't take any chances. He cashed in his debt. Willam passed along the orders to their spies in The Den, who passed along the orders to the spies in the streets, who passed along the orders to the spies around the castle. They would be ready for Lars.

The cosmos wouldn't be.

Chapter Thirty-Three
Emelle

Emelle was shoved into a filthy, rat-infested dungeon. It was dank and dark, and held only a bucket in the corner. Pungent fumes wafted and Emelle fought against a gag. The thought of opening her mouth in this decrepit chamber had her jaw clenched tightly. Rodents skittered into the darkness as she righted herself, leaning against the back wall with a groan. They'd finally cut the binds off her wrists, but the damage was far from healing. Where was that magical healing cave when she really needed it? Shivering, she brought her legs up to her chest and wrapped her arms around her knees.

Her dirty shift hardly covered her body and offered little heat, but she tucked her legs under the skirt anyways. She shook her head to fan her hair around her shoulders, anything to brace against the chill.

Her mind flashed to that first morning in Cloudburne, when Lars took one look at her bird's nest and loved her even fiercer. He hadn't said it, but she felt it. She'd felt the warmth in his gaze, in his hold. In the way he tucked the strands behind her ears and wrapped his body around hers, offering an acceptance she'd desperately been searching for her entire life. He saw through her masks, her defenses. And he loved her still. Not in spite of, but because. She held onto the whisper of that warmth, but it did nothing to protect her against the frigid draft.

And now, the sight of her unkempt hair brought tears to her eyes.

With little else to occupy her, she tried to think how she could escape. How she could save herself. But she'd been taken down two levels underground, and the locks on her cell were intricate.

A constant drip in the corner of her prison kept her company. Minutes, or hours, later, a guard plopped a paltry excuse for a dinner in front of her: more stale bread and a suspicious looking...meat?

Grabbing the loaf, Emelle broke off small chunks and held them on her tongue, hoping to soften them with her saliva. But they didn't give her any water, and her tongue was swollen from dehydration. The harsh edges still scratched on the way down and she coughed from the pain, the dryness.

After finishing her pathetic meal, Emelle shuffled back to her spot near the rear of the cell. Wrapping her bruised and bleeding arms around her body, she began to plot.

☽✶☾

There she remained, in the filthy, freezing cell that dripped grimy water in a maddening rhythm. She was so thirsty, even *that* was starting to appeal. Food was dropped off at seemingly random intervals, and she quickly lost track of time. But at least sleep came easier. She began to welcome the reprieve from her bleak reality.

Starvation finally broke her resolve.

Tentatively eating the mystery meat, Emelle only gagged the first few times. After a few more meals, she was scarfing it down as though it were juicy venison. Hands filthy, she picked up her food without care and ate quickly.

Lars would come for her, she knew that in her bones, but she had to act if she had the opportunity. And she wouldn't lose her chance because she was *starving*.

In the beginning, the guards would take her food away after only a few minutes, so she'd learned to eat fast. Now they leered and laughed at her hunger and desperation.

She didn't care. Let them laugh. If they were in her shoes—the joke almost made her break down into helpless laughter—they would do the same.

Time stretched on. Emelle found a stone and began marking what she thought would be a day on the wall closest to her corner. So far, there were five scratch marks. With each night that bled into another morning, she realized she was going to have to save herself.

Emelle mulled over what she knew, what she'd heard from her lifetime of being invisible. She turned over techniques, but most required a strength she did not possess, especially with the meager meals they tossed at her.

She'd have to outsmart them.

She'd play her part, the distressed damsel who whimpered and needed to be saved.

She'd let them see what they wanted to see, and it would be their downfall.

Her head ached as she licked her chapped lips. They'd finally given her some water, but not nearly as much as her body needed. Mumbling under her breath, Emelle sent a promise into the cosmos as she tilted her head under the leaking rock, catching the filthy water on her tongue.

She would make them regret the moment they set their sights on Emelle St. King.

☽✷☾

"Let's go," someone growled, unlocking her cell. The rusted metal groaned ominously as they opened the gates. It was hauntingly familiar to the squeaking hinges on the door to The Finn. She'd once thought that the tavern, the responsibility that shackled her to Silvermist, was a prison sentence. But this dark and filthy cell was a rude awakening. Oh, what she wouldn't give in this moment to be transported back to her boring, monotonous life running her tavern.

But Emelle had worked out how she'd save herself, so she didn't fight as they stepped into the cell. She needed to play her role and get herself alone with the male who had greeted her, *taunted* her, when she arrived. He was the one in charge, she could tell by the way all of the males deferred to his presence. She needed to swipe a knife, any knife, and she'd carve his fucking eyes from his skull. Then, she'd slip from the palace on silent feet that she'd been training on her entire life.

Was it brutal? Yes. Would she hesitate? Not a chance.

The man stomped into her space, his form towering over her and blocking the light from the tunnel. Emelle flinched, shielding her face with a grimy arm. But he just grabbed her elbow and *yanked*.

Emelle scrambled to her feet, tumbling after the large jester. She could deal with a few more bruises if it kept her alive.

She kept her eyes peeled, scanning her surroundings as they led her like chattel up the many stairwells and through several doors, cataloging every small detail. Anything she could use to her advantage. To aid in her escape.

Details. She imagined Lars saying the word, reminding her what she needed to focus on, and she felt strengthened by it. By what she learned at his side. If only Greer could see her now. Emelle stifled a chuckle. Greer probably wouldn't even recognize her, filthy clothes and broken body aside.

They walked her down one marble hallway that seemed to stretch for miles. Portraits of a familiar man lined the walls, staring at her with increasingly sinister eyes as she passed each canvas. Pieces began falling together.

Each portrait seemed to noticeably darken, evil seeping through the canvas, and the air grew icier with each step down the corridor.

But all too quickly they reached the wooden door at the end, and she was pushed over the threshold. Calloused hands gripped the back of her neck this time, walking her like a feral dog into the spacious room. Finally, her jailer tossed her in the center of a regal room. Her knees slammed onto the floor.

An ornate throne sat on a dais at the back of the room. Ruby red cushions were deceptively inviting, and its golden trim and clawed feet gleamed menacingly in the afternoon sun that streamed in from the high-arched windows, casting a beam of light onto the throne. It was certainly imposing, but just another detail. That was how she needed to think. To stay present, to stay *sane*.

A door opened silently, and in he strode. Emelle hated that she still trembled.

"It is nice to see you again, Emelle," he said as he approached. "I hope you have enjoyed your stay so far." False pretense dripped from each word, while golden light shone against his auburn hair and brightened the room. It should've made the scene less frightening. Wasn't daylight supposed to scare the monsters away?

The man strolled leisurely in front of her, never straying too close, but the threat remained. It was staring down his nose at her.

Emelle stayed silent.

"We are just awaiting the *Wraith of Wells*," he exaggerated with an eye roll. "My men tell me he has finally reached the borders. He did not have the luxury of Celestial travel on his side."

Celestial travel? Was that how they reached Wellsmore in less than half the time it was supposed to take?

The final pieces fell together and it was as though lightning struck her. It was so obvious now.

This was a Celestial trial.

But not for her. No, this was a Celestial trial for *Lars*.

She fought back emotion, refusing to give this man anything against her. Was she predestined to be saved? Did the Cosmic Fates have a plan? Did she just need to play her part and wait to be rescued?

A part of her raged at being a pawn in someone else's destiny, even if that someone was Lars. Merely a plot device in his grand story.

As Emelle sped through her options, she fought to let go of her madly formed plan. But still, what she lacked in physical strength, she made up for in vast knowledge of trials and all the mistakes the Heroes had made. Perhaps she could convince this man of her worth beyond bait for Lars.

Stifling her trembles, Emelle lifted her chin and spoke as clearly as she could manage. "What makes you think Lars will be coming for me?" She made it sound as though she had information they did not possess.

Technically, she did.

A dark chuckle, and then he spoke, scanning over her filthy form. She had to fight her instincts, forcing herself to remain still.

"Because, my dear, I sent him to you. To *find you*. His *mate*. I knew you would be out there somewhere. Whispers in the wind told me you were in the North Forest and we've been tracking the two of you for weeks. I even made sure he was...motivated. All so I could steal you right from under his nose and bring you here. So I could stifle the man who was starting a revolution in my kingdom.

"With your presence, I have single-handedly leashed the Wraith of Wells. My kingdom is *mine* again. And soon, I will conquer the rest of Eralyn. Then Thoryn in the north. And the Wraith will help me every step of the way." The man flashed his perfect teeth, a predatory smile contorting his features.

Emelle's heart sank as his words settled in the air between them.

He wasn't planning to kill her. But somehow...somehow this was much worse. How long would he keep her barely alive, just to wrest his control over Lars?

And...*his* kingdom? This was Lars's father? Winthorpe? Emelle looked the man over, this time with a more careful eye.

His dark auburn hair had the same waves, but Lars must have gotten his color from his mother. They had the same nose, though this man didn't boast a scar slashing the bridge of his. His frame was lankier, less muscular. And his eyes...

His eyes were a blazing red, just like the Celestial beings who'd climbed out of the rift in the vision from the mountain.

Terror sent a chill down her spine as she put the final pieces together. This wasn't just a Celestial trial.

The king *was* a Celestial.

Just as the beasts were Celestial, somehow the same energy had possessed this man. Except this time, they'd fused within a body that had access to vast resources and power and intellect.

Oh, Fates.

How long had he been possessed? The man in front of her had an intelligence the other beasts didn't. How long did it take for the Celestials to fuse their energy into a living, breathing human, before finally drowning anything mortal? Did he even fight their intrusion? Or was the promise of fortune and power too good to pass up?

The walls of the throne room seemed to grow—or maybe she was shrinking—as half-formed thoughts slammed into her one after the other. She felt as though she were tumbling madly down a hole, as if she were in some sort of dreamscape and decidedly late to the most important event in her life. Where everyone was waiting for her to just *catch up*.

The golden throne on the dais darkened as she struggled to stay present, but her vision tunneled, panic threatening to decimate her.

Did Lars know what his father was? He'd said he hadn't been seen outside of his palace in over twenty years. Emelle's heart throbbed, once again reminded of Lars's upbringing. She thought of her own mother, who so easily abandoned them, and how much it stung. And Emelle was already fifteen. Lars was *nine*. So young, and yet thrown into the streets without care. Pressured to build himself into a frightening legend that was apparently a force to be reckoned with amongst the streets of Wellsmore.

As her knees throbbed on the hardened floor, Emelle prayed to whoever was listening. The king's blazing red eyes shimmered with glee, a mad smirk twisting his otherwise attractive features into a sickening impersonation of a person. He looked inhuman. Uncanny.

Evil masquerading as a mere mortal.

The king seemed more than willing to let her squirm, to process his words. With each twitch of her body, each shaky inhale, his eyes sparked with delight.

Surely there must be someone in the palace who leaked information to the common folk. Someone who got this information to Lars. But he never mentioned his father being overtaken by the Celestials. Granted, he didn't know much about the Celestial trials when he arrived in Silvermist, but he had to have a suspicion...right?

Emelle's hands shook as she scanned the room. Sentries lined the walls, the doors. She still needed to get Winthorpe alone, Celestial being or not, and she needed to do it fast. If Lars was on his way, she needed to be ready.

"You said he's...my mate?" she asked, curling her shoulders in on herself. She was the picture of a damsel in distress. And while she'd never been a good liar, if the lives of her mate and quite literally the fate of their continent relied on her deception, she'd make him believe every word she forced through her teeth.

"You did not know?" the king said skeptically, eyebrows raised in disbelief.

She knew she'd felt the cosmic shift that first night at The Finn, but she'd been in denial for weeks as to what it meant. Even when she realized she loved him, that they shared a soul-deep cosmic connection, she did not even *think* he could be her mate.

Fates, even after Ozram told them about the magic of soulmates, she hadn't put it together. So much for being the brightest barkeep in Eralyn.

She remembered the way Lars looked, his eyes wide in discovery after Ozram finished speaking.

Lars *did* know. He knew and he didn't say anything.

Emelle shook her head, not bothering to mask her sadness. "I don't think he knew, either. He would've said something." She wished that weren't a lie. "Truthfully, he didn't even act like he wanted me around. When I finally caught up to him, he did everything he could to shake me off."

She lied for her life, for Lars's life. She willed mist to gather in her eyes, though she didn't have to try very hard. She wanted the unforgiving ground to swallow her whole, to save her from the presence of this evil.

Breaking her heart even further, she willed herself to believe her own words as she continued.

"If he's here...I don't think he's here for me." A solitary tear slipped down her cheek. Sniffling, she shook herself, as though ridding the heartache. "I just want to go home. My parents are injured, and they rely on me. Please, just send me back to Silvermist and you'll never hear about me again."

Her palms grew clammy at the mention of her parents. At the thought of her father, who she prayed she'd get the chance to see again. So she could launch herself into his familiar embrace and tell him she loved him. She never told him about her resentment over her obligations. Maybe he knew, maybe he didn't. But it hadn't been fair to hold onto this anger, this bitterness, when she hadn't ever voiced it. He'd been more than happy to run The Finn. He just assumed she would be too.

And her mother...she could see the signs so clearly now.

Her mother hadn't wanted to be shackled to the tavern, either. The stress of the taxes and the behavior from the travelers who passed through...She couldn't take it anymore and did the only thing she could think of. Did that make her a horrible person? Emelle didn't think so. Her mother had handled it terribly, that was true, but she had only been a couple years older than Emelle was now. Their romance had been a whirlwind, and then she fell pregnant. She moved out of her parents' home and into The Finn by the time she was seventeen. Her mother was flawed, but she was just a woman put in an impossible situation.

And Emelle forgave her. If she wasn't meant to live much longer, she refused to die holding onto any anger.

She wiped her hands on her dirty shift, the worn material scratching her skin and sending a shiver down her spine. Her heart thudded in her ribcage, as if desperate to escape. She was almost afraid it would.

The king scanned a wary eye over Emelle, weighing her words. A bead of sweat trickled down the column of her neck, following the same pesky trail as when she'd worked a long day at the tavern.

"No," he said simply, a cruel smile taunting her. "So you say he does not know you are his mate..." He trailed off. "But once he does, he will do anything to keep you safe. Feelings or not, you are *invaluable* as collateral."

While she had known he wouldn't go for it, she had hoped she could gain some trust from him. By the skeptical look in Winthorpe's eyes, Emelle doubted it had worked.

Head snapping to his commander, the king barked an order: "Take her to my chambers. Get her washed."

Emelle's stomach dropped.

Chapter Thirty-Four
Emelle

Emelle's knees ached from the number of times she'd been shoved to the floor. She was positively sick of arrogant men throwing her around as though she were a possession to toy with. She cringed as her freshly clean knees groaned in pain, waiting for the king's arrival.

Two timid women had scrubbed every inch of her skin, despite her protests. While she was used to being naked around others, it had always been her choice. At least they'd studiously avoided looking, letting their hands blindly run the scratchy cloths over her bruised body.

Her feet and wrists had stung the entire time, but she used the pain to focus herself. To practice building a brick wall between her physical pain and her very soul. She could survive this, she prayed.

After finishing with her skin, they'd dunked her head under the water and Emelle had choked on the suds. Then they'd haphazardly dried her and dressed her in a simple tunic and trousers, which she appreciated more than they would ever know. She'd gripped the thin material between her fingertips as they handed her back to her two favorite guards, before melting into the shadows again, leaving her to be marched to her demise.

Now, Emelle knelt on the frigid marble floor of King

Winthorpe's bedroom as she waited for *His Majesty*. Her lip curled in disgust at the title as she scanned the room.

His four-poster bed sat ominously in the back of the room, with large windows on either side. Heavy draping curtains were tied over the windows, framing the bed as though welcoming her. Beckoning her. She shuddered involuntarily, horrified at the thought of sharing a bed with the king.

To her immediate right, deep sapphire couches provided seating around a crackling fireplace that warmed the room. The couches were elegantly lined with golden threads and sat upon clawed feet, complemented by golden side tables with intricate designs down the legs. Candles flickered on the tables and around the room.

The room itself dripped in wealth. She wasn't surprised, knowing intimately how much the various crowns usually taxed their citizens. But knowing who occupied this space, and knowing who paid for the luxuries, tarnished the obvious beauty. It was hard to even look at. Sweat began to drip down Emelle's neck as she waited. Her new best friends remained silent behind her.

But still, Emelle searched for anything that could give her any sort of advantage. Her heart swelled at a pair of daggers displayed above the fireplace. Though her hopes were swiftly dashed as she noticed the dull edges. She needed something *sharp*, anything that she could use to—

"Well, you certainly clean up *nicely*," Winthorpe purred, sending shivers of disgust down Emelle's back.

Snapping her head straight, Emelle refused to acknowledge the possessed man. Her blood rushed in her ears, dulling the king's soft steps. She'd almost forgotten why he'd want her clean.

The king barked a laugh, as if sensing her fear. "Do not flatter yourself, I have no desire to taste you. For now, at least. Now stand up," he said, a cruel smile following his haunting words.

When he offered his hand, a memory of Lars speaking a similar command in the hot springs flashed in her mind, churning bile in her throat. And though Emelle hated it, she let the king help her to her feet, hoping to maintain the demure and innocent guise for as long as possible. Following him to the overstuffed couch, Emelle tucked herself as far into the corner as she could.

"Why don't you think the Wraith won't do everything in his power to get you back?" A wicked gleam sparked in his eyes, and Emelle knew *this* was his sick pleasure. Taunting the anguish of others, forcing them to witness each painful truth.

Emelle lied through her teeth. "Like you said, he's entered the city, and yet he hasn't come for me. He tried to get rid of me every chance he got. I would assume he is quite relieved that I'm gone." Emelle's heart cracked deeper with each word she forced past her lips. If these were the final days of her life, she hated that she had to lie about her love for Lars, and the love he so clearly had for her.

Winthorpe nodded thoughtfully as she spoke and Emelle willed her heartbeat to slow, to not give her away. She had no idea if he could hear it.

"That may be true. But he will not want you in anyone's possession other than his own, regardless of his feelings for you, or lack thereof."

Emelle figured as much, though she was surprised he'd admitted it out loud.

The glint in his blood red eyes sharpened. "Nevertheless, you shall remain here in my chambers with me. I would not want him to think he could sneak into the dungeons and snatch you away from under my nose." Like he'd done to Lars.

A cruel smile sparkled at her, and Emelle audibly swallowed.

Fuck.

Chapter Thirty-Five

The Wraith of Wells

After spending several hours gathering information from the Sceptres in his network, he made his way to the palace under the blanket of night. In meetings held in shadowed corners and alleys, he discovered that Emelle had been taken by two of the king's commanders.

So he'd snuck into their barracks and found their bunks. Waking them one by one, he extracted answers from the commanders, ruthlessly, mercilessly. With each scream, he gleaned *why* the king had taken Emelle, and how they'd even found them. He cursed at himself for being too wrapped up in Emelle to notice the tail they'd picked up in Cloudburne that somehow evaded his advanced senses.

He then recognized one of the commanders as the man who'd served their ale back in Cloudburne. He made sure his death would be remembered, a warning to those who dared to cross him. A red haze fell over him.

Afterwards, he snuck past the guards standing sentry around the palace, drifting through the dense shadows. Under the cloak of night, he cleared the way to an unsecured window on the second floor of the east side of the palace and climbed the stone wall, slipping in unnoticed. He crouched, unsheathing his dagger as he made his way down the lavish hallway. Long ruby-red runners were plush under his feet, silencing each step, just as they had in his youth.

Rounding the corner, he found himself at the top of a short staircase. He slunk down the few steps, stalking across to a plain wooden door.

Cracking open the door, he surveyed the courtyard in front of him. Crickets chirped, disturbing the otherwise still air. He inhaled deeply. *Citrus and jasmine with a hint of smoky vanilla.*

He inhaled once more.

Blood. Emelle's blood, to be specific.

A murderous calm settled over him. Only his heart thumping in his chest gave away his true emotions. Slipping out of the hallway, he crept along the shadows of the courtyard, evading the few guards patrolling, before slipping into the main door on the north wall.

Her scent was stronger here. Another inhale. It dripped with another scent, something bitter and harsh: *fear.*

The entrance to the palace was exactly the same as in his memory. An enormous marble foyer held a dual-staircase, lining the opulently detailed walls on either side with their grand steps. Wrought-iron rails painted sapphire curled around the stairs, and above the mezzanine, a larger-than-life portrait of the king hung, glowering down at anyone brave enough to enter. He barely recognized the man, the menace that shone behind his eyes somehow captured in the painting.

In his youth, the king had been distant, but never outwardly cruel. Sometimes, he'd catch his father staring from afar, not a menacing look to be found, as he played with the other children in the castle. Just...staring at him, as though wishing he could take a step closer.

He never did.

As he stalked under the stairs and through the long, yawning hallway, more portraits of the king lined the wall. The increasing violence that sparkled in the king's eyes was disturbing to witness, a tangible showcase to the evil that corrupted his father.

Seeing a door barely cracked at the end, he stalked up to it, gripping it so tightly the wood groaned. He promised his wrath upon anyone involved in Emelle's capture.

Pushing the door open more, he peeked through the crack at the empty throne room. Emelle's scent was drenched in fear, and he shook with rage. At the Fates for allowing this. At himself for not stopping it. At his father for taking her. He would peel every inch of skin from the man and feed his living corpse to the rabid dogs of Wellsmore.

Sneaking through the shadows, he spotted two guards conversing near the door on the far side of the throne room. His hands twitched, aching to snap their bones, but the rational part of him knew he needed to gather more information. Wrangling control over the murderous beast inside him, he listened.

"I wouldn't mind guarding her," one chuckled, his tongue practically wagging.

He bit his tongue so hard blood filled his mouth.

"Didn't you hear? She's the Wraith's mate. The king isn't going to let her out of his sight now that the Wraith is back," the other responded. "Don't do anything stupid to fuck this up for me. We're almost next in line."

He wasn't sure what they were in line for, but he didn't care. He slithered behind the first, and slid his dagger between his ribs, clasping his free hand over the fool's mouth. Agonizingly slowly, he twisted the blade as he pulled it out. Sullied blood spilled onto the floor.

The jester whirled around, forced to watch as he slid the dagger across the man's neck. Hot blood poured free.

He shoved the broken body towards the jester, who jumped backwards. Slipping into the shadows, he appeared behind the jester, pulling his head back by his hair as he laid his dagger across his throat.

"Where is my mate?" he growled, voice leaving no room for deceit.

Still, the jester did not answer, so he dug the blade into his skin, blood spilling down his leathers. The man gulped, slicing his skin further, and he scented something acrid in the air. Urine.

"*Where is my mate?*" he repeated through clenched teeth, soul raging at him to drown the jester in his own blood.

"The king's chambe—"

He sliced his dagger through the man's throat, and tossed his body forward before slipping back into the shadows.

He crept through the palace until he reached the king's chambers. Along the way, he dispatched several more of the king's guards. Blood soaked his leathers and his boots left a bloody trail in his wake.

Steeling himself, he prepared for this final trial. For rescuing his princess. Approaching the entrance to the chamber, he paused, eyes widening at the bloodied door hanging wide open. He wasn't prepared for the massacre that awaited him.

Chapter Thirty-Six
Emelle

Emelle remained on high alert as King Winthorpe slept next to her. She kept waiting for him to slide his hands over to yank down her trousers the instant she finally drifted off.

Believing her to be just a tavern barkeep, he'd commanded his guards to stay outside of his chambers entirely. They stood at the end of the long corridor. Far out of hearing range. She wasn't sure how she felt about that. Though, even if they did hear her scream, they would never disobey their king. Perhaps it was better this way.

And Winthorpe wasn't exactly wrong. Lars joked she was the brightest barkeep in Eralyn, but intelligence didn't always win against brute strength.

As she lay on her side facing away from the sleeping man, she scanned the dim room. Her gaze kept returning to the dull daggers displayed above the fireplace, now down to embers. So far, those were her only option.

Could she even make it over there without waking the king up? She had to try anyway.

Slowly rolling onto her back, she tested his reaction. His breath remained stable, snoring softly, even. Emelle fought a scoff.

Keeping her sight on Winthorpe, she slowly pulled one leg out from under the covers and pressed her foot onto the floor. A heartbeat later, she hesitantly pushed herself off the mattress, waiting for him to wake up.

After several seconds of no reaction, Emelle backed away a few paces before slipping towards the dying fireplace on soft feet.

Carefully, she grasped the hilt of one of the daggers. She dared a look back at the sleeping king, watching his chest rise and fall as she gently pulled the dagger from its place of honor.

A snag blocked the dagger from being removed and Emelle whirled her head around, yanking with more force. It budged, but barely. Emelle's panic churned, threatening to escape, but she bit her lip until she tasted blood.

She tugged again, once, twice.

Unprepared, she fell backwards as the weapon came loose in her hand. Catching herself against one of the ornate side tables, Emelle cringed as the melting candle wobbled. She slapped a hand down on the base with a silent curse.

"I am disappointed, Emelle. Truly, I was hoping you would make a less obvious choice."

Emelle's head snapped up as Winthorpe strolled towards her leisurely, not a hint of sleep in his fiery gaze.

Frantically, Emelle realized it had been a test. He'd wanted to see what she'd do the second she had the opportunity, and she fell for it.

Foolish.

She was so incredibly *foolish*.

Tears burned in her eyes, but she refused to let them spill over, refused to give him the satisfaction. Gripping the dagger, Emelle shuffled but did not cower.

As the king strolled closer, she weighed her options. Clearly, he needed her alive in order to use her as collateral against Lars, so that meant he wouldn't kill her...She hoped.

"What were you hoping I would do?" she asked, voice surprisingly firm. She had to do something to stall him.

"Ah, well, I had hoped you would just fall asleep, but you can never do anything the easy way, can you?"

Winthorpe was almost to her. She was running out of time. He might not kill her, but he could certainly drag her right to the edge. A breath, and she knew.

Fates, she wished she'd had more time.

Time with Lars, time with Greer, time to travel and wander the wild adventures offered on this earth...

Raising the dull blade to her throat, Emelle stared down her nose at the approaching king, who slowed with each step. Tears fell, not from fear, but for all of the moments she'd been robbed of. She was grateful for these last two months with Lars, and truly, she wouldn't change her time with him for anything. Whispering a hurried prayer to the Fates, Emelle notched the blade against her carotid.

"Emelle, don't do this," the king warned, eyes widening as they blazed with righteous Celestial power, hands raised in caution. He was almost close enough to stop her, and Emelle felt the hilt of the dagger warm in her palm. Gulped, as she felt the newly sharpened blade against her skin.

It was now or never.

An inhale, and Winthorpe lunged for her.

An exhale, and Emelle whipped her arm in front of her, slicing the king deeply across the abdomen, spilling his tainted blood across the stone floor.

Clutching his mangled stomach, Winthorpe was wholly unprepared for Emelle as she grabbed his head by the hair and tilted his head back to expose his throat.

As the Celestial fire dimmed in his eyes, she could've sworn she saw a hint of relief. But Emelle had no mercy for this man, possessed or not.

"*For Lars,*" she whispered through clenched teeth, slitting his throat open with the blade.

The blade the Cosmic Fates had blessed from her frantic, whispered prayer. It was never about the cleansing: it was about the acknowledgement to the Fates. To their healing power. To the history that had been forgotten.

Erased.

Emelle didn't dare blink until the last breath left the king. Until the light faded from his eyes, the blazing red yielding to dark onyx. After several agonizingly long moments, she finally let his body collapse to the floor, his head hitting the marble with a sickening *squelch*. It was bent at an odd angle, barely attached to the rest of his body, but thankfully facedown.

Emelle fell onto the couch, breathing hard, as if she'd just run for miles. Disbelief had her searching her hands, the bright red blood of her mate's father staining her skin. A manic laugh spilled from her chest as she finally let the tears fall.

She did it. She actually fucking *did it*.

Minutes passed as she sat staring at the regal wallpaper surrounding the fireplace, trying to ignore the cooling body that lingered at the edges of her vision, the blurry lump of clothes that she couldn't quite acknowledge just yet. No one came rushing in. More minutes passed, and shock began to thaw into adrenaline, her skin prickling.

Looking back down at her hands, plain confusion gave way to utter horror as Winthorpe's blood was *absorbed* by her skin. *No*—it was…

Snapping her head up, she realized with terror that she hadn't decapitated Winthorpe, nor did she even think about finishing the ritual. It hadn't even crossed her mind.

Without removing the head and burying the body, the evil was released, but to where?

Standing numbly, Emelle walked over to the polished mirror by the bedroom door and watched in horror as her emerald irises transformed to a blazing, fiery red.

A haze settled over her, the urge to bring carnage and destruction overtaking all other senses. The last things she remembered were the terrified faces of the jesters standing guard over the king's chambers before she tore them limb from limb with her bare hands.

Chapter Thirty-Seven
The Wraith of Wells

Panic overtook him as he crossed the dark, hushed corridor down to the king's bedchambers. Blood splashed on the walls, the floors...Limbs were thrown and chunks of flesh sat in pools of blood.

He couldn't breathe as he ran into Winthorpe's room, scanning for any sign that this blood, this *flesh* wasn't Emelle's.

Seeing a body on the marble, he skidded onto the floor as he realized it was male. Rolling the body over by the shoulder, he choked as he took in the gruesome sight of his father's nearly severed head staring back at him.

"Fates, what happened here?" he whispered, dropping his father without any remorse for his death. He needed to find Emelle.

Standing, he inhaled through his nose, hoping for any clue. There was his mate, and fear, *so much fear,* then...horror. Revulsion. Was Emelle here when this massacre happened? Where was she now?

He stalked around the room, checking behind the curtains, in the bathing chamber, anywhere he could think that his mate might have hidden while the destruction took place.

Not finding her anywhere, he left the chambers. She must have escaped somehow. It was the only truth he could accept in that moment.

Leaving the king's chambers, he stalked down the opposite hallway from which he came. Surely he would've come across Emelle if she'd escaped through the east side of the palace.

Turning the corner, he realized whoever caused this massacre had left a trail of limbs, of pools of blood, leading out the western side of the castle. The ruby-red runners were darkened, almost *black* from how thoroughly they were soaked.

Running into the streets of Wellsmore, he heard nothing but screams from its citizens as whatever caused this damage began to unleash it on the people. The bodies were being shredded, torn apart as though a feral beast had been let loose. It had to be *other*.

Celestial.

No mortal monster could produce this level of carnage.

As he cataloged the bodies, a small part of him was relieved that it appeared to only be killing guards so far. He was extremely relieved that Emelle wasn't any of the bodies either. Did it take her? Or did she escape? The Cosmic Fates better pray to him that was the case.

He refused to accept anything worse.

☽✻☾

He followed the trail of body parts throughout Wellsmore as the sun began to rise. The slaughter didn't seem to have a pattern, apart from the fact the guards were the main target, again and again and again.

He was convinced with each street that the beast had taken Emelle with it. She had to be witnessing each horror. He scented her through each alley, her disgust and fear calling out to him, but he was always one step behind.

His stomach lurched at the thought of her seeing this gore. He knew just how strong she was—he'd seen it firsthand countless times over the last couple of months—but he didn't wish *anyone* to see this.

Finally, after hours of trailing behind this creature, the screams began to fade. An eerie quiet laced through the streets of Wellsmore, and he was struggling to keep his eyes open.

Blinking, he found himself at the door of The Den.

Another blink, and Willam was in front of him.

Another blink, and he was on the ground.

The last thing he remembered was Willam dragging him onto a cot.

Chapter Thirty-Eight
Emelle

Blinking her eyes open, Emelle groaned as she rolled over. A wet *splosh* startled her, and she scrambled upright, hands slipping over the soaked ground.

All around her were torn, bloodied body parts. Arms, legs, torsos, *heads*...She gagged, throwing up right into the pool of blood she'd laid in for Fates knew how long. Flashes of the previous night flooded her, showing her the massacre she'd committed in the streets of Wellsmore.

Horrified, Emelle burst into sobs as she clawed at her arms that had caused so much devastation.

More images assaulted her memory, and Emelle gave herself over to the relief of unconsciousness, passing back out in the shredded remains of her countless victims.

☽✳☾

When she was roused into awareness again, she didn't care how much time had passed. She was starting to go numb towards the terror she'd caused. An alarming thought on its own, but at the same time it was a strange respite.

Moments later, the murderous thirst fell over her senses once again. Before she was forced from control, she gave it the same command, the only one she could issue before being thrown into the recess of her mind: only those with blazing red eyes would meet their final judgment at her hands.

Chapter Thirty-Nine
Lars

Lars's head *pounded* as he tried to sit up. Squinting, his eyes darted around the dim room. He was in his office at The Den. How did he get here?

As if on cue, Willam burst inside carrying a tray of steaming stew and a pitcher of water. Lars's mouth watered, uncaring of his burnt tongue as he slurped the stew straight from the bowl.

"Let it cool, you fool," Willam chastised, but Lars ignored him.

Glancing out his window, he guessed it was nearing dusk. Whipping his head back to Willam, he wasn't shocked when he saw the burly man freeze.

"We tried to wake you earlier but you wouldn't rouse," he explained, as if that made his sleeping all day fine. His *mate* was missing, for fuck's sake.

"Status report," he snapped, shoveling more of the stew in his mouth without tasting a bite. Chugging the water to sooth the burn, he arched a brow at Willam.

"The Sceptres have been out all day searching for the beast that was released last night. We've never seen anything like it. Civilians have been instructed to remain indoors until further notice. We were waiting for you to wake before we held another briefing."

Lars nodded and tossed his empty bowl onto his desk. Crossing over to the bathing room, he began stripping as he glanced back to Willam.

"Gather everyone. Now," he commanded, leaving no room for argument.

Willam left to spread the order as Lars took the quickest bath he'd ever subjected himself to. The freezing water focused him, calmed him. The pain of each icy slice down his skin tunneled his rage into something tangible.

Dressing in spare leathers, Lars cursed the Fates for its lack of sheaths. Stabbing his dagger into his desk, he left his office and stalked into their meeting space, hidden behind the bar. His fingers itched to hold his mate, his mind conjuring horrific scenarios that she was injured, or worse, dead. But he refused to listen to the voice, choosing instead to focus on how he could find her, *save her*. He would feel it if she were dead, a cleaving of his soul.

Elix and Greer were already in the back of the bar, so Lars crossed the darkened room to them. Greer's eyes were shining, arms wrapped around herself. Elix mirrored Lars's murderous rage in his own mossy eyes.

Noticing his approach, Greer threw her arms around Lars, not giving him the option as she crushed him. Mindful of her pregnant belly, Lars held her gingerly.

"You didn't find her," she said dully, more in confirmation than question.

Lars shook his head, and watched helplessly as the last bit of hope Greer had shattered. He did that to her.

"We're going to have a quick meeting about how to handle this threat. Please stay." He spoke as softly as he could manage in that moment before storming over to a worn desk.

Most of his men had been waiting, only a few remained in the quiet streets searching for the beast. They stood shoulder to shoulder in the cramped meeting space that hadn't been designed for a group this large. The stench of sweat and blood permeated the air.

"Sceptres, you all know why you've been called in. The streets run red with blood, shed by what can only be a Celestial monster," he began. He wouldn't be surprised if the king had somehow trapped a beast and kept it locked inside the castle. "The Guard is dead. The few who remain have likely scattered. It is now your duty to protect the citizens of Wellsmore." He scanned the room and locked eyes with men he'd grown up with. Other than Willam and a select few, most he could only trust on a good day. It would have to be enough today.

"The king is dead." He didn't try to hide the elation in his voice. "The same monster who's been let loose on Wellsmore seems to have killed the king. The only thing I'll ever thank it for." No one laughed.

"Your first task is to track this monster," he commanded. Ozram's explanation of how the Fates imbued their power into the Heroes, so they could slay the Celestial beasts in their stead, surged to the front of his mind. Memories of the fight back in Briarshire rushed forward as well, and Lars realized he hadn't imagined the azure glow on the hilt of the dagger. From the very beginning, the Fates had been helping him. "Since it must be Celestial in nature, I am the only one who can slay it. When you find it, you find *me*. Your second task is to the citizens of Wellsmore. Protect them with your life. Is that understood?"

Heads nodded, but it wasn't enough. "I said, *is that understood?*" he repeated, voice blazing with Cosmic power. His hands began to glow atop the desk—no, *his whole body* was glowing in that same azure hue that the worms had in the caves. The same glow they'd seen on the warrior in the vision they were shown atop the mountain.

Stunned silence met his question, before a resounding *Yes, Wraith* was chanted in unison.

Lars nodded, skin returning to its normal dull tone. But the power hadn't left him. No, he could still feel it, simmering under his skin. The thrum was growing louder with each minute.

That could be useful.

Several hours later, dark had fallen completely as Lars was busy marking plots on a map of monster sightings. By all accounts, it appeared to be slowing down and he couldn't fathom why.

He shoved his hands into his pockets, leaning against the wall as he stared at the map on his desk, trying to find a pattern. None of it made any sense, why the beast wasn't trying to leave the borders of Wellsmore. Instead, it circled and backtracked and had no distinguishable pattern apart from the constant attack of guards.

His fingers rolled a small forgotten flint left over from whoever wore these leathers last. His hands ached to kill the Celestial beast and find Emelle, but for now, he busied them in any way he could.

The door to his office slammed open, and Lars glanced up to find a frantic man shivering. Standing abruptly, Lars grabbed his claymore.

"Where is it?" he asked as he followed the man out the door and onto the cobblestone street. Greer saw him leaving and ran to one of the only windows that The Den had in the main taproom.

"Stay here, Greer. Do not leave The Den," he ordered, fixing a look to Elix to protect his mate on his way out the front door.

"She's there." The Sceptre pointed with a shaky finger as the most beautiful woman he'd ever met walked down the street covered in gore, eyes blazing red.

He thought it might have been a trick of the light, but as she slowly walked towards him, bloody body illuminated in the bright moonlight, he knew it was true.

Lars's heart stopped. It was only the pain of bone cracking on stone that made him realize his knees had given out right there in the middle of the cobblestone, but it was nothing compared to his world eclipsing into darkness.

"No..." Denial singed his chest, his heart refusing the truth in front of him. Ripping the last of his soul apart. "Fates, *NO!*" he bellowed, the walls of The Den shaking from the force of his cry.

Tears streamed as he took in her bloody face, her blood-drenched clothes, her poor hands...The nails had been torn from her fingertips, the skin shredded on her wrists and forearms, the blood that pooled around her bare feet as she approached him.

Blazing red eyes met onyx. His mate. She was gone. She was...*Celestial*. She was the monster who'd run the streets red with blood.

He searched her for any recognition, for anything that meant his mate, *his Emelle*, was still in there.

He found nothing.

All those dreams in which he saw her broken and bleeding... They weren't just nightmares. It wasn't just nerves and terror invading his subconscious. They were visions.

This was his *trial*.

Slaying another Celestial beast. Not rescuing Emelle, his *mate*, his *princess*.

A scream shattered the night, and Greer rushed into the street. Elix grabbed her by her shoulders, pulling her with him as he backed them against the wall of The Den.

"Stay back, Greer. Do *not* approach her," Lars ordered.

At his words, the monster that was his mate cocked its head. The blazing eyes took in her hysterics, examining Greer from head to toe.

"No, you do not look at her. You look at me," he said, regaining its attention as he forced himself to his feet.

Its head jerked awkwardly and the beast growled, taking a single step forward. Lars's world narrowed at the sight.

Fates, what was he supposed to do?

As if in answer, a golden male stepped from the shadows of The Den. Light burst around it and Emelle—*the Celestial* screeched in horror, shielding its face with a bloodied arm.

"Alaryk, you know what must be done," the male said softly as it gently touched the hand that held his claymore, revealing the Cosmic energy imbued into the metal. *Into him.*

Lars looked to his sword, and then to Emelle. His mate. He was supposed to...kill her? No, that couldn't be right.

Snapping his head towards the Fate, Lars searched its face for any *other* sort of command, to do *anything* but that.

"No," he whispered, more to himself than anything. "I—can't. I can't kill her. She's my *soulmate*." Tears blurred the iridescent Fate standing in front of him. Lars didn't bother to wipe them away.

"We know, son. We knew it would take one great sacrifice to rid this earth of the evils of Celestial power. An end to this cycle, this pain. We needed someone who could collect the remaining embers of power in this land, absorbing it into one monstrous beast for someone of great power to kill." The Fate shook its head. "We knew it could be you."

Its light was the only thing stopping Emelle from attacking. It burned her every time she got too close. Shrieking, she retreated a few steps.

Sobbing met his ears, Greer still heaving over the realization that her sister was the one who caused all of this destruction. That her soul sister was *gone*. He felt each cry echoed in his soul.

For the second time since he was nine, Lars was in utter shock as he glanced down at his sword and back up to a hissing Emelle.

No—a hissing Celestial.

Pain lanced his heart as he tried to think of *any* way around this. He said he'd let his kingdom burn, but he'd never even considered the fact that she'd be the one who'd light the flames.

She was lost to him.

He could see it was her body, but her mind and soul and everything that made Emelle *Emmy* was gone. Had been for a while, based on the hours upon hours of screaming that had cracked through Wellsmore.

His Sceptres quivered as they hovered along the edges of his sight, terrified of the woman in front of him. Emelle was soaked in blood, fingers and hair dripping with gore, but so was he. From the moment he'd understood what it meant, he'd been bathing in blood. His hands were permanently stained from the years upon decades they'd been spilling the lifeforce. How could he ever fear her, even as she stood in front of him, looking as though she'd swum in a river of blood on her way to him? He was sure he'd drown in the same river just for her.

But even as he thought of all the death, the absolute carnage that had been wrought, he couldn't hate her.

It wasn't Emelle who was killing. It was the Celestial. It may have been her hands, but it wasn't *her*.

And she wouldn't want to live like this. Couldn't live like this. If she hurt him, hurt Greer…Even if she somehow came back to him, she would never forgive herself.

He already had.

And he hated himself, for never taking the chance to tell her he loved her. Because now, he never would. *Never could.*

The moon shone brightly, iridescent light clashing with the bright light from the Fate standing next to him.

She was drifting away, like sand slipping through his fingers. No amount of time with her would ever be enough, but this was especially cruel. To have her snatched from him after such a short time together was wicked. The knot in his throat grew tighter, and he knew.

She was worth all the pain in the cosmos. He would rip out his own beating heart should she ask.

But it wasn't her who was asking.

And for the privilege of knowing her and the honor of etching her claim over his soul, to feel the purest love he'd ever have the chance to embrace, he would do it all again. He'd subject himself to hordes of the Celestial beasts just to have another moment with her, no matter how brief.

Even knowing how it ended, with fresh twin graves dug by Greer and Elix come dawn, he cherished every moment he had with her.

His mate, the one soul he would chase across the cosmos, past time and death itself, to find once more. Their story wasn't over. It was merely pausing for a moment.

Until they reached across the universes to reunite once again.

Lars's soul cleaved in two with each shaky step he took towards his mate. His breath hitched, his body falling into muscle memory for an attack he wasn't sure he could make.

He sobbed, tears falling down his face. He didn't think he could make the first move. How could he lift his sword in anything but protection for his mate? He was certain he would rather die than wet his sword with her blood. To bring her any measure of pain.

Lars slowed, horrified at himself, at the Fates, at the damned cosmos, as the monster possessing his mate's arm raised the dagger from its side.

Chapter Forty
Emelle

Emelle wasn't sure when she was able to swim back into consciousness, but she felt nothing beyond revulsion as the sticky blood dripped down her fingertips and onto the cobblestone. She'd left a trail down the streets, leading anyone who wished straight to her.

As she prowled the abandoned alleys, Emelle caught a scent on the evening air.

Cypress and cedarwood.

Inhaling, she blindly followed the scent of her mate to a dingy corner of Wellsmore.

Apparently, the only thing she could do in her body right now was put one foot in front of the other. But even that was instinct as she followed the scent to her mate.

It hit her belatedly that maybe she shouldn't have brought this monster straight to Lars.

Oh Fates, what if she killed him?

Emelle began to panic, trying to slow each step down but to no avail. A man she didn't recognize ran into the street, pointing in her direction. A breath later, and there he was.

Lars! she tried to scream, but her lips refused to obey her.

Lars, she cried, tears escaping down her bloodied cheeks.

Her mate stared at her, dropping to his knees as he took in her monstrosity. She tried to thrash, to move, to do *anything* that would make this body to retreat so he would be spared. But her body sluggishly moved forward, stuck in its trance, step by slow step.

A scream, and a woman ran into the street. No—not just a woman. *Greer.* Her sister. Why was Greer here?

It was enough. She paused, frozen on the street.

Oh Fates, no. Please, *no.*

She knew deep in her soul that her mate would choose to die with her here tonight. To leave this world together. One soul, cleaved in two, destined to meet but perish only months later. They'd go out together. Their souls would be reunited—maybe not on this earth, not in this life. But in the next one.

At least it was poetic.

She would reach across time and space and *death* to hold onto him. Her stranger. Her Lars.

But she couldn't do that to Greer. She'd sooner die right now than harm a hair on Greer's head.

A noise, and she realized Lars was speaking to her, to this beast she barely held in check. "Do not look at her. You look at me," he said, piercing through her haze.

The Celestial was satiated for now, but Emelle feared the moment the thirst returned. She couldn't be around any of them when that happened. Falling forward a step, Emelle was trapped in her mind as her body betrayed her, a growl splitting from her chest.

Emelle panicked, about to take another step forward when a golden female stepped into the street. Blinding light shone, chasing shadows away as she shielded her eyes. Where her skin touched the light, fire sizzled, *burning her.*

She screamed.

And to her utter surprise, her mouth moved, sound escaping into the darkness. Dizzy from the effort it took, Emelle took one unsteady step back, then another.

But even over her broiling flesh, she heard the female, and she paused. The female she'd sat with in the vision on Mount Haleburne. She listened as the Fate told Lars to *end her*. To destroy the Celestial powers once and for all. After she'd run the kingdom red with blood, absorbing the scattered Celestial energy that was in so many—*too many*—guards, all they needed was for Lars to use their Cosmic powers to send it all hurtling back into the cosmos.

They...From the beginning, they *used her*. She was but a pawn in their Cosmic games her entire life. Destined to be Lars's mate so she could be some...some magical Celestial sponge? All so Lars could kill her, ending the Celestial cycle once and for all.

What was left of Emelle's shredded soul *raged* at the implications.

Lars stepped towards her and the last of her heart shattered, as she watched him raise his glowing sword. Tears were streaming, his pain openly sketched on his beautiful face.

She couldn't break the last of her dying heart and watch him kill her. Having to witness him charge her would surely splinter the last of her already ruined sanity.

Emelle knew she could end this madness. If she could only control her *arms*.

She screeched with the effort it took to move her hand. Her pain was a broken song in the wind that would forget her sacrifice the moment she slipped from this world, just as the rest of the truth had been. Forgotten. Erased. *Manipulated*.

But her fingers twitched, and she forced her hand, one agonizing inch at a time, to raise the dagger she'd used to kill the king.

Looking to Greer for the final time, she tried to apologize but she wasn't sure if her lips moved, if any sound came out. Sending her a look she knew she'd understand, Emelle said goodbye to her longest and greatest friend. The woman she'd spent nearly thirty years with, who held her when she cried after her grandmother passed, who listened when she frantically told her of her crumbling family, who showed her every day that sisters weren't always made from blood, but from their souls recognizing their person. That soulmates weren't always romantic.

A tear slipped down her monstrous cheek. Greer thrashed, screaming at her from where Elix held her back. Seeing Elix behind her gave Emelle some comfort as she finally forced herself to turn away, to face her mate.

Lars was still approaching her, terror laced on his face. Emelle knew he would hate himself for the rest of his days if she let him go through with this.

She wouldn't hate him, though. She could never hate him. As much as it broke her, she understood.

And she forgave him.

Rational thoughts began to slip as the haze slowly settled over her mind again. Blanketing her consciousness. Emelle had destroyed anyone in Wellsmore who had even a drop of Celestial power in them. She was losing control over her functions, her mind. She didn't think she'd be able to climb her way back after this. Not after she killed her mate and Greer.

She wouldn't want to come back.

She looked towards her stranger, her mate, the man who'd given Emelle her childhood dream: the adventure of a lifetime. She just didn't think her lifetime would be over so soon.

That it would be the *only* adventure of her lifetime.

She thought she'd have more time. Time with him, time with Greer, just *time*.

Using the final dredges of her awareness, she whispered the cleansing prayer and the dagger in her bloodied hand glowed once, twice.

More tears pooled, blurring her vision as she looked at Lars. She blinked rapidly, needing to see him clearly, just once more. To preserve his memory, so when the details of his face yielded against the torrent of time and death, she'd at least have these final few heartbeats to hold her until she met him again on the other side.

"You are my soul, Lars. My destiny. And my favorite adventure.

I will love you long after my last breath." She hoped the words would carry on the shadows to him.

"Find me in the next life. I'll be waiting."

By the dawning of horror on his face, Emelle knew her words had reached him.

Lifting the dagger, Emelle drew the blade deeply across her throat, spilling her tainted blood onto the streets of Wellsmore. She felt the Celestial power being banished into the cosmos, nowhere to go but into the skies.

She'd defied the natural order of the powers, creating what would surely be a vacuum that would implode amongst the stars.

A faint smile graced her as she fell, knowing *she'd* been the one to end the Celestial cycle.

Collapsing onto the cobblestone, Emelle St. King drew her final breath. Her last thoughts were of her mate.

It's my time, Lars. Reach for me when it's yours.

Chapter Forty-One
Lars

Someone was screaming. Lars watched in a daze as his mate sliced her throat open. His world reeled to a crawl as her body fell, hitting the stone with a force that shook the cobblestones. Someone was screaming. Who was screaming?

Abandoning his sword, Lars stumbled over to Emelle, dropping numbly to his knees as he reached her. His world went quiet as the Celestial fire in her eyes faded into the emerald he loved so deeply.

But there was no life left behind. Tears fell down his face as he stared in horror at the peaceful smile she wore, even in death.

It was all he could do to not follow her into the cosmos, as a fiery spark of Celestial energy shot out of her chest and into the skies above, an implosion blacking out the glittering stars. As quickly as it began, the darkness winked out, and the night sky twinkled back at him. Emelle had broken all the rules. Obliterated them.

Lars shut down.

Golden light warmed his shoulder, but Lars couldn't look away from his mate growing colder by the second.

If only he could reach his claymore... but he'd dropped it several feet away.

Greer rushed forward, screaming. She's who had been screaming.

Lars could only watch as she grabbed Emelle by her shoulders, trying to lift her body but failing as her head nearly fell off. Greer's screams grew guttural, echoing around the street.

Then Elix was behind his mate, pulling her back into him as she turned, breaking in his arms.

Lars felt nothing.

Sensing the Fate, he waited for it to speak. He wanted to hate this being, but he felt *nothing*. He just wanted to know if they'd fixed the magic so he could follow Emelle into the cosmos.

"You've done well, Alaryk. Now, release our Cosmic energy back into the earth. Set your intentions and bring *life* back home. Bring the Cosmos *home*," the Fate instructed, teeth gleaming brightly as it guided Lars's hand to the stone he knelt on.

The stone stained with his mate's blood.

The blood that was still *warm*.

Lars felt the heat of her lifeforce as his hand hovered over the stone and his chest pumped viciously. Painfully.

How unfair was this pathetic excuse of a life? They'd let this woman, *this wondrous woman,* go through so much pain in her short life. They'd forced her to carry a burden she didn't ask for. Didn't deserve. A burden that was *theirs* to shoulder.

Lars's dam was cracking, emotions flooding back in as the shock wore off. Distantly, he heard Greer still shrieking into her mate's arms.

Time surged back into motion, and Lars realized the world still somehow spun, even after the death of his mate. How was that possible?

His hand, glowing brightly blue, reached for the ground.

This was it. All he'd worked for. All he'd sacrificed for. All his soulmate had sacrificed for. Had *died* for.

How did it all end like this?

A beat, and then—Lars lurched over to Emelle, slamming his palm over her heart.

"Let the Fates try to take you from me," he cried, slashing a frenzied look over to the Fate that watched on with terror.

"*Live!*" he ordered on a scream, sending all of the Cosmic energy he had in his body rushing into Emelle.

Blue light flashed into Emelle, draining from Lars as it encapsulated her body in a blinding cocoon. Lars shielded his eyes and waited breathlessly while the Fate shrieked.

"That was the last of our power!" it screeched, looking at its fading hands, pearly skin leaching of luster and moisture into dull frailty. "We gave you every last drop!"

It cried as it tried, and failed, to approach the blue light surrounding Emelle.

Elix shouted his name, and a moment later Lars caught a sword, planting himself in front of Emelle's body. "Take one more step towards my mate. Watch what happens."

His shadows pushed in on the Fate, suffocating it as it clawed at its neck. The Fate withered before him as the last of its Cosmic power yielded to Lars's command, flowing from the dying Fate and snaking behind him, commanded to *save Emelle*.

He didn't care.

He prowled over to the writhing Fate, and spat next to its head. "You made a mistake choosing *her*. There is not a universe out there where I choose *anyone* or *anything* over her. You were wrong."

Dark eyes blazed bright blue. Raising the sword, Lars brought down his wrath on the frail neck of the Fate, severing its head from its body. The dying light fading in the *Fates'* mortal eyes was the greatest sight he'd witnessed, second only to the first time he laid eyes on his mate.

Lars's chest heaved from exertion as he dragged the body several feet away. He reached into his pocket and pulled out the old forgotten flint, slashing a dense shadow across it and watching with triumph as sparks fell.

Fire caught, burning the Fates' mortal form but no smell wafted from the pyre. Moments later, the body fell to the flames, before extinguishing into a pile of ash. Sending a gust of shadows, Lars watched the ashes blow away into the cosmos.

A gasp sounded behind him, snaking hope deep into his broken soul.

Whipping around, twinkling emerald irises clashed into his.

Sound vanished, time slowed, as his gaze searched her face, down to her delicate neck that boasted a new scar, faint but jagged. It was the only indication of the horrors she'd experienced. Every last drop of blood she'd been drenched in, both hers and others, was cleansed from her as though she'd never lifted a finger.

Lars bolted to her side, crashing onto his knees and gathering a hysterical Emelle. Small hands found his face, pulling him in to kiss once, twice.

"You weren't supposed to follow me! You were supposed to have more time!" Emelle scolded even as she peppered his face with kisses, everywhere she could reach.

Wrapping his arms around her, Lars clung to his mate for several seconds, not yet registering her words.

She was alive.

"Emmy," he said, pulling back from her. "Princess, I'm not dead."

Confusion met his stare as she glanced down at her body. "If you're not dead..." She trailed off, putting the pieces together in her mind.

Head snapping to her left, she searched frantically for something—or rather, *someone*. "Where's Greer?" she cried, eyes searching the darkness for her sister.

"Ellie!" Greer sobbed from behind them, and Emelle spun around. On a cry, Emelle launched herself out of Lars's arms and flung herself into Greer's. The sisters hugged, words spilling out of their mouths faster than Lars could understand.

Motioning to Elix, Lars stood to join the reunion. Lars stared at the women, and couldn't help but poke Emelle in the shoulder. His finger met flesh and bone. When it earned him a glare, he just shrugged.

"Felt too good to be true, princess."

Emelle smiled, the small kind that made his stomach flip, before she turned back to Greer. Finally noticing the protruding belly, Emelle burst into laughter as she dropped to her knees, placing her hands on Greer's belly.

"I know, right?" Greer asked the incredulous Emmy, as tears fell down her cheeks. "You would've known if you'd *read one of the last two months' worth of letters.*" But she couldn't hold even her mock anger for long, falling to her knees to hug Emelle again.

As the first rays of dawn broke, the women rose to their feet—Emelle with more grace than her pregnant friend. Together, they turned to watch the sun rise. The first sun to rise in this new world without any Cosmic Fates or Celestials. And they were *alive*.

Lars walked up behind Emelle, tucking her into his chest. Kissing the crown of her head, Lars bent down to whisper in her ear.

"I love you, too, Emmy," he muttered. "You have been my destiny from my very first breath." His mate whirled, staring up at him with something like shock, but he continued. "I will love you with every breath in our *very* long lives together. And I will love you with every breath after."

"You heard that?" she whispered, twinkling emerald meeting onyx. He'd never take the sight for granted again.

He nodded. Emelle crushed her mouth to his, reuniting their souls after far too long apart.

Clutching his mate, Lars held her face reverently as their kiss turned salty, tears tracking down their cheeks and into their joined mouths. He didn't care.

A cough, and then—

"All right, lovebirds, I don't want to get pregnant twice. That would be weird," Greer jested, and Emelle pulled away from him, face flaming.

"There's that blush I've missed so much," Lars said, brushing her wild bangs behind her ears. A blinding smile met his, and Lars took his first deep breath in what felt like years.

Chapter Forty-Two
Emelle

As they made their way into what Lars called *The Den*, Emelle, Lars, Greer, and Elix crossed into a spacious office with a rumpled cot in one corner. A blush crept onto her mate's cheekbones, the first she'd ever seen.

Not wanting to draw attention to it, Emelle just met his stare for a heartbeat before pointedly looking away. She'd acquaint herself with his blush. *Later.*

Greer was a step behind her as they entered, her hand wrapped around Emelle's arm. Air left Emelle's lungs in a rush as she was pulled into another bone-crushing hug.

"Be careful," she scolded, trying to pull away so she didn't hurt Greer's baby.

"It's fine, if I can still spend my nights with *that* one"—she nodded towards her mate, who sheepishly grinned at Greer with nothing but pride—"a hug won't hurt the babe."

Emelle's eyes misted at the thought of her sister, *pregnant*. Fates, she couldn't wait to meet the child.

Greer nodded, hearing her unspoken words. A watery smile slid onto her beautiful face. "I know, she can't wait to meet you, either."

"*She?*" Emelle's eyes bugged, snapping down to Greer's rounded belly. "How do you know?"

"It's just a feeling I have. He thinks it's a boy," she said with a thumb thrown over her shoulder towards Elix.

"I'll be happy as long as they come into the world screaming," Elix retorted, hands raised in mock defense. Emelle supposed he was very much used to Greer's feisty attitude by now. By the look on his face, he even enjoyed it. Emelle glanced between the two and her heart nearly burst at the love they shared. Maybe the Fates did one thing right in this world.

"I bet it's a girl," Lars said. "You are the brightest barkeep in all of Eralyn, remember?"

Greer snorted, and Emelle smacked her lightly on the arm. "Oh, hush."

Turning to her mate, Emelle pulled him close and laid her head on his chest. It made her words come out muffled, but she knew he heard. "We should...talk. About what happened."

She felt Lars nod, and peeked over to Greer, who was watching her with worry.

Meeting her stare, Greer nodded and pulled Elix out of the room, who glanced between the two with confusion.

"She'll find us later," Greer explained on a whisper, before shutting the door behind them.

Lifting her head from his chest, Emelle studied Lars's face, his overgrown stubble, his long lashes fanning his sun-kissed cheeks. Overwhelmed by the events of the past few months—Fates, even the past few *hours*—Emelle needed to feel her mate. Feel that she was still here, that *he* was still here. Emelle slammed her lips to his, kissing him with all of the words she hadn't gotten to say yet. He kissed back with equal fervor.

When it finally broke, Lars's eyes sparked with desire, and Emelle was sure hers gave away her wanton need for her mate. "Come. Sit," he ordered, an echo of their first night together in Briarwood.

Settling onto the cot, Emelle snuggled into Lars's side, sighing heavily in relief. "So...Alaryk?" she snickered.

A brash laugh, and Emelle joined in.

"Yes, *Alaryk* is the name my mother gave me. It means 'powerful leader,' supposedly," he said, his voice a bit rough. She rested her head on his shoulder, offering comfort the only way she could. "She was the only one who called me that. The king never cared to call me anything but 'that boy,' and even refused my mother when she wanted to give me his surname. So she gave me hers instead. When I was dropped on the streets, I decided to shed the formality, going by my childhood nickname that the staff called me, Lars."

Emelle smiled and brought their joined hands to her lips to kiss the back of his. "I like it. It suits you."

"What happened, princess?" Lars's voice cracked as he spoke. Fresh tears tracked down his face, and it was Emelle's turn to wipe them away. "We tried to find you, but it was..."

When he trailed off, she followed his gaze to a map on the desk. The tacks scattered over it looked horrifyingly familiar. She remembered enough to know what those points meant. He'd tracked her, all through the city, not knowing if she was even alive.

Lars squeezed her hand once, twice in reassurance, bringing her focus back to him.

And so she told him. She told him of waking up in the cart, the speedy days traveling with the handsy commanders, what she later learned was possible with Celestial travel, her time in the dungeons...Emelle recounted her night with the king, not aware of her tears until Lars crushed her to his chest.

"I...I watched myself rip all of those people apart, Lars." She couldn't bear to look at him, at the weight of his judgment. It hurt to breathe, every inhale scraping down her throat only to choke in her lungs.

Suddenly, Lars was on his knees in front of her, holding her face and instructing her to breathe. Following his inhales, Emelle took several moments to calm herself.

"I told it, *only Celestials*, to only go after those with the blazing red eyes. I didn't stop for hours...Lars, there were so many," she whispered, horrified at her actions. At the destruction she'd wrought. "I finally woke up covered in the remains of the people I tore apart. I passed out right in my own vomit, disgusted with the hands that caused so much carnage." She turned her hands over, half-expecting to still see the blood. Her skin was healed, save for faint scars around her wrists from where they'd been bound in rope. Her nails had regrown and were sensitive.

Lars didn't leave her, staying on his knees as memories of the last two days flashed in her mind. She tried to drop her gaze, but Lars stopped her with a gentle hand under her chin. She was safe. *He* was safe. It still felt surreal.

"Then I scented *you*. My mate. And it wanted you. I didn't realize until later that I should've fought harder. I should've stayed away from you. I didn't know what it was going to do..."

Lars leaned forward, dropping his forehead to her lap and wrapping his arms around her body. It settled something in her, made it easier to continue.

"I—I heard what the Fate had said. That I was born for this moment. To collect the Celestial energy so you could vanquish the evil for good. And I knew it would kill you if you had to be the one to end me. With Greer there...I couldn't take that risk. I *needed* you both to be safe, so I made a decision. I couldn't let you be the one to end me. So I..." When she hiccupped, Lars stood, pulling her up with him, strong arms wrapping around her sobbing frame.

"I was ready," he started, voice quiet. "To follow you. But my sword was so far away and I had left my dagger inside The Den. I couldn't live what would've been a husk of a life without you."

Emelle sobbed harder, clutching Lars as he shook.

"I'd follow you anywhere, Emelle. Even into death."

"I know," she whispered. "I'd hold the curtain open for you. But only when it's your time."

"Who said I'll let you go first?" he joked, forcing a sharp laugh from Emelle.

Eyes wet with emotion, Lars pulled back. Words failed her, her love for this man too great to form any proper sentence. But she had time. And she would use her final breaths to tell him one last time, whenever that day may come. Though she was certain it wouldn't be soon.

Stepping away, he swiped something off his desk, too quick for her to see. His steps were soft against the wood floor and Emelle took the opportunity to scan his form. She didn't recognize his leathers, though they were nondescript. And he didn't appear to be injured, which she was grateful for. That was all that mattered right now.

Returning to her, dark onyx eyes once again captivated her. Commanded her.

"This...is for you," he whispered, setting the offering in her hands.

Emelle glanced down, a smile wobbling across her mouth at the emerald handkerchief. A lone tear dripped onto the silk, darkening the fabric.

"This is yours," she replied.

"You can hold onto it for me. I have no intention of letting you go so easily."

Emelle smiled and gently placed the handkerchief onto the small table next to the small bed, then crushed their lips together. She pushed Lars onto the cot and settled astride him, grinding herself over his hardening cock.

"Fuck, don't ever do that again, all right, princess? I think you shaved ten years off my life," Lars said between kisses. Emelle yelped as Lars flipped her over before yanking her tunic over her head. Greedy eyes scanned her unbound breasts, before he dipped low to lick and suck on her sensitive flesh.

Groaning, Emelle arched her chest into his hungry mouth.

"Yes, Fates, please don't stop," she whimpered, earning a bite on her nipple, her flesh stinging before Lars lapped at the pain.

"The Fates no longer exist, princess. You'll have to beg me from now on," Lars said, voice sensual and dripping with wanton need.

She would beg for him any day of the week.

Lars slunk down the bed, taking her trousers with her. Shadows slipped from his body, wrapping around her thighs to spread her open as he sat back on his haunches, staring at her apex with carnal desire. Lars licked his lips before pressing his face to her cunt, fucking her with his tongue as he ground his nose on her clit. Crying out, Emelle clutched his head, grinding her dripping sex into Lars's face.

He smiled into her cunt, and thrust two fingers into her core. Finding her weak spot, Lars suckled on her throbbing clit, creating a maddening rhythm that threatened to obliterate her. His other hand snaked around to press on her abdomen, commanding her body to his will with each stroke.

"Stay still for me, princess."

More shadows fell, pulling her arms above her head and securing them with a surprisingly firm hold. Another drifted down her chest, whispering over her peaked nipples, teasing them to the point of pain. Emelle shuddered, overstimulated and ready to fall.

"That's right. Ride my hand, princess. Fuck this mouth of yours," he said, breath hot against her pussy.

"Come for me, mate," he ordered.

Emelle obeyed.

Aftershocks kept his mouth lapping at her leaking sex as she finally came down.

Lars crawled back up her body, naked already. When he'd shed his clothes, she didn't care. When their eyes met, he raised a brow and she nodded, needing him inside her. Lining himself up, Lars thrust into her with one powerful snap of his hips, a groan escaping his wet mouth. The shadows around her wrists dissipated, sliding down her body to strum her clit.

Emelle captured his face and kissed him, tasting her own release with a hazy moan. Lars moved inside of her in an achingly slow pace, one that dragged her higher and higher with each stroke. His shadows matched his tempo, while one tendril curled into her sex, thrusting along his cock. Emelle's sight went dark at the fullness.

"Fuck, princess, you feel so fucking good," he whispered next to her ear. "You were fucking made for me, for my cock."

Emelle panted, meeting him thrust for thrust as they built towards that peak again, this time together. Yes, she was made for him, much to the Cosmic Fates' demise.

The shadow inside her slipped down to her rear, thinning as it entered her before it thickened to an impossible girth. She'd only had a few men back there, but she'd never been filled in both holes at the same time.

She loved it.

Emelle wrapped her arms around Lars's neck, burrowing into him as he wrung every drop of pleasure from her. But Lars pulled back, staring into her eyes as he thrust inside her, their lips brushing. She felt their souls embracing after so long apart. And she knew he felt the same.

"I need to come in you, princess. Are you ready?" Lars groaned into her mouth. "Let me hear you. You can take it."

Emelle nodded and reached for Lars's chin, forcing him to look at her.

"Fill me, mate," she ordered.

Lars obeyed.

Emelle cried out, coming harder than she ever had before on her mate's hard cock.

It took what felt like years for their bodies to slow, for their breaths to settle as Lars rested his glistening forehead on Emelle's. With a smile, he kissed Emelle quickly before slithering down her body. She gasped as his cock and shadows slipped from her. Lars sat back to look down at her, hunger still lingering in his gaze.

Emelle raised herself onto her elbows, arching her brow.

"I can't just leave you like this, now, can I?" he snarked, licking his lips. "I need to clean my mate up."

Ducking back into her cunt, Lars lapped around her wet sex, shoving his tongue inside of her to taste their mixed release. Shadows wrapped around her wrists again, but this time they brought her hands to his head, forcing her to grip his hair and hold him against her sex. He groaned loudly against her, rutting his hips into the cot as he thoroughly enjoyed cleaning her. As he thoroughly enjoyed Emelle's fingers grasping his inky waves while she ground her sex against his mouth.

"You look so pretty like this, all trussed up and leaking with our cum."

Emelle blushed from his filthy words. She loved it. She loved *him*. And Fates, she loved his tongue.

Another taste, and Lars raised his head, sticking his tongue out to present her with their combined cum before swallowing it on a moan. Doubling down, Lars dove back into her folds, licking and sucking her to another unexpected, but explosive, orgasm. His shadows ensured she was captive to his ministrations.

As her aftershocks finally eased, Lars licked his lips, savoring the last of her orgasm. Wiping his mouth with his forearm, Lars crawled back up, lifting Emelle onto his body as they laid together. The shadows dissipated, and she surprised herself by missing them. She'd grown fond of the hazy comfort they provided. Of the pleasure they wrung from her body.

Emelle's pulse hammered as she lounged on Lars's bare chest, idly running her fingertips over his skin, drawing obscure patterns.

"I will love you always, princess," he murmured into her hair. "Even after we are fading stardust in the cosmos, your soul will claim ownership over mine. Every mangled scrap of me is yours."

"I will love you for even longer, stranger," Emelle replied, kissing the space above his heart. "Until we're stardust, then."

"Even after," he vowed.

☽✷☾

The next morning, Emelle and Lars slept in until the sun was high in the sky, before spending the rest of the day with Greer and Elix to catch up on all that had happened over the last several months.

Emelle was shocked to learn that the story Lars had told her all those weeks ago about the woman he saved from being abducted was *Greer*. And she laughed when she found out Elix was the man Lars had recovered missing funds for after Anders swindled them. What were the chances their fates had all been so carefully woven together?

Her mood soured at the thought of the Cosmic Fates, but she shook it away. She wouldn't let the Fates hold her captive any longer.

Emelle and Lars settled in that night, doing anything *but* sleep for hours. And when there was no more pleasure to be wrung from them, Emelle drifted off in the warm embrace of his strong arms, peace filling her as she closed her eyes.

They were alive.

And she planned to *live*.

CHAPTER FORTY-THREE

Lars

Over the next few days, Lars and Emelle got to work in rebuilding Wellsmore. The Sceptres had been hard at work, washing the streets and disposing of what remained of the bodies. Some of the stains were stubborn, as if the earth itself refused to let this part of history be erased.

He didn't envy the job.

Lars declined to ascend the throne, opting instead to hold an election between a few selective people from the royal council who hadn't been tainted by the Celestial power. A fierce woman by the name of Quinn Baxter won the election, and she quickly formed a tiered plan to get the kingdom back to rights. Lars felt confident she'd do a competent job, and it was with relief that the weight of the throne was lifted from his shoulders.

He knew Emelle understood the words he couldn't say, at least in that moment—that he felt some lingering guilt over the lack of desire to ascend the throne. Over the crushing relief that he didn't have to rule.

After two decades of working towards a singular goal, the sizable shift in trajectory created somewhat of an absence in him. He let Willam take over as leader of the Sceptres, and he spent his

THE FOOL'S ERRAND

abundance of free time with his mate and with her sister. He found a friend in Elix, too, and they stayed up one night while the women had a sleepover. Emelle had all but slammed the door in his face, muttering something about girl time. Elix and Lars drank late into the night, and Lars began to remember how to be a friend again. He was *alive*, and so was she. They'd learn how to live in this new world together.

They would walk this life together. And the next.

But not for quite some time.

About a week after Baxter's inauguration, a messenger delivered a letter to The Den to Lars's surprise. Apparently the location was no longer secret after recent events. He'd let Willam find the new nexus for the Sceptres; after Lars and Emelle would leave, they had no intention of returning to Wellsmore. At least, not anytime soon.

Gathering into his office—as it was still his office for now—Lars and Emelle sat at his desk to read the curious letter together. On the casing of the scroll, Lars was shocked to see it addressed to *Alaryk Winthorpe*. It appeared aged, as if it hadn't seen the sun in many years.

Alaryk,

If you are reading this, then I have finally been set free. You have no reason to trust my words, but know that I love you.

When I found out Bria was in labor, I almost fell over from excitement. I did not know she was with child; she had only told me she was sick. I had been worried over her absence, of course, but was ultimately occupied by my political duties. When I was told she was in the birthing room, my world went dark. I remembered I had already been infected, had been for over a year after making a deal I now greatly regret, and terror had me racing to the birthing room. When you arrived into this world with eyes black as night, I had hoped that meant you were spared from the Celestial energy I had been slowly succumbing to. The thought was too terrifying so after your birth, I ensured I could bear no further heirs.

As you grew older, inexplicable shadows began to pour from your tiny body. I stayed away as best I could, terrified that my Celestial power could somehow transfer to you. I know you believe it was because I did not care for you, but it is entirely the opposite. You and Bria have my heart, and because of that, I had to stay away. For your sake.

Your ninth birthday was yesterday, and it breaks me, but I need you safe. Safe from me. You already have a connection with the Celestials, but they have begun whispering their plans. They believe they've found how to sew kernels of their powers into the jesters and fools, and intend to slowly infect the population before overthrowing the rest of Eralyn. And from there...I shudder to think of the possibilities.

I am too weak to stop them, having spent almost a decade under their thrall. I am using the last of my willpower to write this to you, in hopes that one day I will be free of this tainted power and you will know the truth.

I think they have finally figured out how to smother the last of my consciousness, my soul. I will be but a vessel soon, and I could not bear it if my fate befalls you.

If you are reading this, I can only hope that means you have found a way to stop the Celestials. To do what I never could. I am sorry I have made this your burden. I made a dreadful deal, trading my soul for political gain, the promise of ruling all of Eralyn too great, and the only thing I regret more is not being a part of your life.

Live well, Alaryk. You have always been my greatest joy. With the last of my soul, you and Bria will be my final thoughts.

Goodbye, son.

~ Wexley Winthorpe

Lars stared at the letter, too stunned to move, to think, to even breathe. It felt as if the world had gone quiet around him. It was only when a teardrop landed on the parchment, bleeding over the word "son," that he realized he was still here, at this desk, in The Den, with Emelle at his side. She gently gathered the scroll before climbing into his lap, wrapping her arms around him.

"That was...a lot," she offered.

Lars gulped, and his shimmering eyes searched hers.

"He...knew," Lars breathed. "He made a deal with the Celestials, and he was *infected* with them for years. But he knew I was...made from Celestial power too. Where my shadows came from. And he..." Lars trailed off, at a loss for words, his mouth opening, then shutting. The office's closed windows made it hard to breathe.

Emelle nodded. "He sent you away to save you. The last of his willpower was *choosing you.*"

"I don't know if I can forgive him," Lars rasped as his shadows wrapped around them. Cocooned them in their safety.

Inspecting the tendrils, Emelle ran a hand through one. "You don't have to, Lars. Maybe one day, if you want, but he made the decision all those years ago that put you on this path. You're allowed to feel however you want to feel about it."

Lars only nodded.

☽✻☾

Several days later, it was finally time to make their goodbyes. Greer and Elix had left a little over two weeks ago, wanting to return to Thoryn before Greer got too far in her pregnancy, and Elix had to return to his crown. He became King Elwood once they'd returned to the north all those months ago, and he'd been away for too long, he'd said.

After they packed their belongings, Emelle and Lars took one final walk through Wellsmore. He wasn't certain he would ever want to return, so they made sure to take their time while Emelle asked questions about his life growing up here. With each story, she appeared equal parts fascinated and horrified by what he had to endure.

Walking through the market, Emelle searched through the unique offerings each vendor had. Seeing the bustling shops and wares through her eyes, Lars took in the people, the *scents*, as the familiarity of the scene washed over him.

Wellsmore was massive, and people traveled from all over to visit their market. Some even came and sold their own items, setting up shop for a while until they ran out. And it seemed, in the wake of all that had happened, that wouldn't change—people were determined to carry on with their lives. The vendors lined the cobblestone, twisting and turning to fit each stall, and Emelle took her time through each. People milled about, their collective voices loud as they haggled over prices and chatted with neighbors. Emelle took a particularly long few minutes ruffling through a vendor who sold old leather books, speaking softly with the merchant as Lars leaned against the table. There was a spark in her eyes as the merchant shared which stories he had for sale.

His heart was full when, a few moments later, Emelle asked him to close his eyes and hold out his hands. Happy to follow her orders, Lars did as she asked.

Upon opening his eyes, he found a small leatherbound book with an intricate design on the cover. Flipping through the pages, there was only blank parchment staring back at him. He looked to his mate, one brow raised.

"For our new adventures," she said with a smile. "To write *ours* down, instead of reading others."

Wrapping her in a hug, he rasped, "We might need more than one."

On their way back to The Den, Emelle tripped, but Lars caught her with an arm around her waist. Looking down in tandem, they realized her boots had finally given up on her, the sole having ripped apart on a cobblestone. Emelle pitched over, breaking into laughter over the boots *almost* making it through the entire journey.

"Come on, up you go," he commanded with a nod towards his back.

A giddy laugh escaped her as she hopped on his back. Lars carried her the rest of the way to The Den.

They may not return to Wellsmore again, but they'd certainly never forget their time here.

There was so much pain in these streets. They'd suffered immensely in this kingdom. But they'd also found each other. They'd reunited their souls here. They'd defied the odds and carved their own destiny, rebuking the Cosmic Fates right to their faces.

So no, they would never forget Wellsmore, even though the nightmares made them wish they could.

Epilogue
Emelle

Making their way back to Silvermist was thankfully an uneventful journey. They may be searching for an adventure, but they certainly weren't looking to save the earth from Cosmic forces or Celestial beings again.

Lars spat on the ground when Emelle asked if he was considered a Hero now, technically.

"If I'm a Hero, you're a Hero, since you solved the riddle *and* ended Winthorpe *and* vanquished the Celestial powers," he'd insisted, scoffing. The childlike part of Emelle was exhilarated at her Hero status, despite knowing the Fates had created the accolades with ulterior motives.

"Does that make me royalty now?" she'd asked.

"You've always been my princess," he'd answered plainly, as though it should have been obvious.

Passing into Mistwood, Lars and Emelle stopped in Meggie's Place briefly. Emelle was pleased to see that with the release of the Celestial forces, Meggie no longer had to deal with Celestial-charged drunks.

Meggie had also mysteriously disappeared, replaced by a woman who seemed vaguely familiar to Emelle. She had a kind smile but a firm hand. Emelle was sure she'd whip the place into good shape. Perhaps she'd even change the name.

Finally stepping into Silvermist after sixteen days of travel and so long away, Emelle turned her face to the sun, unable to help a smile. She swore the languid wind slipped around her body, welcoming her home.

Their first stop was The Finn, and Emelle looked over the space with new eyes. Somehow the building felt smaller, the cracked walls and stained floors more obvious than before. The bar she spent her life behind looked less like a shackle now.

It was just a bar.

And she remembered. There, in the corner, she'd drawn a field of orchids on the wall, a few feet below one of the largest cracks in the walls. The flowers were faded now, but she could still see a few outlines. Her grandmother had snickered the entire time, keeping an eye out for her parents while she taught her how to draw the petals. Emelle had thought it would make them feel better about the crack they couldn't afford to fix. It did. Eventually they covered it with a tapestry and called it a day, but Emelle knew they were always there.

And there, in her office, where she used to sit and listen to the stories her grandmother told. One night, they'd been up late and she'd spilled an entire plate of melted wax onto the floor. It stained the wood in an ugly shape that had her father sighing as he added it to the list of countless spills from over the years.

She saw the long tables and remembered the times when Greer's family would come over for the winter solstice. Her family helped fill each and every mismatched seat. And Greer and Emelle always sat on the end closest to the door, too eager to run out after supper to bother cherishing the memories in the moment they were being made.

Too young to understand, she supposed. How fleeting time was. How quickly it sped past you when you were too busy looking to the future, dreaming of life on your own, not realizing you already were.

Her gaze traveled to the staircase, the steps she'd run up and down thousands of times. The stairs she'd spent so much of her life hating.

It was there, at the top, where she secretly eavesdropped on her parents. And there, near the middle, where her teenage heart broke apart after Greer had told her about Lonnie. And on that very first step, where her mother held her after her grandmother died, sitting with her all night.

Yes, she'd outgrown this place, these rooms. But it was never a shackle. It was just a tavern.

She'd carry the memories with her, tucked in her pockets like a letter she'd pull out to read whenever she needed to feel closer to the person who wrote it.

Someone slammed into Emelle, knocking her free of her memories. Emelle hugged Janie back, surprised by how much she had missed her.

"The Finn is yours," Emelle said after Janie poured them a few ales. She could see Janie had blossomed while she was gone, thriving in her own space. It was clear in the way she carried herself, the way she ran The Finn. She didn't think Janie was magically cured, but every time Janie peeked at a pretty traveler lingering in the corner—finger tracing the lip of her stein, eyes following the movement as if to hide the fact her attention wasn't focused on them—Emelle was confident with time she would be.

Janie just stared at her slack-jawed until a patron tapped his empty stein on the bartop. Hurrying to help her customer, Janie arched a brow that promised pain if Emelle didn't explain later. She would. Emelle needed to hear more about the woman who apparently hadn't left in over a week.

Rushing up the stairs, Emelle searched for Evie. Her furry baby usually stayed away from the noise, and she found her sunbathing next to the window in her room. Evie peeked an eye open, uninterested in a blubbering Emelle. She didn't even move from her spot.

Of course, the ungrateful brat.

Emelle scooped the cat into her arms all the same, planting kiss after kiss onto her furry face, no matter how hard she tried to escape.

Typical. Lars entered her room close behind, and chuckled at the sight.

"She's still coming with us. Don't believe this act for a second. She missed me," Emelle cooed, snuggling deeper into the fur of her baby.

"Oh, I wouldn't dare," he chucked, crossing over to pet the small creature's head. Evie leaned into his palm and batted at the curl over his brow.

Emelle scoffed before twisting away and plopping onto the bed, forcing the feline into some much-needed cuddles. It lasted for about thirty seconds before Evie wrestled out of her hold.

After grabbing an open room, Emelle and Lars spent the next several days tying up her loose ends in Silvermist. Emelle took advantage of the privacy and decided maybe she didn't hate mornings, if it meant waking up each day next to her mate. It still took them hours to get out of bed, though, much to Evie's dismay.

One night, Emelle stayed up with Janie, telling her all about her adventures. Janie was in tears by the time she got to that fateful night, Janie's eyes glued to Emelle's new scar. Hugging her fiercely, they wept together.

Then Janie told her about working at Meggie's Place. How she had to brush off more than a few wandering hands and lewd comments. How Meggie turned a blind eye when an extra coin was tossed her way. Janie told her about the other women who no longer had any life behind their eyes. How the crowd began to take liberties with her, and she was terrified for the day when her spirit faded behind her own because the money was too good. Tears misted in the young woman's eyes with each word. Emelle slipped her hand into Janie's and squeezed hard, offering what comfort she could.

After another fierce hug, Emelle's tears turned joyful as Janie told her about Mara, the woman who kept finding excuses to stay. A soft azure glow wove around Janie's hair, so subtle Emelle might have dismissed it as a trick of the light. But after learning what she had about soulmates, Emelle encouraged Janie to follow her heart.

She didn't say much more than that, fearful of meddling too much. Of anyone, Janie deserved all the happiness the world could offer.

On their last day, Emelle gathered Janie into her arms, and dropped a pouch of coins into her hands—all she'd tucked away from the bag Lars had left so very long ago. Certainly more coins than either of them had ever seen before.

"Hire some help, fix this place up the way I never could. You can do this." Emelle smiled softly as she looked at her dear friend. And then she winked. "Mara might need work if she's to stay in Silvermist."

Janie's face flamed as her eyes darted to the woman who was trying, and failing, not to stare in their direction. Her olive skin and long, rich brown hair shimmered in the morning light as she tucked a few strands behind one ear. It revealed the tip turning dark with a blush.

Janie turned back to Emelle, a single tear slipping down her cheek. "I can do this," Janie affirmed, throwing her arms around Emelle once again.

☽✻☾

With the morning sun, they left The Flushed Finn. Emelle had one last stop to make: a house that had seen better days, tucked on the outskirts of town, close to the hot springs. Knocking on the worn wooden door, she waited with sweaty palms for an answer. Lars stood at her back, offering silent support.

The door creaked open, and Emelle gaped at the strong man in front of her.

"Dad?" Her voice was incredulous as she took in his stance, no cane in sight. "How?"

A light blush crept onto the older man's weathered skin as he scrubbed the back of his neck with one hand. "I've been working on it. A healer stopped through the market a few weeks ago, and she had some foul-smelling cream that helped with the inflammation. I can't stand for long, but each day I'm getting stronger. We've even managed to make a few trips to the hot springs." His eyes shone with pride.

Emelle peeked over to Lars, wondering if he was thinking the same thing...The hot springs certainly still held some raw magic in them then. They'd known the earth had inherent magic, but they weren't sure what it looked like now that the Cosmic Fates and the Celestials were gone.

A seemingly kind woman with a deep golden complexion walked up to the door, placing a soft hand on her father's arm. Emelle's heart warmed at the emotion shimmering between the two. Her father would be all right.

"I've left The Finn to Janie," she blurted.

A shadow of something passed through her father's eyes, but it quickly vanished as he smiled. "It's time for your great adventure, right? You've been itching to leave Silvermist your whole life. I can see that now. You look...happy. Go on one for me, will ya?"

Emelle released the last of her guilt and anger, throwing her arms around her father and promising she would.

As they walked through her village one last time, Emelle pointed out all of the little details of her life, showing Lars where she grew up. The bakery that should have permanent stains on the glass from how often Greer and Emelle pressed their noses to the windows; the small school she attended; the bookstore she used to sneak out to. Lars asked her every question he could think of, leaving them in stitches as she retold stories of her and Greer's misbehaving antics.

Weaving through Silvermist's humble market, only a few vendors were scattered around the small clearing, and the wares were dismal this late in the week. Still, she took his hand and introduced him to her neighbors. A part of her was giddy to be leaving them with juicy gossip.

As they left the market for the last time, her gaze caught on an older woman with strawberry hair tucked into a knot atop her head, one hand shielding her eyes from the sun as she browsed the wares the vendor sold. Next to her stood a lanky teenager who seemed more interested in inspecting the teenage boy running the stall.

Emelle's heart skipped only a beat at the sight of her mother, the first she'd seen of her in a very long time. And as if she sensed someone watching her, her mother scanned the market before her eyes alighted on Emelle. She was far enough away, but Emelle thought something akin to regret passed over her mother's face. Emelle gave her a polite nod before looking at her younger sister one last time. She hoped her mother was better to her than she had been to Emelle. Waving a hand in goodbye, Emelle turned away from the village she'd spent her entire life in.

She was ready.

Leaving Silvermist with her grandmother's dress, her handkerchiefs, and Evie in a basket hooked over one arm, Emelle paused at the border and whispered thanks to her village. This Chapter of her life would always hold a special place in her heart.

The week's trip to the West Docks flew by, and before they knew it, they were boarding a ship to Thoryn. Three weeks later, they were greeted by Greer and Elix. Emelle hugged her fiercely but angled her hips so she didn't crush the baby.

They agreed to stay in Ashwyck until after the birth, but then...Then Lars would take her on all of the adventures she'd dreamed of as a little girl. She couldn't wait.

Two weeks later, a screaming baby girl entered the world. Emelle and Greer sobbed together, sweaty foreheads resting on each other as the little girl shrieked her fury.

"Her name is Lemmie," Greer whispered.

"Named after two of the most important people in our life. Her auntie and uncle," Elix choked, voice gruff with emotion. Lars crushed Elix into a hug, before falling into excited laughter.

"Lemmie?" Emelle whispered, her own tears threatening to fall.

Greer nodded, sharing a bright smile, and Emelle collapsed into a fit of crying. That is, until Lemmie woke up and joined in.

Staying for another six months, Lars and Emelle fell more in love with not only Lemmie, but the Kingdom of Ashwyck. The people, the lush agriculture, the food, the beaches, the *freedom*...

Life was slower here, the people content to savor each day. Many days they spent at a beach of warm sand kissed by crisp blue water, and Emelle had the joy of watching Lars's defined muscles glisten each time he emerged from the waves. She encountered new animals, one that actually swung between the vines of the jungle. Lars just chuckled and told her they were called monkeys. Emelle's eyes bugged when he explained the Babau he slayed all that time ago looked similar to the cute primate—though much larger. And far more harrowing.

As if by fate, though Emelle wasn't quite sure how much she believed in the notion anymore, Lars found a grove of trees with orchids of all colors outside Elix's palace. Emelle's eyes burned when he showed her.

And Emelle loved to tease Greer, now the Queen of Ashwyck. Greer smacked her every time she said it and flushed every time she curtsied in greeting. It didn't stop Emelle from baiting her best friend.

Lars had also forgiven his father. At least, he'd forgiven the scared young man who'd made a woeful decision that set him on a dreadful course he never could have imagined. He still didn't agree with the decisions his father made, but he no longer wished to hold any anger in his heart. There wasn't room for it anymore. After all, he never would have left the borders of Wellsmore in search of a trial, never would have found *her*, without his father setting the board.

She had never been more grateful that Lars had been mad enough to weave his own destiny. To challenge the Fates themselves. His dedication was one of the things she loved most about him. She hoped the Sable sisters, and anyone who dared to dream for *something* bigger, never gave up, either. They'd proven that the only people who were needed to bless a destiny were themselves.

Fuck destiny. Weave your own future.

Together, they'd agreed that when they were done with their travels, when they'd filled their books, they'd return here. This was their home. This was where they'd meet the cosmos together.

Beaming, Lars and Emelle Winter waved to a crying Greer, a smiling Elix, a babbling Lemmie, and an uninterested Evie as they set off on their next grand adventure. The ship left the harbor, charted to head northeast over the Wildlands and into the Theston Gulf and beyond.

Emelle looked to Lars, squeezing his hand once, twice. A gleam of fierce love and devotion shone back in his onyx eyes. Their life together was only just beginning.

And so she learned: Be so *incredibly* foolish. It may just work out in your favor.

Finn

Acknowledgments

Thank you to everyone who gave my debut novel, The Fool's Errand, a shot. It has been such a whirlwind writing and falling in love with this world and these characters, and I hope you enjoyed the time you spent with them. I'm sure you're sick of hearing this from every author, but if you could leave an honest review on the usual platforms, I would be so appreciative. As an indie author, it helps more than you know!

Now, onto my many, many thanks I have to give.

I'm not sure if I'm the only one, but I truly did not realize exactly how much went into writing a book when I first opened my Google Doc. My fingers flew across the keyboard, crafting a story that I quickly fell in love with, but only through the support and expertise of others is this book in front of you today.

To Becca and Bethany, my best friends who have never read a fantasy novel in their life (until now) and yet listened to every rant, every excitement, every hurdle that I overcame and were so excited for me. Thank you for always being my hype women. Thank you for being the ones who taught me soulmates weren't always romantic.

To Taylor, my friend who read my roughest draft and gave me such positive feedback and direction. I am so appreciative of your thorough comments, guiding questions, and constructive criticism that helped shape the jagged edges of this novel. For your continued support and endless answers to my random questions, I am eternally grateful for you.

To Emily and Katie, my editors who answered my tireless questions and helped transform this from a Google Doc to an actual, legible novel. Without your expertise, I fear this passion project would've never left my own computer. From the bottom of my heart, thank you.

To Giulia, my amazing cover artist who worked tirelessly with me to ensure I had the cover of my dreams. I am in awe of the design and cannot thank you enough.

To Chelsea, my extremely talented artist who brought Emelle and Lars to life. Seeing my characters exist outside of my head is wild, and I have you to thank for that. You may as well have downloaded the images from my brain and I am so grateful.

To Rusty, my map artist who worked with me back and forth on creating Eralyn and was so patient with my requests. You understood my vision and the map you created is exactly how I pictured this world I dreamt up. Thank you.

To Lorna, my formatter who helped me when I quickly became overwhelmed at creating my actual books. I appreciate your attention to detail and ability to bring my vision to life.

And finally, to six-year-old Katie, the little girl who dreamed of writing a novel one day. You did it, babe. I'm so proud of you. (Don't read this though, it's not for you)

About the Author

Katherine Carter lives in Arizona, USA with her 3 cats and approximately 142 book boyfriends she's collected over the years. As an avid reader, Katherine loves to escape between the pages, losing herself in the adventures and fantasy and romance. She'd always dreamed of writing, but had always thought it too out of reach.

And then she realized, the only one stopping her was herself.

Her debut novel, The Fool's Errand, is the culmination of her childhood dream to become an author and the years she spent thinking up mismatched characters and adventures. This passion project was born out of a spark that quickly blazed into a full-blown inferno that took over her every waking thought. She can't thank you enough for giving her a chance.

Stay tuned on her socials for information on her future works! Katherine loves dark romance, rom-coms, fantasy, and basically anything with a romance subplot, so who knows what her next project will be... :)

TikTok @KatherineCarterAuthor
Instagram @KatherineCarterAuthor
www.KatherineCarterAuthor.com
KatherineCarterAuthor@gmail.com

Content & Trigger Warnings

Content Warnings: explicit sex and mature language

Trigger Warnings: murder/death (on page), blood/gore (on page), suicide (as a sacrifice), suicidal ideation (vague, on page), slaying of mythical beasts (vaguely graphic, on page), reference to possible past SA (side character, brief/vague on page reference), concern for possible SA of FMC (on page, very brief and vague, more of a passing thought), small incidental injuries, drugging, abduction.

All depictions of sexual acts are consensual.

Made in the USA
Monee, IL
19 February 2025